"Shelly Lange. . . . years. . . ."

Her partner's words caused pity and anger to churn in Meg's belly. "That's what McNeil guessed. She lived next door to him years ago."

"And he remembered her well enough to recognize her now?" Skepticism edged Ben Shea's voice.

"It wasn't like that." Oh, hell. It sounded as if she was being defensive. Maybe she was. She didn't want to think of Scott McNeil as a suspect. She'd have to, of course. Why *had* he remembered a neighbor's daughter so well? But she didn't believe he was a murderer. She'd seen too much tenderness on his face when he talked about the baby, too much anger and abhorrence when he speculated on who might have left her out in the cold. She would have sworn he wasn't faking that.

Unless he was a heck of an actor.

What she really meant, Meg thought wryly, was that she didn't want to believe she could be attracted to a man capable of such a brutal crime.

Dear Reader,

Here we are on the second book of my trilogy! I've got to tell you, writing this one was the hardest in some respects. My mom (also an author) reads every word I write. She had to keep saying, "Um, Janice, your heroine is Meg, not Renee." I didn't want to shift gears. I'd been with Renee for a long time and grown fond of her. Who the heck was Meg?

So I fiddled, and fiddled some more, and found out who Meg was. She became as individual as Renee, and gave me the added pleasure of looking at my story world through different eyes. The oldest of the three sisters, Meg was able to untie many of the tangled threads of their pasts.

As always, I wrote about family in *The Baby and the Badge*. Sisters, mothers, fathers. They're what really count, aren't they? And after all, where else does a love story lead? A man and woman taking that walk down the aisle do tend to become parents.

Here's keeping my fingers crossed that you enjoy this book as much as I did the challenging task of writing it!

Sincerely,

Janice Kay Johnson

THE BABY AND THE BADGE
Janice
Kay
Johnson

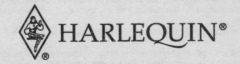

HARLEQUIN®

TORONTO • NEW YORK • LONDON
AMSTERDAM • PARIS • SYDNEY • HAMBURG
STOCKHOLM • ATHENS • TOKYO • MILAN • MADRID
PRAGUE • WARSAW • BUDAPEST • AUCKLAND

ISBN 0-373-70860-2

THE BABY AND THE BADGE

Copyright © 1999 by Janice Kay Johnson.

This edition published by arrangement with Harlequin Books S.A.

® and TM are trademarks of the publisher. Trademarks indicated with ® are registered in the United States Patent and Trademark Office, the Canadian Trade Marks Office and in other countries.

Visit us at www.romance.net

Printed in U.S.A.

To the members of my writers' group,
all good friends and kind critics.

PROLOGUE

"JOHNNY!" Meg Patton protested. She batted at his hand, cupping her breast. "Stop! We don't have time."

And she had to talk to him. Talk, not…well, do *this*. She'd asked him specially to slip away from campus at lunchtime and come home with her. She had to be alone with him. To tell him.

"Come on," her boyfriend coaxed. "What's the big deal? So what if we're five minutes late to class? Like they're going to call our parents or something."

If he'd been intending to reassure her, he failed. She shuddered at the very idea. "No, really," she said, grabbing his wrist. "Besides, what if my dad came home and caught us?"

"In the middle of the day?" Johnny grinned, his warm brown eyes soft with desire for her. "You said yourself he never does."

"Yes, but…" She closed her eyes when he kissed her.

Oh, the way he kissed! His lips were needy, and the feel of his tongue inside her mouth always melted her knees. How could she help but kiss him back?

He peeled off her shirt, unhooked her bra.

"We should…at least…go up to my bedroom,"

she whispered, her head falling back as he nibbled on her neck. "In case…"

"In case what?" He sucked on her breast and held her up when her legs buckled.

"In case…" She couldn't think.

"Your dad's not coming home." He scooped up the hem of her little short skirt and whisked down her panties.

Oh, this wouldn't take long, Meg told herself. And it felt so good. She unbuttoned the fly of his jeans, feeling his weight bump against her. So good.

"Here," he said, depositing her on the couch. Johnny dropped to his knees in front of her.

Meg felt him nudging at her and closed her eyes. "Yes," she whispered. "Like this."

She heard something outside—a car door slamming?—but it didn't matter. Only this mattered. Not until footsteps sounded heavy on the porch, a key scraped the lock, did the fire of terror burn away the fog of sexual desire.

"Oh, my God!" she cried. "Johnny…!"

He'd heard, too. He was falling away from her, yanking his jeans up, when Meg's father walked into the living room.

In his uniform, with the wide black belt and the gun at his hip, he looked ten feet tall and near as wide, filling the living room with silent rage.

Meg pulled down her skirt and crossed her arms over her breasts. Her shirt, she saw with a frantic glance, was out of reach.

Johnny had gotten to his feet and was trying to button his jeans over his erection. Her father stared at it with violence in his eyes.

His gaze turned to her and she shrank back. "Get dressed."

She couldn't seem to move.

"Get dressed!" her father shouted. "I won't have a whore sitting here naked in my living room!"

"Sir, I..." Johnny's voice squeaked, broke. He was still fumbling with his fly. "It's not her fault. I..."

Her father crossed the room. His fist smashed into Johnny's face. Her boyfriend fell across the coffee table right in front of her. Blood splattered his face, and she screamed.

Her father went after him. His boot lashed out, and Meg heard Johnny's rib snap. He curled on the floor in a fetal position.

She was screaming still, screaming, screaming. Her father backhanded her, and pain exploded across her cheek.

"Get up!" he ordered. He kicked Johnny again. "Get up. Face me like a man."

Through her tears she saw Johnny push himself to his knees, then shakily rise to his feet. He wiped blood and tears from his face with his forearm.

"How do you feel about my daughter?" her father asked coldly.

"I..." Johnny swallowed. "I don't know."

Meg stared in disbelief, the pain in her cheek nothing compared to the agony in her chest.

"Are you ever going to touch her again?"

Johnny didn't look at her. "No, sir."

"Call her?"

Johnny shook his head.

"See her?"

His eye was almost swollen shut. He closed the other one. "No," he whispered.

Out of nowhere, her father punched him again, his fist connecting with the swollen eye. Johnny screamed and went down again.

"What if she calls you?"

Johnny, her Johnny—the football player, the jock, whose swagger had every girl in school swooning—began crawling toward the front door.

Her father kicked him, his voice a crack like a rifle shot. "What if she calls you?"

"I'll hang up!"

One more kick. "Then get the hell out of here!" Ed Patton snarled.

Johnny staggered to his feet and ran, swaying. Meg heard the front door open and close, and a moment later the sound of a car engine, the screech of tires.

A sixteen-year-old girl, she was left alone to face her father, the man she hated and feared with every fiber of her being.

He must never know. Whatever she did, her father must never find out what she hadn't had time to tell Johnny.

She lifted her chin and waited for the first blow.

CHAPTER ONE

Meg had never been so scared in her life, not even facing down her father. Not even in boot camp, when she'd been sure she wouldn't make it through but had no idea how else she'd survive and support her infant son.

But he was fourteen now, and Meg would die before she'd let her son see her stark terror.

"Well." She gazed at the modern red-brick public safety building that stood across the snow-covered street from where she'd parked. An American flag fluttered on a pole in front. Leafless trees stood at attention like soldiers along the sidewalk, shoveled bare. "Here we are."

"Cool!" Her son unsnapped his seat belt. "Let's go in."

She wanted to sit here and think about this some more. Lots more. Maybe for half an hour. Maybe until it was time to get a hotel room for the night.

But she took a deep breath, reached for her purse and said, "Right behind you."

As she trailed him across the street, minding her footing so she didn't slip and fall, her heart was a knot of longing and fear, her stomach a ball of nausea. Oh, God, why was she doing this? She'd had a good life! After thirteen years in the Army, she'd been respected, well-established in her career, financially solvent. She was raising a terrific kid with no help, thank you. Why try to fix something that wasn't broken?

But she knew the answer perfectly well: because she thought about her sisters every day, wondered what kind of women they'd grown into, suffered guilt because she wasn't there to help them.

Because her son had the right to meet his father. For better or worse. But not, please God, today. She could face Renee, even if her sister hated her, but not Johnny, too.

Brass letters on brick above the double doors formed the words Elk Springs Police Department. No more old granite building; she'd gone there first, but it was an antique mall now. She'd have to check it out one of these days. After she and Will had gotten settled.

Settled. Her stomach took another dive. What if Renee and Abby didn't want her back in their lives? Meg wouldn't blame them.

Fresh panic roiled. She shouldn't have burned her bridges. She should have made this a visit, not a permanent move.

Too late.

Ahead of her, Will pushed open one of the doors, then remembered his manners long enough to hold it so that it didn't swing shut in her face. A true gentleman.

At fourteen, he was starting to look uncomfortably like a man. Just in the past few months, he'd begun to shave. Only once in a while, but the milestone had come nonetheless. She was used to his height—he'd passed her by the age of twelve—but now his shoulders were developing bulk, too, and his voice was deepening.

Scary.

Was this the worst of all times to make such a major change in their lives? Meg worried. Hormones were going to cause enough trouble without him being rejected by his father, too. Or what if...

His nudge jarred her back to the here and now. They were already inside the police station, looking around a lobby that could have belonged to a doctor's office: shining vinyl floor, rows of comfortable chairs, magazines strewn on low tables. A middle-age couple sat together, murmuring to each other; a sulky teenage girl slouched at the far end, staring down at her feet. Behind a long counter waited a uniformed officer.

"May I help you, ma'am?"

"Yes. I'm looking for Renee Patton."

"Renee?" His expression changed. "Hey, aren't you...?"

"Yes." She forced a smile. "I'm her sister."

"Well!" He looked pleased. "Isn't that something?"

Agonizing impatience warred with gratitude at the reprieve chatting with him gave her. "Yes," she agreed meaninglessly.

"Did you think she used her maiden name on the job?" he asked, resting his elbows comfortably on the counter.

Maiden name? That meant... She mentally gulped. Her scrawny little sister was *married?*

Meg gave her head a bemused shake. "Yes, I..." She backtracked, unwilling to admit she didn't know her own sister was married. Didn't know anything about her sister since she'd been fourteen years old, except that she'd become a cop. "Well, no. It was just...habit. We've been Pattons a long time."

He chuckled. "Yeah. I can see how that would happen."

Will stirred.

"Um...is she here?" Meg asked.

"What? Oh, yeah. Sure. Far as I know, she's in her office." He turned. "What the heck, here she comes now."

Forgetting to breathe, Meg stared. Absorbed in conversation, two police officers were coming down the long hall toward the lobby. One was so downy-cheeked he had to be a recruit. The other...

Even in uniform, Renee was beautiful and unmistakably a Patton. Her cheeks had fleshed out, her hips rounded, she had *breasts*. Meg had a flash, remembering her sister, the little kid, vowing never to get breasts.

"They're gross!" she'd proclaimed, scrunching up her face. "They bounce up and down, and you have to wear a stupid bra, and they stick out."

Rolling her eyes, Meg had told her, "You can't just decide something like that. I mean, you either get big ones or you don't."

"If I do, I'll...I'll bind them!" Renee had declared fiercely. "Like Deborah Sampson. You know, that girl who pretended to be a boy and fought in the Revolutionary war. I read about her the other day. She just wrapped this cloth around her chest." Renee demonstrated. "And *flattened* them."

"You do that," Meg had agreed, humoring her little sister. "Whatever makes you happy."

For a while there, Renee's resolve had seemed to work; she was still skinny and flat at fourteen when Meg ran away from home.

Well, Renee had breasts now, Meg observed, and immediately felt foolish. What, she thought her sister really would figure out how not to mature physically?

Renee still hadn't noticed her. Why should she? Meg reminded herself. Think how she must have changed, too!

"Is that Aunt Renee?" Will whispered.

Heart cramped, Meg couldn't have answered to save her life. She suddenly wanted to bolt. What if Renee recognized her and deliberately turned away? What if she didn't care, hadn't missed her big sister? What if anger was stronger than love?

Will said something. She didn't hear because Renee had spotted her.

Her sister stopped, just froze midstride. "Meg?"

Hot tears burned Meg's eyes. She didn't cry. She'd always figured she'd run out of tears, all those years ago when she'd used so many.

"Renee." Her voice choked, cracked.

"Meg." Renee couldn't seem to say anything else. She only stared, as Meg had done a moment before. And then she was crying, too.

They met at a waist-high swinging door at one end of the counter. They hugged so hard the door cut into Meg's stomach, but she didn't care. She was crying on her sister's uniform collar, but she didn't care about that, either.

Her skinny little sister was a woman now, but somehow she still felt the same. Smelled the same, a hint of vanilla that seemed to go with her white, white skin and pale blond hair.

"I've missed you so much," Meg mumbled.

"Have you?" Abruptly Renee pushed her away. Her face was soaked with tears, her eyes red, puffy. She gave an angry swipe at her wet cheeks. "Then why didn't you call? Write? Not even once? Why the hell did you...did you..." Her mouth worked, but she couldn't seem to finish. Fresh tears were pouring out.

"Desert you?"

Stilling the hands wiping her cheeks, her sister nodded.

"I... It's a long story." Understatement of the century. She glanced back to check on Will, who hadn't moved. "I need to blow my nose."

"Me, too." Renee sniffed. "Let's go back to my office. No... I'll just take the rest of the day off. You'll come home with me, won't you?"

"Home isn't still..." She hadn't driven by, however tempted. Her sisters first.

"No. I've gotten married and sold the house."

"Anybody I know?"

"Daniel Barnard. You went to school with him."

"I remember." She'd had a brief crush on him in about eighth grade. He'd been a foot taller than everyone else, so awkward he was always tripping over his own feet, but those eyes! So blue they looked like heaven. "He was nice," she said.

Her sister grinned. "Still is. He's cuter now, too." Her smile faded. "Are you married?"

"No, but..." Meg turned. "I have a son."

Renee's breath caught as her gaze followed

Meg's. "Dear Lord," she whispered. "He could be Jack. You were *pregnant?*"

It wasn't so much a question as an exclamation, but Meg answered, anyway. "Yes. If Dad had known…"

Her sister gave her a single, horrified glance.

What she'd said finally caught up with Meg. "Why does he call himself Jack now?"

"I don't know. He has pretty much since you left. He was different after that." Renee shrugged helplessly. "I figured it had to do with you going. You did know he's the police chief, didn't you? I can check to see if he's in if you want…."

"No." Meg had to call on every grain of self-will she possessed not to bolt. "No. I knew he was police chief. But I'm not ready… I hoped we wouldn't run into him today. Eventually I'll have to tell him, but…"

Renee touched her arm. "It's okay. He won't come out here." A frown crinkled her brow. "But how did you know?"

"The same way I knew Dad was dead. I ran into Pete Branagh. I'd taken Will and some of his buddies to Disneyland. Can you believe it? Just out of the blue."

She still remembered the shock, her first instinct to pretend she wasn't Meg Patton, that he was mistaken. But the pharmacist—retired now—had been a nice guy, and there wasn't any reason to hide anymore. Nobody was going to take Will away from her. And so they'd talked about the old Elk Springs and the new.

"Are you going to introduce me to your son?"

Meg gave herself a shake. After a surreptitious

glance toward that long hall—empty—she said, "I'm sorry. Of course I am. Will?"

He came to her side, his head ducked shyly.

"Meet your aunt Renee."

Across the counter, Renee extended her hand. "It's a pleasure, Will."

He took it, a flush running across his cheekbones.

Meg stole another glance at the hall.

Renee tore her bemused gaze from Will. "Let me check out and we'll go home. You can, um, see other old friends another time."

"Bless you," Meg said, meaning it. "Can we drive by the old place, or is that out of the way?"

"Not by much. You bet."

"I'll have to follow you. I'm not sure I could find it from here. This town has grown."

"Big time," her sister said. "You know about the new ski area?" Her expression changed. "Oh, my gosh. Abby. Shall I call her? Or do you want to do it yourself?"

"She's still here, too? In Elk Springs?" At Renee's nod, Meg felt more tears spring to her eyes. Will stared at her in astonishment. He'd think she'd morphed into some sitcom mother if she didn't watch out. She blinked, sniffed, came to a decision. "I'll do it. When I get to your place."

Renee leaned awkwardly over the counter, gave her another quick, hard hug, then retreated, looking embarrassed. "I'm parked out back—four-by-four with a rack of lights."

"Gotcha. Red Subaru station wagon," Meg said over her shoulder, steering Will toward the door. The hall behind them was still deserted; in her ea-

gerness to make good her escape, she marched Will
out double-time.

"But Mom! *He* might be here." *His* identity was
no secret. "Why do we have to go so quick?"

Because I'm not ready to run into your father.
How did she explain that one? Will wanted more
than anything in the world to meet his father. As far
as he was concerned, Johnny Murray was why
they'd come to Elk Springs.

"He doesn't know you exist. We shouldn't spring
it on him in public. Especially in front of the people
who work for him."

The look he gave her over the roof of the car told
her he knew she was making excuses, but he waited
until they were buckled in to say, "But he might be
here."

The thought was enough to make Meg break out
in a cold sweat. She was all too aware that Johnny
might be looking out one of those windows right
now.

Take a deep breath. Don't hyperventilate, she told
herself.

She met her son's eyes. "Will. Not yet. Please.
Let me…let me find out what Renee and Abby think
first. This is…a big step for me."

His outrage shifted into perplexity. "Aunt Renee
was happy to see you."

"Maybe. But it won't be that easy." She swallowed. "I abandoned them. 'I'm sorry' won't be
good enough. When they find out I'm trying to horn
my way back in to the family, I may get the cold
shoulder. That will…hurt."

"Here she comes," he said.

A Bronco topped with police lights pulled onto

the street. Behind the wheel, Renee waved. Meg jockeyed out of the parking spot and fell in behind her.

"Mom." Will swallowed. "Aunt Renee will understand. I mean, she *loves* you."

Tears stung Meg's eyes again and she felt as if her heart might burst. She had him; that was enough.

But she hoped it wouldn't have to be. *He* needed more.

"Thank you," Meg said when she could. She blinked hard a couple of times and made herself look around at the new buildings on every side. Fancy stoplights had replaced signs at every intersection. "I don't know where anything is," she said, trying her best to sound like the mom he knew. "This was a little town. Now it looks like Southern California! There's an espresso stand on every corner, and a mall. A mall! Who the heck shops there?"

"Mom." Will gave her a look. "Elk Springs doesn't look like L.A. Trust me. This is Podunk, U.S.A. I can't believe it didn't *have* a mall."

Meg hardly listened. "I knew they put in a ski area, but jeez!" Main Street used to have a Woolworth's and a Sears catalog store. Now... With her head swiveling she had to brake sharply when the light changed ahead, feeling the tires slip on the packed snow. Careless. She was too used to sunshine. But her thoughts reverted to the astonishing sight of her hometown.

"Art galleries," she muttered. "Designer clothes. And what's that?" With difficulty, she made out the script. "Holistic health!"

"Cool-looking bookstore," Will observed.

She hardly heard him. "And the restaurants! I can't believe it."

"You know," her son said, "it's been like, fifteen years since you've been here. Did you think you were time traveling or something?"

Wisdom from a teenager. One of life's little miracles.

"Okay, okay," she agreed, putting the Subaru in gear now that the light had turned green. "You're right. Time marches on. My waistline isn't quite what it was fifteen years ago, either. But still. This was an isolated ranching community. Suddenly, it's Aspen, Colorado, transported a few states west."

"Not suddenly."

"Are you trying to make me feel old?"

"You *are* old."

"Brat," she said amiably, and he grinned.

A right turn and they were crossing the Deschutes on a bridge she remembered. The thick concrete railing had been dated September 1939; the bridge was the work of WPA workers during the Depression.

How many times had she walked over that bridge on her way to town to hang out with friends or buy an ice cream cone or just get out of the house? She remembered how hot the rough concrete got under the summer sun as she rested her arms on it and dreamed, mesmerized by the slow, swirling current below. Just downstream the ducks and swans gathered at the park, hoping for handouts. There the willows dangled fingers of green in the water. She could smell it now, though it was January, the whole landscape snowy white and the car windows rolled up: the pines and grass, new-mown, and the river and the red volcanic dirt. Home. Her throat closed.

"Mom?"

She blinked.

"Are you crying again?"

"No." Meg cleared her throat. "Don't be silly. I was just...remembering something."

Will bounced in his seat like an impatient toddler. "Are we almost there?"

"Yep. We're almost there."

The neighborhood had changed hardly at all. The houses were still gracious, the yards well-groomed, the shade trees mature, though bare of leaf. Whoever shopped at the boutiques along Main Street, they didn't live here. These were old-time residents, people she might have known. Ones who probably didn't know what "holistic" meant and didn't care.

"There," she said, tension entering her voice. The brake lights flickered ahead as Renee slowed. "There's where I grew up."

Will turned his head as they passed, studying the white house with a wide porch, the picket fence and snowy sweep of yard, green in summer, that went right down to the riverbank. Now a tire swing hung from a huge old sycamore and a child's pink bike, spoke-deep in snow, blocked the paved walkway. A wooden sled leaned against the porch.

Her father must be rolling over in his grave, Meg thought with pleasure.

"It's not that big," Will said.

"Big?" she echoed, surprised.

"Well... You made it sound like some haunted house. You know. This huge dark place with lots of empty rooms where you had to tiptoe around because something might jump out at you. Boo! Like that."

In her memory, the house was bigger. But her father was the only one who'd jump out. They *had* tiptoed. Always. If Dad heard you... If Dad found out... If Dad even *guessed*...

"No, it's a perfectly ordinary house," Meg said to her son. Who never tiptoed. "A nice house. There are four bedrooms, but no family room. They didn't build 'em in those days. With different people living there, it could even be a cheerful house."

Giving it a last, lingering look in the rearview mirror, she thought maybe it *was* cheerful now, that it liked having a tire swing and a little girl's bike cluttering up the sidewalk.

And *she* liked the idea of her father forever restless in his grave.

Renee led them out of town down Butte Road toward the red volcanic cinder cone that held memories for every local teenager. She and Johnny had climbed and slid down, laughing hysterically. They'd parked there and necked and drank illicit beer, feeling like rebels, like grown-ups. While proving, she thought now, that they definitely weren't.

She remembered passing the gates of the Triple B, although she'd never been to Daniel Barnard's home. Renee's Bronco turned under the peeled pole arch with the ranch name burned into the crosspiece, the Subaru right behind it. A crushed cinder lane divided dry high-desert scrub: stunted junipers and sagebrush, everything gray-green but the dirt and the traces of snow. At a Y, Renee bore to the left and headed up a lava ridge to a gorgeous new Craftsman-style house commanding the ranch.

Meg parked beside her sister's vehicle and

climbed out, looking below at the sprawling barns and green pastures. Mountains one direction, the working ranch and vast dry land beyond. She bet the sunrises and sunsets were really something here.

"Horses," Will said eagerly from beside her. "Do you think I could ride?"

Having joined them, Renee said without hesitation, "Are you kidding? Daniel—my husband—trains world-class cutting horses. He'll be thrilled if someone else in the family is interested."

"Cool!" Will said.

To Meg's relief, he'd apparently accepted the delay in meeting his father. His aunt and uncle were enough.

"Daniel's mother lives in the original house," Renee said, waving at the white clapboard place set among cottonwoods along a creek. "She's a sweetie. I'm lucky."

"I vaguely remember her from school." Meg frowned, thinking back. "She volunteered in the library, I think. I liked her better than the librarian."

As they started up the porch steps, Renee asked, "How long are you here for? We have plenty of room for you. You will stay, won't you?"

"Tonight we will," Meg agreed. "Actually..." Why was this so hard to say? "Well, we're here for good."

Renee stopped, staring with her mouth opening and closing like a puffer fish's. "For good? You're moving back here?"

"Yeah." Meg tried for nonchalance with her shrug, but defensiveness crept into her tone. "Why so surprised? Once I heard that Dad had died, I just…thought it was time to come home. This wasn't a bad place to raise a kid, you know.''

"But…what will you *do?* For a living? There aren't that many good jobs here…''

Renee didn't want her here. Meg heard the truth, loud and clear. It hurt. Oh, God, it hurt.

"I already have a job.'' She was terribly conscious of the anxiety on Will's face. Of the burned bridges behind her. "I start Monday.''

"You applied for a job here, and you didn't even call me?'' Renee's expression closed and her voice chilled. "Well, it's your business. Don't feel you have to stay tonight if you've already rented a place.''

"I was hoping you'd help me find a house,'' Meg said quietly. "I didn't come for an interview. They hired me sight unseen.''

Her sister was unlocking the front door. "Oh?'' she said distantly. "What will you be doing?''

"Law enforcement.'' As Renee turned back to her in shock, Meg smiled. "I'm a cop, too. Apparently, it runs in the family. I'll be a county sheriff's deputy. The guy who hired me knew Dad.''

Renee looked as if a grenade had knocked her flat. Even so, she said, "But not like we did.''

"No,'' Meg agreed, her smile twisting. "Not like we did.''

Her little sister shook her head in dazed disbelief one more time before stepping into a slate-floored entry. Spreading her arms wide, she said, "My house is yours, and all that.'' At last, at last, her voice softened. "Welcome home, Meg.''

AFTER DINNER Will went off to the barn with his newly discovered uncle Daniel, and the three sisters finally had time to talk.

Meg couldn't stop looking at them. Renee drinking coffee, Abby tea, they sat on opposite ends of the gorgeous, deep-cushioned leather sofa in the Barnard living room. Their postures mimicked each other; both had tucked their feet under them, lounging with the boneless comfort of two slender cats who were nonetheless aware of every sound, every movement.

It seemed fitting, Meg thought, that she was in the easy chair facing them, the coffee table a barrier symbolizing the years since she had seen them, the silence nobody wanted to talk about even now that they could.

How old had they been? Abby eleven and Renee fourteen when she left that terrible day? Girls. Skinny and blond and unfinished. Renee burying her anger, Abby so sweet even their father had been soft on her. *They would be all right,* she'd told herself, unable to let herself believe anything else. She couldn't stay, not pregnant, not once Johnny had betrayed her. Even if he hadn't, she recognized now, she wouldn't dare have stayed. For the baby she'd already carried, she had to go.

Would her sisters understand?

They gazed at her, Renee's eyes green-gold, Abby's sky-blue like Meg's, both curious but wary, as well. Their pleasure in seeing her was genuine, Meg thought, but they felt other emotions, too, that they couldn't yet articulate. Renee had asked just the once why Meg had never called or written; she had been careful since not to let the conversation wander close to the subject.

"I was only a girl," Meg said, startling them. "I didn't know what to do."

"What *did* you do?" asked Abby over the rim of her teacup.

"I packed." Meg looked at Renee. "You remember. You helped."

Her middle sister nodded.

"I stole money from Dad."

"Really?" Renee's eyes widened, as though the idea of doing so was unimaginable.

As it had once been for Meg. Only desperation so deep, she'd known there was no alternative, had sent her creeping into her father's bedroom. Hands shaking, she'd opened first the drawers in his nightstand, then his bureau. One had jammed, she remembered. She had battered it with her hands, her tears falling hot and wet on his undershirts. She could still see those splotches on the pristine white knit, and even though she was there to do something much worse, she'd been terrified at how angry he'd be that his shirts would have to be washed again.

In the bottom drawer, she'd found a gun, and the money.

"A thousand dollars," she said now. "Ten hundred-dollar bills in an envelope. I don't know why he kept so much in cash. It was between the folds of a shirt he never wore, not like he'd just been to the bank. This was hidden."

They exchanged unreadable glances, her sisters, then gazed back at her, still watchful, still expectant.

"And then you...hitchhiked? Took a bus?" Abby prodded.

"No." She looked back at them, feeling oddly detached. "I did take a bus, but first... After I made

Renee go to her friend's house, I searched Dad's closet.''

''Why?'' Renee asked simply.

''Because I thought he might have something that would tell me where Mom had gone. So that I could find her.''

Their expressions didn't change. ''But he didn't,'' Renee said. ''I went through all his stuff after he died.''

Meg took a breath. ''Then, he'd thrown away her letters. So you couldn't find them, too.''

''Too?'' they echoed in unison.

''You mean,'' Abby said, very carefully, ''she wrote to him?''

''To us,'' Meg corrected. The box had sat on the shelf in the back corner of his closet. Inside, the flap ripped open, were the photographs of their mother the girls had hungered for. A wedding picture. An album filled with photos of her with first one baby, then a toddler and a second baby, and finally all three daughters. Dad must have snapped them himself, because he was never in any.

Though the letters were on top, Meg had looked at the pictures first, because Mom's face was already fading in her memory, first softening around the edges, then becoming fuzzy, until she couldn't bring it into focus at all. But here she was, blond and slender with Renee's eyes, and a million memories rushed back, one image after another like old-fashioned cards that you flipped through to create animation.

At last she'd picked up the letters, all addressed to them. Abby and Renee and Meg. Dozens and dozens of envelopes, all unopened.

Why had he kept them? She would never know.

She had sat cross-legged on the floor, tearing them open, reading as many as she dared in the time she thought she had. The addresses neatly written in the upper left-hand corner of each envelope had changed as the years passed. The letters had come further and further apart, unless he hadn't kept them all. They had finally stopped a year before.

She'd taken that one, though she had also memorized the address in San Jose, California.

"So, you went looking for her. For Mom," Renee said in a voice like glass, as though she didn't quite believe it.

The dreaded moment had come, but Meg wouldn't let herself shirk.

"Yes," she said, meeting their eyes. Her sisters, who would never know their mother. "And I found her."

CHAPTER TWO

AS USUAL, he was the last one left in the vast dark lodge.

Scott McNeil flicked off his computer, stretching while the screen went dark. Nothing he'd been doing was particularly urgent; it could have waited. But why should it? His empty house didn't exactly beckon.

Frowning at the realization—not new—that he was hiding out in his office, Scott grabbed his parka, locked the door behind him and headed down the stairs.

The huge lodge was silent, the night lighting dim. During the day, ski boots thumped up and down the broad, battered wooden stairs. Goggles and parkas and gloves heaped the tables and floors as skiers ate chili or hamburgers from the café, warmed their hands on foam cups of cocoa or espresso, before hitting the slopes again.

Racks of clothing made hulking silhouettes in the ski shop, locked and dark but for the night-light. The banks of lockers were all closed.

Scott turned down a narrow hallway and went out an employee entrance into the cold. He rattled the door to be sure it locked. From a distance away, a flashlight was trained on him. Scott lifted a hand. "Good night."

Two security officers patrolled after-hours. The one who'd spotted him called, "'Night, Boss."

The path to the employee lot was trampled between banks of deep snow. A cloud veiled the moon, making the night pitch-black except for the sickly yellow glow from the sodium lights in the parking lot.

He was a hundred yards away when he saw that something pale sat beside the driver's door of his Jeep Grand Cherokee. He squinted, trying to make out the shape. Looked like a tall box. Strange. If somebody wanted to leave something for him, why hadn't they come by his office?

He'd covered half the distance when he identified the shape. A car seat. It was a baby's car seat, just resting upright on the packed snow where someone had set it. The back was to him as he approached.

There wouldn't be a kid in it. He didn't know why he felt his gut tightening. Somebody was junking a broken car seat. That's all. Nobody would set a kid down and forget him.

And then he heard...a whimper. Followed by a thin sad wail that lifted the hairs on the back of his neck.

"Oh, my God."

In a couple of running steps, he reached the child seat and dropped to his knees on the snow. Tiny mittened hands flapped and the cry increased in intensity. The baby was alive and well—couldn't have been out here long, because even earlier, in the sun of the afternoon, the mercury hadn't risen above freezing.

"It's okay," he murmured, rage whistling through him like an icy wind scouring the mountain summit. "We'll get you inside. We'll find your mommy or daddy."

Back to the lodge? But he had nothing there to feed this baby. If he called 9-1-1, it would take someone half an hour to get here, another half hour to turn around and head back to town. The ski resort was on Forest Service land, so no condos or inns clustered at the base of the mountain. The nearest private land was twenty miles down the road.

Making a decision, Scott scooped up the whole car seat and hurried to the passenger side of his Jeep. He buckled the child seat in, under the dome light finally able to see the baby better.

Six months old, give or take a few weeks. Nose and round cheeks red from the cold. Huge dark eyes staring at him, a fringe of brown hair beneath a knitted hat. A yellow hat, green snowsuit, orange mittens, which didn't help him guess gender. Nice clothes, as if someone had cared.

"Who left you?" Scott murmured. "Your mommy or daddy? Would they do something like that?"

The kid opened its mouth and screamed. Who could blame him/her?

Even so, Scott grabbed his flashlight from the glove compartment and took a minute to scan the area. No note he could see, nothing left but the baby.

God Almighty. He—she—couldn't be simply forgotten, as sometimes happened when parents got confused about who had which kid. Skiers would have had no business in this parking lot. Besides, the lifts had shut down hours ago. Anybody would have realized long since that the baby was missing.

He shone the light around for a moment more,

then gave up. If there were tracks worth spotting, they'd still be here tomorrow, frozen solid. Snow wasn't expected tonight.

He backed out, then despite the ascending cry, took a fast sweep through the area parking lots. Not a single vehicle was here that shouldn't be.

Why, in God's name, would you leave a baby sitting out in the cold? What if he'd decided to bunk down in the lodge, as he did occasionally?

At the very thought, fury and a kind of agony crushed his chest. How could anybody do something like this?

He'd had pleasanter drives. His passenger cried for the entire half hour, going from sad gulping sobs to window shattering screams. The kid could hit a hell of a high note. And sustain it. He'd forgotten…

Don't go there, he told himself on a clench of pain. Think about this baby. Not… But he didn't let the name form.

He passed his own road. A couple miles farther was a resort with condos, a classy restaurant, sporting goods, an ice skating rink and a small store where he sometimes picked up milk or a six-pack. Scott assumed guests must occasionally need baby formula.

He left the child in the car and hurried in. Thank God he was right; a selection of plastic bottles in neon colors, packages of nipples and three brands of formula shared a shelf. He chose some of each, plus a pacifier. Maybe he could plug that mouth temporarily. On the shelf below were diapers, which now seemed to come in girl and boy varieties, not to mention sizes. He grabbed the one package that wasn't gender specific.

The clerk rang it all up without comment.

Back in the car, Scott ripped open the packaging and popped that pacifier right in. After the smallest hesitation, the rosebud mouth closed around it and began sucking so hard, it rocked up and down like a fishing bob.

In the blessed near silence, Scott drove home. Feed the baby, then call the cops, he figured. First things first.

By the time he rolled to a stop in his garage, the pacifier hurtled out hard enough to hit the dashboard and the siren began again.

"Not getting any milk, huh?" Garage door closed, Scott went around and unbuckled the baby, leaving the seat where it was. Expertly, he lifted the kid to his shoulder and jiggled. "Pretty frustrating, I know. Just give me a minute, and we can do something about it."

He spread a lap quilt on the leather couch, laid the baby on it, and began unpeeling layers of outerwear. Inside were cute pink overalls, soaking wet, and a tiny turtleneck with pink and yellow butterflies all over it. Lifting the little butt, he took off the overalls and the soggy diaper.

Definitely a girl. For reasons he didn't let himself analyze, that was a relief. No rash, so he didn't do anything but pat her dry and put on a clean diaper. That momentarily silenced her.

Formula warmed in the microwave, he tucked her in the crook of his arm and popped that nipple right in her mouth. She sucked with fierce concentration. He'd never seen the level in a bottle go down so quick.

Okay, she hadn't been out in the cold long, but she hadn't been fed in hours.

The whole thing didn't make sense. Where were her parents? Had she been snatched, and then the kidnapper panicked?

About the time she hit the bottom of the bottle, her eyelids got heavy. He rocked gently, murmuring a nearly forgotten song. At last the nipple fell from her slack mouth and he'd have sworn a tiny snore emerged.

Moving as carefully as if he were traversing an avalanche slope, Scott eased down the hall, grabbing some blankets from the linen closet on the way. In his bedroom, he set her on the bed, then pulled a drawer from his bureau and dumped its contents on the floor. Putting it down beside the bed, he padded it carefully, nestled her on her back inside it and tucked a quilt around her. Exhausted, she didn't even stir.

Babies slept as wholeheartedly as they did everything else. He'd forgotten. Nate had always frowned...

Scott bit off an obscenity and retreated, switching off the light as he went. Outside the bedroom, he stopped, then swore again and went back. Light from the hall fell in a band across the floor, touching her with pale grace.

He crouched beside the drawer and watched, waiting for her to puff out a breath, move, do *something* to show life. Her face was still, soft and pale. Tension rose in him until he couldn't bear it and had to lift the quilt. Her small chest rose and fell, rose and fell, and his anxiety quieted. He gently tucked the bedding back around her and slipped out of the room.

In the kitchen he went straight to the telephone, dialed 9-1-1 and told the dispatcher, ''I found a baby.''

MEG DISCOVERED how much of a coward she really was when the end of her shift neared and, instead of groaning, she was relieved to have to go out on a call. Relieved, so she didn't have to go home.

Because if she went home, Will would want her to phone Jack.

Her son wasn't alone in his opinion. Renee would probably call—again—to nag.

''You *have* to do it,'' she'd said yesterday evening. ''He knows you're back. What if somebody mentions Will? Even if nobody says anything about the resemblance, once Jack finds out Will's age, he'll know. Wouldn't you rather tell him?''

''Yes,'' Meg had agreed meekly. ''Of course you're right. I know I have to. I just thought it'd be nice to get settled in first.''

''You *are* settled in,'' Renee said crisply. ''Tell him about Will. Soon. You've got me slinking around the police station hoping I don't see him, because he'll ask me about you, and something might slip out, or he might be able to tell I'm hiding something... For Pete's sake, I did *traffic* duty yesterday, just to be sure Jack couldn't corner me.''

''Tomorrow, when I get home from work,'' Meg had promised. And she'd meant it.

But now, if she was lucky, this would take a while, and by the time she got home and had something to eat and listened to Will talk about his day, it would be too late to call Jack.

The duty officer had given her the option of going home. It was, after all, her first day as a Butte County sheriff's deputy and her shift was over. Meg had been hired, however, to work part-time in Investigations and part-time as a "youth" officer. Juvenile crime was rising; the sheriff's department was being asked to go into the schools for preventive programs and to crack down on drug use and fighting. Child abuse and neglect was an increasing problem in rural areas of the county as well as in Elk Springs itself. It so happened that the high school was outside the Elk Springs city limits, making it a county sheriff's department problem. When the sheriff got funding for one new officer, he'd chosen to have one who'd specialize in kids. That one was Meg.

So there she was, about to walk out the door, and a call comes in from a guy who says he's found a baby. How could she say, "Oh, just let a patrolman handle it"?

Trouble was, she'd never been good at deceiving herself. And she knew perfectly well she would have seized any excuse that came her way to procrastinate for one more day.

The address was on a dead-end road off the mountain loop highway. The road itself hadn't existed fifteen years ago. Meg hadn't been up that way yet, but she'd heard about the fancy houses that were springing up like seeds scattered by the ski area. This must be one of them. It wouldn't be hard to find, even in the dark.

She gave Will a quick call, squelched his protests

and set out. The sheriff's office was out in the flat desert scrub east of town. Tonight she passed within a few blocks of her old neighborhood and crossed the Deschutes River on that Depression era concrete bridge where she had once dreamed.

About Jack.

Meg scowled. *Okay, be honest,* she told herself. She'd come home partly so that Will could know his father. So why the foot-dragging?

Maybe because she could handle only one emotional issue at a time. And the one that mattered to her right now was reconciling with her sisters.

After Meg had dropped her bombshell that first evening, Renee had stared at her for a long moment, face blank with shock, and then leaped to her feet. Unnoticed, her mug tilted and spilled coffee down the leather arm of the sofa.

"You never told us? You let us think she was *dead?*" Her voice quivered with a sense of betrayal. "How could you do that, Meg?"

Meg bit her lip so hard she tasted blood. "Mom *is* dead. She was dying when I found her. She'd had breast cancer, and apparently when she had the lumpectomy they didn't get it all, because it came back a year later. And then it was in her lymph nodes, and…" She stopped.

"But we could have seen her," Renee wailed with the distress of a child. "Said goodbye."

"Would we have wanted to?" Abby blurted out unexpectedly. "She never said goodbye to us!"

Renee whirled on her sister. "But she wrote! You heard Meg."

"She could have done more." Abby's tone was unforgiving. "Say what you want about Dad, but at least he was *there.* He fed us and raised us and came to school stuff. He didn't just walk away and never come back.''

''Mom knew he'd never let go of anything that was *his,*'' Renee countered bitterly. ''Whatever he felt, it wasn't love.''

''How do you know?'' Abby snapped. ''Maybe he just didn't know how to express what he felt! Maybe his parents were jerks. Maybe he did the best he could.''

''Oh, yeah, he always was the softest on you,'' Renee jeered. ''It figures you'd defend him.''

''Guys…'' Meg began.

Both sisters turned. Abby was the one to speak. ''But we should have had the choice of whether we wanted to see Mom again. Why didn't you give us that choice, Meg? You, of all people. You knew how much we wondered about her. How much not having her hurt. How could you be just like him?''

Meg tried to explain. Mom had begged her not to tell the younger girls. It was better if they were angry at her, she'd said. Anything was better than her daughters remembering her as a frail extension of the machines that gave her a semblance of life.

''Later, sometime, tell them that I know I was a coward. I should have fought for you. All of you. But I was being crushed.'' Her eyes were huge, pathetic, pleading. ''Sometimes I couldn't breathe. It was like…like running from an avalanche. Your body says run and you do, and then afterwards you worry about the people you were with. Only then it's too late.''

Once she was a parent herself, Meg had remembered and tried to imagine herself running from that avalanche and leaving a child behind. Responding to instinct that said, *Go!* And she had concluded with fierce certainty that a stronger instinct would have had her frantically hunting for her son, throwing her body over his to save him from the crushing weight of snow. She had run once, but to save him; she would never have run if it had meant leaving him.

But she wasn't her mother. Perhaps, for the strength that Jolene Patton had lacked, Meg, Abby and Renee had their father to thank.

Oh, how she hated to be grateful to him for anything.

Meg had tried to convey some of what she knew and felt, but she sensed that her sisters didn't really hear any of it, didn't want to hear it. She was no longer to be trusted. In their opinion, who was she to pass judgment on their mother? Or perhaps they just didn't want to believe that their sainted mother had been flawed.

Renee had calmed down enough to notice the spilled coffee and grab a dish towel from the kitchen to wipe it up.

Then she sat. "Okay, you honored your promise to Mom." Her tone was hard, unforgiving. "How about later? Couldn't you have let us know after the funeral? Told us she was dead? You were okay? Would one phone call have been so tough?"

Meg gazed back at them and remembered herself, eight months' pregnant, walking across the springy grass at the cemetery, leaving behind her mother's open grave. She had let the symbolic handful of dirt trickle from her fingers onto the shiny casket, listened across the vast distance of the open hole in the ground to the minister who had not even known her mother as he mouthed the traditional send-off. She was alone. Completely alone. She wanted desperately to pick up a phone, hear her sister's voices, even her father's. She wanted to buy a bus ticket and go home. She could not bear to be so alone and so frightened.

But inside Will had somersaulted and poked her as if to say, *Don't forget me,* and she had known she couldn't go home. Like it or not, she wasn't really alone. She had a child. Although barely seventeen years old, *she* was the mom now.

If she called her sisters, they would dump their fear, their grief, their longing on her, and her own was almost overwhelming.

Now, facing them after the passage of so many years, she closed her eyes, which felt gritty. If only she could cry. In a voice that felt like shattered glass, she said, "One phone call might have killed me. If you'd begged me to come home…"

"We would have understood," Renee said.

"Would you?" She looked from one to the other, and found no understanding now. How could she have hoped for it then, when they were children? "Think back. What if I'd called and said, 'I found Mom, I just buried her, and I can't come home? If Dad hits you…well, deal.' Would that have comforted you?"

"You could have called regularly." Renee stared at her with dislike. Hatred? "Checked on us. Let us know you were all right."

"I had to cope on my own. Every phone call home would have left me feeling guilty all over again because I couldn't help you. I had to focus everything I had on going forward.''

Abby spoke for both. ''But we were the ones you left behind.''

What more was there to say? What more would there ever be to say? She'd come home fifteen years too late. She'd saved her son by abandoning her sisters. No wonder they couldn't forgive her.

Oh, they were adult enough to lay a veneer over the raw emotion, to pretend that they still loved her, but conversations since that first night had been rocky ground where each foot had to be placed with exquisite care so as not to slice skin and draw blood.

Toward Will, Renee and Abby were warm and welcoming. Daniel Barnard's sister was coming soon for a visit with her young son, which made Will feel as if he even had a cousin.

But he did have first cousins, Meg knew; Renee had told her. Jack's older brother was married. He had two girls, nine and eleven. Jack's mother nudged him often toward marriage, telling him he had to give her grandchildren, too, according to Renee. How would she feel about Will?

Assuming Jack ever told her about the son he hadn't known about.

And that, Meg thought ruefully, was assuming *she* ever told him about the son he *still* didn't know he had.

Which she'd be doing right now if she weren't driving up the mountain loop highway in the dark, instead slowing every time she saw a road turnoff so that she could peer at the small street signs. The highway itself was plowed bare, although snow still lay under the ponderosa pines that became denser as the elevation rose.

She passed the Sunrise Resort, where she could see a lighted ice-skating rink and the aqua glow of a swimming pool with steam rising into the cold night air above it. Another half mile and she at last spotted Sumac Drive. Making a left, Meg followed the road past half a dozen driveways to the end. The number on the mailbox was right.

The driveway curved between pines and manzanita. She drove carefully, following the tracks other vehicles had made. In front of the garage, she set her parking brake and turned off the ignition.

The house was sharp angles and steep roof, glass and window boxes. It reminded her of Alpine villages, although she could see none of the cute shutters or gingerbread that characterized the Swiss chalets. A porch light was on.

She got out, crunched through the snow, and gingerly climbed the steps, shoveled bare but still icy. After ringing the doorbell, Meg didn't have long to wait. The house was too well-insulated for her to hear footsteps; the first she knew was the click of a dead bolt being released. Then the door opened and a large man filled the opening.

He wore cords and a turtleneck; his dark auburn hair was cut severely short. And he was built—six foot two or three, broad-shouldered, with the easy grace of a natural athlete. But it was his face that made her heart give a peculiar little bump. Handsome, she could have resisted. Handsome, she wouldn't have trusted. But, no, his face was like his house, all angles and planes, so bony it might have been homely if the lines weren't so clean and strong.

His eyes were light blue or gray, she couldn't tell; tiny white creases beside them betrayed how often he must squint against the sun.

"Mr. McNeil?" she inquired.

"That's me," he agreed, voice low, deep. He was studying her with as much interest as she was him. Or so she thought, until he said brusquely, "Come in. You're here about the baby?"

"Yes. A little girl, I'm told?"

"That's right." As she stepped across the threshold, he said, "I assume you were told I found her up at Juanita Butte. Right next to my Jeep, as if she'd been left for me. Have you sent anyone up there yet?"

"I'd like to see the baby first," she said levelly. "If you don't mind."

Irritation flickered in his eyes. "And your name is…?"

Embarrassed, she said, "I'm sorry. Deputy Patton. Margaret Patton."

"Patton," he mused. "Any relation to Abby Patton? A firefighter, I think?"

What was this? Twenty questions? Was he dawdling for some reason? "Yes. She's my sister."

"Ah." He frowned at her, seeming to brood over something.

Waiting, Meg felt the stir of an uncomfortable, edgy awareness of him and of their isolation.

McNeil appeared to make up his mind. His decision did nothing to soothe her disquiet.

He nodded into the depths of the dimly lit house. "The baby's in my bedroom."

Come in, said the spider to the fly.

Meg hesitated only a second, then followed at a wary distance.

CHAPTER THREE

LEADING THE WAY across the tiled entry, Scott was disconcerted by the second odd turn his evening had taken.

She was damned pretty, this policewoman. Pretty, hell. She was sexy. Blond, blue-eyed, with a rich, full mouth. Long legs beneath an olive-green county sheriff's department parka that hid her curves. His first reaction to her had been an uncomfortable one.

Good God, Scott thought in horror. He wasn't a horny adolescent anymore. He *never* got turned on like this, at first sight.

It was having a baby in the house, he told himself. That had taken him back to another time, another life. A time when he'd had a pretty, blond wife and thought it would last forever. What he was having now was...hell, a flashback was a good way to think of it. This woman just reminded him of Penny.

He glanced back as he switched on the hall light, only to have his theory blown to smithereens. Except for the superficial resemblance because of coloring, the policewoman didn't really look like his ex-wife. Her face was more interesting than sweet, her eyes too guarded.

He saw that she was keeping a wary distance, which riled him plenty. You called a cop, and they immediately assumed you were some kind of crazed murderer?

The door stood ajar. He pushed it open further, until the ribbon of light fell across the maple floor and touched the sleeping infant.

"Smart place to put her," the officer murmured, and brushed past him, crouching as he had to look down at the little girl. After a moment she rose and came back to his side, nodding.

He eased the door partially shut again and led her to the living room. "Here's her clothes. There's nothing to identify her, but if you want to look…"

She did. She examined each piece thoroughly, probing pockets on the snowsuit and overalls, even running her finger inside the mittens.

"Okay," she said at last. "Where's the car seat?"

"I'll get it." He straightened from where he'd been half sitting on the arm of the couch. "It's still buckled in my Jeep."

"I hope you had on gloves when you handled it."

Fingerprints. Now, there was an idea. "Yeah. I'll put them on again."

"Don't touch it anywhere you normally would."

"Yeah, I get it," he agreed.

Her head was still bent over the clothes when he returned. Barely glancing up, she asked, "This was all she was wearing?"

"She still has on a turtleneck and undershirt. And little booties." He rubbed his jaw as he envisioned the layers as he'd removed them. "Knit by hand, I think. Uh…mittens. But you saw them."

"Diaper?"

"Paper. Pink. Sopping wet. She hadn't been

changed for hours, it looked like. Diaper's still in the kitchen garbage, if you want to see it.''

Her sharp glance told him she recognized a dig when she heard it. ''Thank you, but that's not necessary.''

After he'd set down the car seat, she went over it as carefully, tipping it forward with one finger on an edge, but it had no name on the back, no phone number, no convenient note saying, ''Return to 313 Main Street.''

Finally sinking back on her heels, she stared into space for a long moment. ''Odd,'' she concluded.

''No kidding.''

''A doctor should look at her. She might have frostbite.''

He shook his head. ''No. She's fine. I'll bet she hadn't been out there five minutes.''

''If you're not a medical expert…''

''I manage the ski area. We know frostbite when we see it.''

She dipped her head, conceding the point. ''All right. Tell me exactly where you found her.''

He described the spot, telling her he'd taken a quick detour through the mile-long parking lot that bordered the highway. ''I've already called my security people to tell them what happened, have them keep an eye out for anything unusual.''

''I'll drive on up there, anyway,'' she said. ''It may be hard to tell much before daylight, but I might as well try, just in case it snows.''

''It won't.''

She opened her mouth, then closed it, evidently realizing that he had better sources than the daily paper with its little drawings of sunshine, clouds and snowflakes.

"It's damned cold out there," he said, the words just coming. "Sometimes I spend the night at the lodge. I have a cot. If I hadn't decided to come home…"

Their eyes met in mutual horror.

"How could somebody just leave her?" Deputy Patton said. Asked. But she wasn't really asking; no one with any conscience could have given a reasonable answer.

Unless…

"She was safer there than wherever her mother or father was going," Scott said slowly.

Her nostrils flared, like an animal catching an alarming scent. "How many people work at the ski area?"

"You're suggesting one of them deserted his kid?" Instinctively he shook ·his head. "I can't imagine…"

"Somebody did. You said yourself it was as if she'd been left for you. Your employees seem likeliest to assume you'd come out and find her."

He felt sick at the idea. How could somebody have taken that kind of chance?

Making himself consider it, Scott said, "There are two lodges. Eleven lifts. A ski shop. Rental shop. Food services. Instructors, snow removal, mechanical… Over a thousand people work at Juanita Butte. This is Monday, our slowest. No night skiing. Maybe half of those wouldn't have been working. Almost everyone had gone home a couple hours before I did."

Surprise showed in her eyes; she hadn't realized skiing was quite that big a business.

"You're sure you've never seen this child before?"

"Positive."

"Do you know anyone with one this age? Maybe someone who's showed you pictures, talked about her...?" She spread her hands.

"I don't think so." He'd have tuned out if someone had. Pretended to look at the picture. But he didn't remember having to do that recently.

"Okay," she said, rising to her feet. "It's somewhere to start. I'm going to head on up there now. I hope you don't mind waiting up for me. I'll collect her—" she nodded in the direction of the bedroom "—on my way back down."

Voice rough, he said, "Drive carefully. The road's slippery tonight. I'll put on some coffee."

"I can taste it already." She gave him a quick, rueful smile. "I'm not used to this climate yet."

He hoped she was used to driving snowy roads.

More waiting. He'd never been very good at it. He was a man who preferred to take charge. Not being able to do anything useful drove him crazy.

He had another look-in at the baby, as sound asleep as ever. He put on the coffee. Paced. Went back to the newspaper but found he didn't give a damn about the high school basketball team or the city council's debate about zoning. Half an hour passed. Forty-five minutes.

Finally, in desperation, Scott grabbed a pencil and went to work on the crossword puzzle. He was three-quarters done, his scrawl near illegible, when the doorbell rang.

The policewoman didn't wait for an invitation this time. She scooted in, shivering, her cheeks rosy red.

"I need new long johns!"

"It's only January. In this country, that means a lot of winter left."

"I just came from Southern California."

"Ah." He wanted to ask her personal questions, but a driving need overcame his casual curiosity. "Did you find out anything?"

She shook her head. "Met your security people. Neither of them saw anything, which isn't surprising because they weren't around."

"Not around?" Scott echoed sharply.

"One had been down at the other lodge during the half hour before you left tonight, and the other was inside warming up."

He grunted.

"We're not going to be able to isolate any tire tracks with the parking lot frozen so solid," she continued, reaching for her zipper. "That coffee ready?"

"Sure. Hang up your jacket." A Danish oil-finished coat tree stood in the slate-floored entry. A couple of jackets were already heaped on it.

He left her shrugging out of her parka and went into the kitchen. By the time she got there he'd taken cream from the refrigerator and a sugar bowl from the cupboard.

She used both. He took his coffee black. She perched on a wrought-iron stool pulled up to the eating bar, he leaned back against the counter. They looked at each other in silence that shivered with awareness having nothing to do with the baby in the bedroom.

Okay, he thought. *Why not?*

"What's your name?" Scott asked. "I mean, what do friends call you? Margaret?"

"Meg." A faint smile. "No shortcut to Scott, is there?"

"Nope." He didn't want to talk about himself. "Why were you in Southern California?"

"I was career Army. An MP." She looked down at her steaming mug. "I just hung it up, came home to Elk Springs."

"How long ago?"

This smile was wry. "Thursday. Today was my first day of work." On her easily read face, the collage of expressions was amusing. "Which isn't to say," she added, "that I don't know what I'm doing. I was hired because of my experience."

"I assumed that." He kept his voice grave. "I don't suppose policing an Army base is any different than doing the same thing here."

"Not much." The policewoman—Meg—shrugged. "In fact, I get the impression things are tamer here. Some of the Army bases are pretty tough territory. I investigated an ugly series of rapes last year."

"Why'd you come home?"

Those crystalline-blue eyes contemplated him. "You're nosy."

He could think of a couple of ways to answer that. Chose one. "Are you curious about me?"

She nibbled on that luscious lower lip. "Maybe," she conceded.

"So?"

Her answer was blunt. "I heard my father was dead. He was why I'd stayed away."

"Ed Patton?"

"Yep."

Scott made a noncommittal noise in the back of his throat. Interesting. Already he wanted to know more, but he was reasonably sure she wouldn't answer right now. Not yet.

"Married?" he asked.

"No." Her gaze challenged him. "You?"

"Divorced. Kids?"

"I have a teenage son. You?"

"None." He'd gotten used to saying that as if it were the entire truth, as if the emptiness of it didn't matter.

"But you knew what to buy for her." Meg nodded toward the bedroom.

He looked away. "How hard is it?"

She accepted his nonanswer, but he was aware of speculation in her eyes. She was a cop, all right, with the sixth sense to let her know he was hiding something.

Well, let her wonder.

"What will you do now?" he asked. "About locating her parents?"

"Check into missing babies." She anticipated his questions. "There aren't any locally. Believe me, we'd be looking hard if there were. But, shoot, someone could have driven over from Portland, or down from Washington..."

"And then dumped her at night up on the mountain?"

"I didn't say it made sense."

"No." He scrubbed a hand over his face in frustration. "Have you found a place for her yet?"

"Not my department." She sipped her coffee.

"Don't worry. They'll come up with a receiving home."

"I wasn't worried." The idea of the poor kid being dragged back out into the night disturbed him. "I don't mind having her here. My housekeeper is coming in the morning to take care of her."

He'd called Marjorie right after talking to the police dispatcher earlier. Shocked and indignant when he explained how he'd found the baby, she professed delight at coming to his rescue. Or at the idea of playing grandma for the day, he wasn't sure which.

"I'll call if they take her away before then," he'd said. "I just thought, since she's comfortable now, and I've read that they never have enough foster homes…" Feeling like an idiot, he'd trailed off. If he babbled on, Marjorie would be thinking he wanted to keep this baby.

"Well, we'll take good care of her," his fiftyish housekeeper had said firmly. "Until they find her mother."

Assuming they did. Or that it wasn't her mother—or father—who'd left her out there in the dark parking lot on a freezing-cold night.

Meg Patton looked thoughtful. "We're pretty short of receiving homes right now, I'm told. Did you read about that mess over in Milton?"

"Mess?"

"This couple had been featured nationally for providing a home to so many unwanted children. They just kept adopting them. I'm told an allegation of abuse was received six weeks or so ago. Last Wednesday, the children were all taken away from the adoptive parents. Twelve of them were under three. Our system isn't designed to take that kind of onslaught.''

''I did read about it.'' But skimming was all he'd let himself do. Had the parents really been well-meaning? he'd wondered. The children in diapers had rashes so bad they looked like bedsores, according to an anonymous source. Scott didn't like reading about things like that. How could you be lucky enough to have a little boy or girl who trusted you, then be so neglectful? The article had concluded that the county was going to be pressed for foster homes to accommodate these children, ranging in age from three months to twelve years. That article was where he'd gotten the idea, he realized now.

''You know,'' he said, ''she's fine here. I mean it. She can stay for a while.''

''You'd have to get licensed.''

''I don't mind.'' Was he nuts? he wondered incredulously. How would a baby fit into his twelve-fifteen-hour workdays? Marjorie wouldn't be able to stay that long; she had a husband and a home of her own.

''Well, then,'' Meg said, setting down her empty coffee cup, ''a social worker will be contacting you in the morning. They'll want to interview you and your housekeeper. If you've changed your mind by then, we'll find someplace for her.''

He saw her to the door, watched her bundle up and take the child's seat in an awkward grip presumably meant to avoid smudging any prints. ''Will I see you in the morning, too?''

''Yep. I'm going to want to talk to employees.

Starting with supervisory personnel. I assume I should get up there well before the lifts open?''

"You might want to go as early as seven.''

Thanks to his big mouth, *he* would be home baby-sitting. Damn it, he ought to be there; those were his people, the ski area was his responsibility. The little girl was not.

Trouble was, he seemed to have been elected.

Meg nodded at the time he'd suggested. "If I see any reason, I might co-opt the ski patrol to mount a search.''

"That's what they're there for.'' That, and reining in stupidity. He held open the door for her.

She hesitated, finally coming out with, "Good night, Mr. McNeil.''

His surname almost stuck in her throat. Well, good. That meant she'd wanted to call him by his first name.

"I'll see you tomorrow, Deputy Patton.'' He emphasized her title. "Take care.''

"I *can* drive.'' The note of acerbity in her voice was probably not aroused by anything he'd actually said.

"I'm sure you can,'' he soothed.

Heading out the door and down the porch steps, she chose not to respond. He watched her go without pushing for a dinner date or any other kind of step toward a personal relationship he wasn't sure he wanted, however intriguing and appealing a woman she was.

Time for him to get to bed. He needed his rest in preparation for those middle-of-the night feedings he had a strong forboding were going to be his lot.

He could see it now: just him and the baby, a

still, dark house around them, and memories of other nights, of another trusting, warm child, long since cold in the frozen ground.

Scott's face contorted and he swore softly. He was a goddamned fool, setting himself up like this.

But he would still comfort her when she awakened, cuddle her close, walk with her if he had to, sing lullabies.

And he would not cry when he laid her back to sleep.

"SIX-MONTH-OLD BABY." The ski area Chief of Operations frowned. "Nobody that I know of has one." He sounded unapologetic. "The kids that sign on here are too young."

Meg had borrowed Scott McNeil's office today—after all, *he* hadn't needed it this morning—and interviewed dozens of employees, mostly supervisors, but also a random selection of lift operators, mechanics, ski instructors and cooks.

Five minutes ago, Mark Robillard had stuck his head in and said, "You wanted to see me?"

He hadn't offered anything she hadn't heard a dozen times already.

Although his manner thus far had been dour, enthusiasm sparked when she asked if he had children of his own. "You bet," he agreed, whipping out his wallet and displaying school pictures of a second-grade girl and a boy in fourth, both well-scrubbed, cheerful and earnest. The boy could have been Will or any of his friends at that age. Those annual fall school portraits had a sameness that was strangely reassuring.

Meg repressed a sigh, asked further about the people who worked directly under Mark at Juanita Butte, and then thanked him for his time.

He wished her luck and left, one of the rare workers here—underling or supervisory—who wasn't a tanned Nordic god or goddess. Medium height, whipcord lean, Mark Robillard did have the weathered look of a man who spent time out of doors. She'd have thought him harsh and verging on uncooperative if he hadn't warmed at the mention of his children. Or, heck, maybe the man was just too busy to waste time gossiping about a young woman he wouldn't have had any reason to know well.

Frustrated, Meg picked up her list and leaned back in the desk chair, studying it.

She hadn't learned a thing. Not from the head honchos like Mark Robillard, not from the random selection of underlings she'd chosen. Just before him, she'd talked to a fresh-faced, nineteen-year-old girl who worked in the rental shop.

Neither of them knew any more than did the… fifty-two other people she'd interviewed, which included the heads of food services, building maintenance, snow removal and marketing. Nobody had an infant daughter or knew anything about anyone who did. Which would seem highly improbable, except for the fact that about ninety percent of the workers here were in their early twenties and unmarried. They worked so they could ski, she had heard. Over and over. They didn't mind the seasonal nature of the work. Summers, some of them headed for the beach, surfed, lifeguarded; others stayed around town, waiting tables or working the dude ranch or river-rafting gigs waiting for snow to fall.

These were not people ready to settle down and have children.

Suppose, Meg thought, staring into space, one of these young women had gotten pregnant and had the baby—say, because of moral objections to abortion. Or the mother of the baby had dumped it on one of the guys who lived this nomadic existence. The change in life-style would have been drastic. So drastic he or she would have abandoned the baby?

At the moment this particular scenario was Meg's front runner. In part she liked it because of Scott McNeil's involvement. He seemed solid and trustworthy, a man you knew would take care of any problem. Leaving the baby next to his car made sense.

Meg muttered a mild profanity, all she allowed herself so that she didn't slip in front of Will.

Leaving the kid there made sense—except for one little problem. Scott claimed everyone who worked at Juanita Butte knew he bunked down in the lodge sometimes. Once or twice a week, he said. He'd thought about it last night.

Whoever had left the baby had taken an enormous chance.

Unless he—or she—had been lurking to make sure Scott did find her.

But then, why hadn't he spotted another vehicle? Why hadn't the security men seen anyone?

This was a big place, Meg reminded herself. Forest Service roads ran like spiderwebs through these woods, used by logging trucks, hikers and fishermen in the summer. None of them was plowed during the winter, but that didn't seem to stop what looked like regular traffic from the tracks she'd noticed on her way up the mountain that morning. Cross-country skiers drove in half a mile, parked and skied into the silent wilderness. Families who just wanted to take the kids sledding did the same. Snowmobilers had their favorite roads.

Whoever abandoned the baby could have headed down the mountain, turned into the first logging road and waited for Scott's Jeep to pass. If it didn't, he or she could go back.

Okay, that worked, Meg told herself. It was cold-blooded as all get-out, but it worked. Now all she had to do was figure out which of these tanned youths with gleaming white teeth and an aura of joy had done such a thing.

She rubbed the back of her neck, then rotated her head a few times. Maybe she'd forget it for the day; after not getting much sleep last night, she'd been here since seven this morning, and her butt and her mind were both going numb. Overwork induced paranoia, which might be why this crawly feeling of apprehension kept raising goose bumps on her arms. She smelled something worse than child abandonment in this case, something…evil.

Meg made a disgusted sound. For crying out loud! Yeah, cops were given to hunches. But only some of them turned out to be right. She had nothing to go on, no reason to think that baby's mother was in trouble or dead.

Nothing but the way a shiver walked down her spine.

To distract herself, she glanced around. The office was remarkably spare, with one window overlooking the ski area, the only personal touch an extraordinary Northwest Coast Indian mask depicting a bear with its mouth open in a snarl. Beyond that, the walls were bare but for an enormous whiteboard calendar covered with scrawled notes. The piles of paperwork were meticulously organized in cubbies and the computer desk was clean. Meg wrinkled her nose, comparing it to what her own desk would look like once she'd occupied it for more than a few weeks.

But if you were going to run a business on the scale of this ski area, maybe you couldn't afford to misplace notes or file something wrong.

Truthfully, she'd had no idea a ski area was a huge operation. Juanita Butte was now officially the largest single employer in Butte County, she'd learned. When Scott came in to work at ten or so that morning, she'd asked a few questions.

Looking faintly amused, he had answered willingly enough. She'd known they groomed the slopes, but not that the grooming machines cost between $170,000 and 200,000 each. And a heck of a lot besides skiing and boarding went on here. Building maintenance alone was a big department. The mechanics department had to keep more than sixty vehicles running. Marketing, strategic planning, ticket sales, rentals... For Pete's sake, they employed two hundred instructors alone!

The numbers boggled the mind. But the one that had really stuck was liability insurance: $400,000 a year.

"Mostly," Scott had growled, "because we get too many reckless fools on the slopes. They ski too fast, they won't stay inside the marked areas, they get drunk, they try to do jumps or flips because they saw it on TV and they figure it's easy..." He shook his head. "They break their idiot necks or they clobber some poor woman stemming her way down the hill. Or they disappear over the ridge and we have to mount a two-day search and bring the poor bastard in with frostbite and a broken leg."

Although she sympathized—she felt the same way about idiot drivers—she couldn't resist challenging him. "Come on, didn't you get into this because you were a skier? You can't tell me you came down the hill like an old lady when you were eighteen and cocky."

"What makes you think I was ever either?"

She'd grinned. "It's a natural progression."

It was the first time she'd seen him smile. His mouth didn't do that much, just twitched at one corner, deepening a groove in that cheek. The smile was all in his eyes, which held a world of laughter and kindness and mischief.

He'd taken her breath away.

Again.

By the time she'd left his place last night, she'd caught herself mumbling an incoherent prayer that this incredibly sexy man not be a criminal. Or involved with a woman, please.

This from someone with no interest whatsoever in becoming involved herself. A new man, a new job and a teenage son didn't mix.

And then there was her reluctant admission to herself that she seemed able to handle only one emotional issue at a time. She couldn't even deal with calling Johnny Murray. She sure as heck wasn't going to start dating. However tempting Scott McNeil's smile, however honestly he'd expressed an interest in her last night.

She just wished she could be sure there wasn't too good a reason that he'd been the one to find that baby.

Like, for example, he was her father.

But why would he have called 9-1-1 if the baby was his, even if he didn't want to be saddled with her?

Another part that didn't make sense. Meg sighed and stretched again. When someone knocked on the door, she called, "It's open."

"Hi." Abby stuck her head inside. "I heard you were here. Busy?"

Taken by surprise, Meg quit scrabbling for her notes. "No. Not right now. Just thinking. What on earth are you doing here?"

Her sister slipped in and closed the door behind her. "Skiing. What else?"

Sexy in a stretchy bodysuit, she wore her shoulder-length blond hair in a perky ponytail. The bulky boots just made her legs look longer and slimmer than ever. Cheeks pink from the cold, eyes sparkling, she'd stepped right out of an ad for the sport.

Meg felt old just looking at her little sister.

"But don't you have to work?" Meg asked.

Abby slouched bonelessly in the extra chair. "We've gone to ten-hour shifts at the fire department. I work Sunday/Monday and Wednesday/Thursday. Leaves me lots of time to ski." Her smile was catlike in its smugness.

"I can see that it would," Meg said wryly. "Jeez, you look just like everyone else up here."

"Meaning?"

"Young, tanned, fit, irresponsible."

Her sister arched a brow. "I could take offense at that."

"None intended." Meg grimaced. "You know why I'm here?"

Abby propped one booted foot on the other. "Nope. You've got everyone buzzing out there. A cop's here, she's asking everyone about babies. Can you tell me what it's about?"

Why not? From Scott's discovery of the baby to Meg's ungrounded disquiet took about five minutes.

Abby gave her a disconcertingly sharp look. "You just don't want to think anyone could abandon their own kid."

So, they were going to get personal. "No," Meg said evenly, "I didn't say that. Babies are abandoned all the time. But usually not under such dangerous circumstances."

"I read just the other day about a newborn someone had tried to bury alive."

"Newborns are a different story." How did you explain instinctive understanding to someone who'd never had a child of her own? "Those are usually left by young girls who panic. The baby isn't real to them. It's just a disaster. They think if they can get rid of it, they can go on as if the whole thing never happened."

Abby's expression was exaggeratedly patient. "Isn't that what probably happened here?"

"It's different with kids even a few weeks old. People care, at least enough to abandon the child somewhere safe. At Grandma's, at the baby-sitter's, at a neighbor's. Sometimes they have to work their way up to the complete severing of ties. They'll leave the child for a few days, then come back. Do it again, maybe stay away longer. Until finally one time they don't come back.''

"You're saying no parent ever dumps a kid someplace that might not be completely safe?'' Abby didn't bother hiding her skepticism.

"I didn't say 'never.' Just rarely. This time doesn't settle with me.''

Abby gave an unconcerned shrug. "What I'm saying is, don't let your personal feelings about a parent walking out on her kids warp your perception.''

Annoyance edged Meg's voice. "What makes you think I am? You and Renee are the ones still hot and bothered by Mom leaving us.''

Abby should have been ticked. Meg was vaguely shocked when she only gave another of those bored, nonchalant shrugs. "Renee is. I'm not. I hardly remember Mom. And Dad wasn't that bad. Renee rubbed him the wrong way. I swear she *tried*.''

Meg said cautiously, "But you were mad the other night, too.''

"I was mad at *you*. You should have let us in on the secret. That's all.'' She sounded so indifferent. As if Meg's disclosures had been mildly interesting, possibly a little irritating, but basically no big deal.

Now Meg had something else to feel unsettled about.

"Do you miss Dad?'' she asked.

"Miss him?'' Abby sounded surprised. "Not especially. It wasn't like we were buddies. I got along with him okay, that's all. I mean, you just had to know how to get around him. I'd try to tell Renee, but she wouldn't listen.''

"Maybe she had too much pride to 'get around him.'"

"Oh, pride." Abby rose lithely. "Why make life rougher than it has to be?"

"Because he was a bastard," Meg said harshly. "Because I'd rather feel the back of his hand any day than knuckle under."

"I thought we were talking about Renee."

"She and I have something in common."

"Yeah, you're both bullheaded." Malicious amusement glinted in Abby's eyes. "Maybe you got that from him."

Meg began hotly, "I didn't get anything from…" Remembering yesterday's meditations, she had to stop. Bullheadedness and pride and strength of character all went hand in hand. Their mother hadn't possessed a one of them. Once again, Meg had to overcome her revulsion to concede that maybe she did have something to thank Ed Patton for.

Her sister watched her mockingly. Meg couldn't help thinking that, despite the loss of their mother early, life had come too easily to Abby, the baby of the family. With her looks and brains, her run of luck might continue. But it was also possible that one of these days she'd butt up against someone who couldn't be wound around her little finger, and then she might discover pride was a more reliable prop than tears or wheedling smiles.

Meg was ashamed to discover that she almost hoped so.

"Well, I'll leave you to your business," Abby said. Her eyes met Meg's, and for a moment they held genuine caring. "I hope you're wrong. About the baby's mother. I hope the little girl was kidnapped, and someone is dying to welcome her home.''

Meg tried to smile. ''Yeah. I hope so, too.''

But when her sister was gone, Meg couldn't help wishing Abby had chosen a better turn of phrase. Someone dying was exactly what had Meg worried.

CHAPTER FOUR

WILL WAS ONE OF THE FIRST to burst out the front door of the school after the bell rang. *He* had nothing to hang around for.

He'd been okay with the idea of the move; hey, he'd moved every few years all his life. Everyone he knew did. What was different this time was that the other kids in this school weren't used to newcomers. It wasn't like a high school near a base, where three-quarters of the students were Army brats.

Most of the other freshman boys were just ignoring him. A bunch of the girls weren't, and he almost wished they would. He liked looking, but he wasn't ready to go out with one. He'd rather hang with his buddies. If he had any.

"Hey, Will!" a girl called from behind him.

He pretended he didn't hear. Jenna Marsh and that dinky friend of hers—Erika, yeah, that was it—they just didn't get the message.

Shoving his hands into the pockets of his parka, Will thought, *and I don't like the cold, either.* He walked faster, hearing some giggles behind him. School had let out at 2:20, and yesterday he'd gone straight home. Today he had other plans.

Will gave a hunted look over his shoulder. It

wasn't just Jenna and Erika; a whole pack of girls trailed him, and they were getting closer.

Reaching the corner, he turned and broke into a run. He hit the next corner and went around it before they appeared. After that he slowed down. He was pretty sure they wouldn't go so far as to track him; they had to pretend whichever way he went was the way they were really going.

What he'd decided to do was visit Aunt Renee at the police station. He wouldn't talk to his father or anything, because that would make Mom mad, but she hadn't said he couldn't go there at all. Like, to see Aunt Renee's office, ask if she'd let him ride along with her sometime. And if he just happened to catch a glimpse of his father... Well, it wasn't like he'd know who Will was, anyway.

Mom said she needed to talk to Will's father first. Only, she kept saying that, but she didn't do it. She had all kinds of excuses, but they'd been in Elk Springs practically a week, and she *still* hadn't called him. All Will wanted was just to *see* his dad. Just to know what he looked like.

Will stopped across the street from the red brick public safety building. His father was probably inside it. Weird.

The red Don't Walk hand stopped him, even though there was no traffic.

He had trouble believing he was going to meet his own, real father. Aunt Renee said they looked alike. Most kids were used to people saying they looked like their mom or dad. But Will had never gotten that, because nobody would even guess he and Mom were related. He'd always thought maybe he'd inherited his dark hair and eyes and the shape of his face from his grandfather or grandmother. Mom didn't have any pictures of her father. But Aunt Renee did, and now he could see that nothing about him was from the Pattons.

He was a Murray.

Aunt Renee knew Jack Murray really well. She said his mom and dad were still alive, and that he had a brother who had two girls. But Will's father wasn't married, and he didn't have any other kids.

Will had tried to hide how he felt when Renee said that, about his dad not being married. Had he been, like, waiting for Will's mom all these years? *She* hadn't married anyone else, either.

But Will didn't let himself think too far ahead.

Instead he wondered: once his father knew about Will, would he tell his family? Will tried to convince himself he didn't care that much; he and Mom were fine by themselves, weren't they? But he knew the truth. He did care. It would feel really crummy to have his own father not want to bother with him. And those were the only grandparents he'd ever have.

The light turned green. Again. Will didn't move.

Maybe this was a dumb idea. Maybe he should wait, the way Mom wanted him to.

But what could it hurt, just to see what his father looked like? Aunt Renee would understand.

His feet were moving, he discovered, even though the Walk sign had been replaced again by the red hand. Nobody was going to run out of the police station to ticket him. With the snowy streets, what cars were out were driving real slow.

He walked in the front doors and asked the desk

sergeant if Aunt Renee was in. The guy sent him back.

"Third door on the right," he said, holding open that swinging gate at the end of the counter.

Will went. He passed a couple uniformed cops and stole peeks in the offices he passed. Nobody looked like his father.

"Will!" Aunt Renee said when he appeared. She tapped a key and her computer screen went dark. "Is something wrong?"

"Nah." He shrugged, trying to look cool. "I just thought I'd stop by. See where you work. I don't have any friends to hang with yet. It's kinda boring with Mom working. You know?"

She rose to her feet. "Yes, but I'm not sure this is the best place for you. Your mom hasn't called Jack yet, has she?"

"She didn't get home till really late last night," he said. "Somebody found a baby, and she went to check it out. And then she left even before me this morning."

Single-minded, Aunt Renee stuck to the point. "I just think your father should have some warning before he comes face-to-face with you."

"I didn't think he'd even be here."

The lift of her eyebrow told him she knew a fib when she heard one. "He's here," she said, sounding grim. "It's not that I mind having you visit. Normally that would be great. But let's wait until the fireworks are over, okay?"

"But why would he even know who I am?" Will said stubbornly.

"Oh, he'll know." She gripped his arm and steered him out of the office. "Go home, Will."

Another woman cop hailed them in the hall. "Renee! Is this your nephew?" Her voice seemed awfully loud.

"Yes," Aunt Renee said tightly. "But he has to go home now. I'll give him the grand tour another day."

Behind her another uniformed officer appeared in a doorway. A big, dark man, his eyes met Will's, and Will felt icy cold and then hot like when he'd had the flu. On the man's face was pure shock. The moment seemed to stretch on forever. Will was vaguely conscious of Aunt Renee turning, of curious looks from the other woman, but all he really clearly saw was his father, who backed up and quietly closed his office door.

"Oh, jeez," Aunt Renee whispered.

Will swallowed. "I gotta go," he blurted, and stumbled backward.

"Here." Aunt Renee took his arm again. "You can go out this way."

He let her propel him toward the back. The hall took a turn and ended up at a gray steel door that led out to a plowed parking lot where some police cars were parked in a line.

"I'm sorry," he said, giving his aunt a desperate look.

He expected her to be mad, but her smile comforted him. "Don't worry. I wouldn't have chosen to do it this way, but your mother shouldn't have procrastinated, either. Jack's a nice guy. Really. It'll be all right."

He felt shaky, dizzy. He knew he'd done something terrible. "I wish I hadn't come."

"Don't worry," she said again. "Just go home. I'll lie and tell your mom it was my fault."

He couldn't let her do that. "No. She already thinks you're mad at her. I'll tell her the truth."

Aunt Renee got a quizzical expression on her face, but he was walking away backward. "I gotta go," he said again, and turned around.

Her voice floated after him. "'Bye, Will."

When he heard the steel door shut, he stopped and closed his eyes, trying to slow his racing heartbeat. Mom was going to be so ticked. And his father…his father would *hate* him! Surprising him in front of other people had been so stupid!

It must have been a minute or more before he calmed himself enough to start trudging across the parking lot. Gol, Mom was going to kill him. He was dumb, dumb, dumb…

The back door of the police station opened again, and his heart jerked. He really, really, didn't want to look, even though it wouldn't be—couldn't be…

"Will." Only a cop could make one word—a name—into a command. The voice was deep, male.

Will stopped, cheeks flushing again. He swallowed, turned… And faced the total stranger who happened to be his biological father.

"You didn't have to run away."

Without thinking, Will blurted the truth. "Mom'll be mad at me."

The eyes narrowed a flicker. "She wants you to stay away from me?"

"She said she should talk to you first." His voice squeaked in the middle, making Will angry. Just when he needed to act cool.

"I see." Unreadably, the man continued to study him. "But you didn't agree."

Will hunched his shoulders, feeling his cheeks burn. "I was just curious. And I wanted to visit Aunt Renee."

Jack Murray bent his head in acknowledgment. "I'll wait to hear from your mother." He didn't sound as if he was going to be especially friendly to her.

"Why did you come out?" Will asked daringly.

"Maybe I was curious, too." His father scrutinized him. "What's she told you about me?"

"That you're my father. That you never knew she was pregnant."

"Did she say why..." He stopped, shaking his head. "Never mind. That's between your mother and me."

Will answered anyway. "She said you were just kids. That you couldn't have helped her. And she was scared of her father."

A muscle jerked in Jack Murray's cheek. "I won't argue about any of that. Except the part about not helping. I wouldn't have abandoned her."

Will didn't know what to say.

"How do you feel about this?"

"I just wanted to know what you were like. That's all."

He wished that were the truth, but it wasn't. He had all these dumb dreams of having a father who took him fishing and came to his basketball games and talked to him about girls. He'd seen some of his friends with their dads. But those fathers had been there all along. They weren't men whose girlfriends had never told them they even had a son.

"Fair enough," Jack Murray said.

What did that mean? Will swallowed. "You believe I'm your son?"

His father got this weird expression on his face. "All I had to do was set eyes on you."

Will nodded. It was true. He wondered why Mom had never told him. He hadn't believed her when she said she'd forgotten what his father looked like. How could you? Unless you tried really hard to forget.

And why would she do that? It was one of the mysteries Will was determined to solve.

"It's cold out here. You'd better get on home."

Will shoved his hands into his pockets. "Um. I shouldn't have come today. I mean, like this." He struggled for words. "So you had to find out about me in front of other people. I'm...well, I'm sorry."

His father half smiled. "Your mom and I'll talk soon."

"Do you need my phone number?" Will began eagerly, starting back.

A lifted hand stopped him. "I'll get it from Renee. Now, scoot."

Will backed up. "Okay. Uh...'bye."

His father waved and went back inside. Will turned and ran, part of him scared at what he'd done, part feeling as high as if he'd sunk a three-pointer to win a championship game.

Maybe he didn't have that dream father. But at least he did *have* a father. He didn't seem like that bad a guy.

And he wasn't married.

Will leaped into the air and slam-dunked an invisible basketball. This might turn out cool. Really cool.

MEG'S NEXT VISITOR was Scott McNeil.

"Wanting your office back?" she asked.

He sat on the corner of the desk, and she couldn't resist a quick peek at the way the stretch fabric of his ski pants outlined the long, powerful muscles in his thigh.

When her gaze lifted, his eyebrows had a quirk that suggested he'd seen her looking. "Find out anything?" he asked.

She chose to assume he was talking about her investigation and not her perusal of his physique.

"No." Meg sighed. "They're all so...young."

The twitch of his mouth quickened her pulse. "You must have had your son when you were at least that young."

"Seventeen," Meg admitted.

"Tough," he said without expression.

"Yes, it was." She had a flash of memory, herself hardly more than a child yet so fiercely protective of the vulnerable baby she held.

The little girl he'd found had been dressed with such loving care. Would a woman do that, and then just leave her tiny daughter in a frozen parking lot on a bitterly cold night? Would a father do that any more than a mother?

The squirrely sensation drove her to her feet, set her to moving restlessly. "I have a bad feeling about this," she said. "The ski patrol did the sweep I requested?"

"And didn't find a thing." He followed her to the window.

Volcanic in origin, Juanita Butte was smaller than Bachelor or Mt. Hood, but shared their conical form, ideal for skiing. Four lifts started here, and another three half a mile away by the East Lodge. Above them, still others rose toward the summit. From here, Meg could see the ticket booths, people heading down toward the parking lots, the lift lines— short on a Tuesday afternoon—and skiers and snowboarders enjoying the meticulously groomed slopes above. It was all innocent and fun.

If you didn't think about that massive liability insurance. Or the baby abandoned last night.

"What did you expect them to find?" Scott asked.

Meg started. She'd almost forgotten he stood at her shoulder.

"Expect is too strong a word," she said reluctantly. "I just can't help wondering…"

"What do you *wonder* if you'll find?"

"The baby's mother." She turned to face him. "Dead."

His expression was first surprised, then perturbed. "What makes you think that?"

"The baby's clothes. Everything was clean, reasonably new, cute. Coordinated. She looked…loved."

"Nice clothes don't equal love."

"No, I know that. I just…" She focused on the scene outside the window abruptly, alarm quickening her voice. "Did I just see a snowflake?"

He stared out, too. Another tiny white flake floated past the window. Then another. "I'm afraid so. We're expecting four or five inches tonight."

"If there are tracks anywhere, they'll be gone."

"We've looked." He faced her. "What do you have in mind?"

"I was just thinking about those Forest Service roads." Grabbing her list and notes, she headed for the door. "I'm checking some of them out."

"Do you have experience driving under that kind of condition? Those roads aren't plowed."

"I'll manage," she snapped.

"You could get stuck."

Impatient, she whirled back. "Well, what do you suggest? They'll be buried by tomorrow."

Buried. Another unfortunate choice of words.

"If a woman was dumped, too, she's dead," he said quietly. "You know how cold it was last night."

"If she was dressed warmly enough..."

"Then why not leave her in the parking lot, too?"

"Because she could have called for help." *Weak.* His huff of breath might have been a snort.

"I'm going to look. I have snow tires and four-wheel drive."

"Will you let me come?"

"You mean, drive?"

He didn't say anything, just waited.

She thought quickly. His presence might compromise a crime scene. She worried about his motives in wanting to go with her. On the other hand, Meg wasn't anxious to find herself stranded a mile up a deserted logging road with snow falling and night coming.

Yeah, Meg mocked herself, *you'd rather be stranded with him, wouldn't you?*

"Fine," she said ungraciously, then tried to improve on it. "Thank you."

They took his Jeep Cherokee. "Which way?" he asked as he backed out.

"Towards town," she decided. "Isn't the road closed for the winter a few miles farther on? Would he have wanted to backtrack?"

"Maybe not, but there'd have been less chance of being seen coming out..." Scott shook his auburn head impatiently. "Hell, it was dark. With no night skiing, there wasn't any traffic, anyway. East it is."

They traveled close to ten miles before coming to the first turnoff that appeared driveable. Logging roads higher on the mountain had vanished for the winter under twenty feet of snow. But the size of the snowbanks beside the road dropped with the altitude.

Scott slowed, then stepped on the gas again. "Nobody's been up there since the last snowfall."

The second one showed several recent sets of tire tracks. A green sign peeked above the snow: Lake Martha Trailhead, 1 Mile.

Scott turned. "I'll look to the left, you to the right," he suggested.

Cars had gone as far as the trailhead, where a nice little slope was obviously a favorite with sledders. Snowmobile tracks vanished into the trees, their deep green the only color in this white landscape. Even down here snowflakes drifted from a pale sky in silent, slow motion.

"If he had a snowmobile..."

"Murder is usually committed on impulse," Meg said. "Even murder in the first degree is rarely planned way ahead."

He grunted. "Shall we look around?"

"Yeah."

They followed half a dozen tracks made by feet rather than skis or sleds. Most ended abruptly and returned to the parking lot. A couple yellow spots in the snow signaled the reason for the trek.

At last she said, "Let's go."

They got nowhere with the next wilderness road, either. The snow was falling harder, making a white veil. Meg glanced at her watch—three-thirty in the afternoon. Darkness wasn't that far away. Common sense told her this was a wild-goose chase. That itch, that certainty something was *wrong,* kept her quiet.

Maybe it was contagious. Scott, driving more slowly as the visibility worsened, didn't suggest giving up. His face was tight, frowning, as he peered ahead. Tension hummed through him. Meg didn't know if the source was him or her. She was glad, suddenly, not to be alone.

"Crap," he muttered, braking. "Forgot this one was here."

The Jeep fishtailed and came to a near stop. He wrestled with the wheel and they swung onto another Forest Service road.

"I didn't see a sign…"

"Must've been buried. This is the Puma Lake trailhead."

The name triggered memories: wildflowers and murmuring brooks running over the stony trail. The blue-green lake water, so astonishingly clear that she could lie on her stomach on a big rock that stuck out and watch the shadows of trout ten feet down. Her sisters' high girlish voices pierced the mountain quiet. Her mother was part of those memories, laying out the picnic lunch as Meg's father cast his line for the fish. Meg would feel the sun hot on her back and drowsily hope he didn't catch any. Mom had brought plenty to eat without, and Meg didn't like watching her father bash in the trouts' heads after he'd pulled them flopping onto the shore.

His hand would be a blur, and she'd hear the crunch, see the rock come away smeared with blood...

She shivered.

Scott gave her a sharp look. "Ghost tap you on the shoulder?"

"Something like that." She didn't elaborate.

This parking lot had been used less heavily. With no good sledding hill, families on a Sunday outing didn't come here in winter. Through the falling snow Meg couldn't see tire tracks at all.

"Let's get out and circle," she suggested.

Ski tracks led up the trail and disappeared. Meg blinked away the snowflakes sticking to her lashes and peered into the woods. Pine branches were weighted from the last snowfall. Wells around each trunk were deep enough that scrambling out would have been difficult. She'd heard of skiers off the marked runs falling into one and dying, unable to escape by themselves.

"Meg!" Scott called. He'd gotten fifteen or twenty feet ahead while she meditated.

Feet sinking deep with each step, she hurried to his side. He pointed. Two sets of tracks disappeared into the trees, the individual footsteps oddly jumbled and smeared. Several places, a compression in the snow suggested someone had fallen.

Only one set of footprints came back.

Instincts kicking into high, Meg said, "We'll circle wide. Stay right behind me."

Once under the trees, the snowfall thinned, the tiny flakes floating individually to the forest floor. Meg walked parallel to the tracks, which continued a couple hundred feet into the woods. Except for the squeak and scrunch of the snow beneath their feet, the puff of Scott's breath, all was completely still and silent. Her own breath came out in visible clouds, the cold biting at her cheeks and nose.

The tracks ended at a well circling a huge ponderosa pine.

Moving carefully, Meg closed in on it. A few feet away, she saw the first blood splatters, the vivid scarlet already muted by the fine coating of fresh snow.

Scott made a sound.

"Stay back," Meg said harshly.

The last few steps, and she sucked in an icy lungful of air. A woman lay in a broken heap against the rough tree trunk. Blood was frozen beneath her like a cherry snow cone. Lividity had settled in the cheek that rested on the snow, but her face was tragically young and pretty.

A strangled obscenity brought Meg whipping around.

Scott had followed her and was staring down at the girl.

"Oh, my God," he said hoarsely. "I know her."

CHAPTER FIVE

"I'M SORRY." The cold plastic of the cell phone to her ear, Meg glanced over her shoulder at the floodlights and the half dozen police cars, the medic units, the yellow tape and the huddled officers. "I'll be another couple hours," she told Will. "Are you okay?"

"Mo-om!"

"I'm doing my best. You know I always do." She was freezing her butt off and she had a dead girl not that many years older than her son lying in the snow with a bullet through the head. Meg was not in the mood for anyone's whining but her own.

"I saw my dad today."

Not just the words but the defiance in his voice snapped her out of her self-pity. "You *what?*"

"I mean..." Will gulped. "I was bored, you know. So I went to see Aunt Renee. For something to do. Only he saw me, and he recognized me, and..."

Her stomach did a somersault so tight she was suddenly nauseated.

"I can't believe you went to the police station when Jack didn't even know you existed yet."

"Yeah, but he never would have known if I'd left it up to you."

Snotty, but possibly true.

"The thing is, he wants to talk to you."

Meg just bet he did.

"I made it sound like you'd call tonight," her son continued. "And now you're not going to be here."

"I wish I were." Little as she wanted to talk to Jack, she meant it. Lord, how she meant it. "I found a body, Will. I can't simply come home because it's five o'clock."

"Yeah, I know, but..."

"If Jack calls, tell him I'm sorry but I'll have to talk to him tomorrow," she said firmly. "Now, I've got to go. I'll be home as quick as I can." She hung up before he had a chance to protest further.

Stowing her phone back in its case, she crunched through the snow toward where the body still lay. Tugging her fleece hat back over her now icy ear, she tried to bury her chin inside the collar of her parka. Damn, it was cold!

Her mind was the only part of her warm enough to be working at top speed: annoyingly, on several levels at once.

Jack had talked to Will. What did that mean? Would he acknowledge him? Try to spend some time with her—no, *their*—son? Or had Will put him on the spot and he hadn't wanted to say, "Leave me alone, kid"?

At the same time as she worried about Will, she was aware of the scene ahead, canopied in blue plastic, brilliantly lit by a floodlight set up under the dark looming pines. Several police officers stood in a clump ahead, staring downward. The falling snow made a filmy curtain that isolated her from the activity ahead and behind.

She imagined herself as the victim, falling, begging, pleading, the snow sucking at each foot and keeping her from running. Just as important, she tried to see what had happened through the murderer's eyes, and found herself consumed by anger but also preternaturally alert, listening for the sound of a car engine, a snowmobile, the whisper of skis— anything to warn of the arrival of a witness. Her imaginary replays were so real, so personal, she was shaken. Sometimes she wished her imagination wasn't quite so vivid.

Just as Meg arrived at the murder scene, Ben Shea, a detective from the investigations unit, gave a hand to the coroner and boosted him out of the well surrounding the tree. Meg hadn't handled enough murders to get over her squeamishness, if anyone ever did. She tried not to look at the body, concentrating on the coroner's face.

"No surprises," he said briskly. "It's hard as hell to see much, but she's been shot in the head twice, close quarters. I'd guess eighteen- to twenty-four inches away. She was probably standing. Small caliber. There's one exit wound. You might look for the bullet."

"We already have." Meg pointed at the fresh hole torn in the tree trunk. "At least, we think so. We'll dig it out once we're done with the scene."

The coroner glanced, made some mental calculations, then nodded with satisfaction. "Height looks about right if she was standing when she was shot, which seems likely. I'll tell you more after the autopsy."

Meg had met Bobby Sanchez, the elected county coroner, for the first time tonight. She wasn't sure she'd recognize him if they met face-to-face tomorrow. Not much but his eyes and nose showed between his blood—no, strawberry—red wool hat and the plaid muffler tucked under the collar of his bulky parka. They knew how to dress in this country; she was probably the only one here who had to clench her jaw to keep her teeth from chattering. At two degrees, the cold sank into her bones.

Long underwear, she reminded herself. A muffler. Or would one of those face masks be even better? Definitely new wool socks. Maybe silk gloves to add another layer.

How could she have forgotten how cold winters were in central Oregon? Or how long? Her father used to say that in Elk Springs, winters lasted nine months and summer took up the other three. But she was sure there'd been a spring. Please God, let there be a spring.

"Patton?" Ben Shea's voice penetrated her misery. "What do you think?"

"Think?"

Not much of his face showed, either, but she saw one eyebrow lift sardonically. "Shall we go ahead and move the body?"

"Uh…" It was unavoidable at last. Meg, too, turned and gazed at the dead girl. "Did we get enough pictures?"

She *had* gotten to know the evidence technicians tonight, and been pleasantly surprised at their efficiency and knowledge. They'd measured, photographed and searched under her direction for any evidence dropped along the trail of footprints.

Hansel and Gretel, she had thought. *We should be so lucky.* Of course, they hadn't been.

"Sheila says yes," Ben told her. "She could do

better in daylight, but with snow coming down this heavy, I don't know if we want to leave it out here all night.''

Meg tried to hide her shudder. ''No. We don't. Is this your case now?''

''Nope. I'm just here to back you up.''

Did everyone have to sound so cheerful?

''Yeah, okay,'' she said. ''Well, let's take a look.''

They had, of course, already studied the body and surroundings, planning a search pattern just in case the murderer had thrown the gun into the woods, figuring it would stay buried in snow until spring. But now, with the coroner's okay, they'd take a more detailed look at the body itself and ready it for transportation to the morgue where Sanchez would do an autopsy.

Fighting her repugnance, Meg slid down into the well and heard Ben doing the same. Both crouched over the dead woman.

Meg checked pockets. Nothing. She unzipped the parka. Beneath was a waist-pack. Inside it she found a wallet and keys attached to a fuzzy ball. Lipstick. Comb. Hairclip.

Each item went into a separate paper evidence bag held out by Ben, who swore under his breath as he awkwardly jotted the whats, wheres, and whens on tags. Meg sympathized; she wasn't sure she'd be able to read her own notes tomorrow. Writing with ski gloves on was a challenge.

Meg patted down the girl's jean pockets, then struggled to roll her. She hated this stage. Between rigor mortis and the freezing temperature, the body was so stiff that moving it was like trying to wrestle a one hundred and twenty pound store mannequin.

Nothing in the back pockets, nothing beneath her. Meg glanced up. Ron Wczniewski, the head of the crime-scene techs, stood waiting.

"Let's shovel up this top inch or two of snow and dirt," Meg ordered. "We can let it melt, then check for trace evidence."

"Up here, too?" He nodded toward the jumbled footsteps where first victim and then murderer had stood.

"Definitely there."

"Shelly Lange." Ben was flipping through the wallet. "That the name you were told?"

"Yep."

"Nineteen years old."

Pity and anger churning in her belly, Meg rose to her feet. "That's what McNeil guessed," she agreed. "Shelly lived next door to him years ago. When she was thirteen or fourteen."

"And he remembered her well enough to recognize her now? Looking like this?" Skepticism edged Ben's gravelly voice.

"She worked at the ski area last year, too."

"And he just happened to lead you to her body."

"It wasn't like that." Oh, hell. She sounded as if she was being defensive. Maybe she was. She didn't want to think of Scott McNeil as a suspect. She'd have to, of course; why *had* he remembered a neighbor's teenage daughter so well? Tomorrow she'd ask him. But she didn't believe he was a murderer. Damn it, she'd seen too much tenderness on his face when he talked about the baby, too much anger and abhorrence when he speculated on who might have left her out there in the cold. And she'd seen his shock and horror this afternoon when he saw the dead woman's face. She would be willing to swear in a court of law that he hadn't known what they would find at the end of the jumbled trail.

Unless he was a heck of an actor. Some of the worst serial murderers were.

What she really meant, Meg thought wryly, was that she didn't want to believe she could be attracted to a man capable of such a brutal crime.

Good thing Ben would be with her tomorrow when she interviewed Scott. Obviously, she needed help staying dispassionate.

But still… She kept her voice even, unemotional. "Checking out these back roads was my idea. He drove because he was convinced that on my own I'd end up in a snowbank and somebody would find me out here come June."

"He might have a point. You don't have that much experience in snow country, do you?"

"I was stationed in Germany for three years."

He grunted. "Here's a picture of a baby girl."

Meg looked at the pretty, smiling baby wearing a red velvet dress trimmed with white lace. She felt a squeeze of pain and grief. "That's her."

"Good enough." Ben nodded toward the body. "We done here?"

He was prodding more than asking, she guessed. Meg waved her agreement and took a hand proferred by one of the other cops to boost her out of the well. She was a little surprised when Ben did the same. She'd barely met him the other day but had the impression that he was the macho type, not much for admitting that he needed help.

But then, she was going on appearances, and she knew better.

She and Ben stood back and watched as the body was bagged and hoisted out of the tree well, then loaded onto a gurney and carried toward the ambulance back in the parking lot. Taking a last look at the blood soaking the dark frozen earth and the snow, Meg ignored a fresh surge of nausea.

Pulling a trigger...now, that was nice and quick and almost impersonal. Anyone might be able to do it, given the right motivation. But making the victim come out into the woods, with her knowing the whole way that she was going to die... What could be crueler?

The murderer wouldn't have seen it that way. It certainly had been faster, more efficient, to force Shelly Lange to walk to her grave. Footsteps, assuming they were spotted before January snows filled them in, weren't likely to excite attention if a snowmobiler happened to notice them, but marks left by a bloody body dragged through the snow would be. Conceivably the murderer had even been angry enough to enjoy her terror.

"We'll search the perimeter in daylight," Meg said.

Nods all around.

"Have we made casts of the footprints yet?"

"We're working on it," Ron said.

"Any hope?" she asked.

"Damn straight." The twenty-something evidence technician became animated as he described how he'd prepared the best couple impressions by sifting layers of powdered plaster in, reinforcing them with sticks and then slowly soaking the plaster with water. "Works better in snow than the usual shellac solution and talc," he insisted.

On being asked, Sheila agreed that she'd taken photographs of every tire track in the parking lot. She didn't sound optimistic. The falling snow had blurred any clear definition, and it looked as though half a dozen vehicles had been in here within the past ten hours.

Scott had long since gone. Meg's impression had been that he was pretty shaken up, although like any man he tried to hide it. Knowing that securing the scene would drag into hours, Meg had insisted that he leave. Tomorrow would be soon enough to talk to him further.

Now she followed Ben Shea back to the parking lot and had the unwelcome realization that she had no car.

"Can you give me a ride back up to the ski area?" she asked.

"Sure. I'm parked over here." He jerked his head. When she fell into step beside him, Ben asked, "We going to talk to the parents next?"

"I don't see how we can put it off." However much she would have liked to.

During the drive up the winding, snowbanked highway, she asked whether Ben knew the Langes. "Or aren't you a local?"

"Nah, I come from Portland." A dark, intense man, he had to be younger than she was, but seemed to have nothing in common with the rootless twenty-five-year-olds she'd talked to that morning at Juanita Butte. "I asked around," he continued. "Ron thinks the victim's old man is a member of some crazy religious sect. They were in the news a while back for beating a kid bloody when he fainted during Wednesday prayer meeting. Around about the third hour of being on his knees.''

All Meg could think was, good thing her own father hadn't gotten religion. That would have been his brand of it.

Ben dropped her beside her Bronco in the Juanita Butte parking lot. Tonight there was night skiing; the hill blazed surreally white, skiers and boarders riding the chairlift up and coming down as if it were noon instead of 10:00 p.m.

Shaking her head—in some ways Meg had to admit to being a conservative—she backed out and accelerated carefully. Incredible to think she'd arrived at seven this morning. Fifteen hours ago. She was tired, but too wired to fall asleep even if she had the chance. Too wired to be hungry, either.

Ben's headlights stayed in her rearview mirror all the way down the mountain. Receiving confirmation on the police radio that Kenneth and Alice Lange resided on 12th Street, Scott's old neighborhood, Meg was able to drive straight there even though she couldn't make out street signs through the falling snow. She knew this part of town on a level deeper than memory. It was part of her, one of the reasons Elk Springs would forever be *home*.

But once she'd pulled up at the curb in front of the brick house blurred by the snow, Meg didn't get out immediately. She hated looking at bodies, but she'd take that any day over having to tell a mother and father their daughter was dead.

She couldn't procrastinate forever, though; Ben waited on the sidewalk, a dark, patient figure hunched against the weather.

Meg joined him. "I hate doing this."

Both picked their way carefully up the walk, icy pavement beneath the fresh inches of snow. Meg had a sudden picture of Shelly Lange's father out here shovelling tomorrow, working despite his grief. Or perhaps because of it.

"I can tell them," Ben offered, his glance unreadable.

Tempting, but she couldn't take him up on it. She'd feel like a coward. And, new as Meg was in the department, she didn't dare appear weak. Women cops had to be stronger than the men in ways that had nothing to do with muscle mass.

"I found her." Stepping onto the small porch, Meg pressed the doorbell. "But thank you."

The porch light came on, and she faced the door as it opened. Scowling at her was a short, husky man with a receding hairline, still dressed as if he'd just stepped in the door from work in an office—he hadn't even loosened his tie. "Do you know how late it is?" he was growling before he saw who stood on his doorstep.

"Mr. Lange?" she asked.

Wariness replaced his irritation. "That's right."

"We're police officers." She showed her ID. "We need to talk to you."

He continued to block the opening. Behind him a television set murmured and a woman asked whether something was wrong. The man ignored her. "What's this about?"

"Your daughter."

"I don't have a daughter." He started to shut the door.

Quicker than Meg, Ben inserted a foot.

"Mr. Lange," Meg said bluntly, "your daughter is dead."

Through the crack she saw no visible reaction on his face. He said nothing.

"We do need to speak to you and your wife."

For a moment he still made no move, although a muscle jumped along his jaw. At last he grunted and stood back. "Come in, then. If you insist."

Meg and Ben trailed him across a small entry into a dark living room. As they entered, a woman leaped to her feet and scurried behind one of a pair of recliners. Only one lamp at the far end of the room was on; the television set glowed a hypnotic blue-white. Out of the corner of her eye, Meg noticed that it was tuned to an evening soap opera aimed at older teens and notorious for sex and scandal.

Kenneth Lange went to the TV and switched it off. "Trash," he muttered. "I'm watching for the good of the youth in my church."

"Right," Ben breathed in Meg's ear.

She poked him with an elbow. "May I turn on this light, Mr. Lange?"

He mumbled what she took as assent. The illumination from the second lamp let Meg really see the woman hovering to one side, her hands clasped and her entire body language radiating anxiety.

Alice Lange would have been a pretty woman still if she'd worn makeup and been more relaxed. But tiny lines etched beside her eyes and mouth looked as if they'd been formed by a lifetime of worries, like earth worn down by trickles of water rather than torrents. Her face was bare, her uncolored brown hair graying in streaks accentuated by the tight bun. Her housedress was shapeless and faded.

"What is it?" she asked timidly.

"Mrs. Lange," Meg focused on her alone, "I'm afraid your daughter Shelly is dead."

Shock made Alice Lange's face go blank; agony crumpled it a second later. She sucked in a breath that was also a moan.

Her husband didn't even look at her. "We've already said our goodbyes," he said brusquely. "Whatever she's gotten herself into has nothing to do with us."

Ben stirred. "What makes you think she's 'gotten herself into' anything?"

Uncertainty flickered in Lange's eyes. "Why... your attitude. Coming here like this. Confronting us. Instead of just bringing word."

"As it happens," Ben said coldly, "you're right. She was murdered."

Shelly's mother let out a keening sound that made Meg ache to comfort her. But she couldn't. Not in these circumstances, not with this odd reaction to news that should have brought pain to both parents.

"How long has it been since you've seen your daughter?" Meg asked, looking at Kenneth Lange.

"A year." His mouth puckered, as though even so much of an answer tasted sour. "She defiled my name. She made her own bed."

Meg imagined the young woman being forced to walk through snow, falling into the tree well, trying to scramble out, begging for her life, the crack of the gun, the bullet shattering her skull....

"Not this one." Her own tone was harsh. "Nobody deserved this one."

A muscle tic below his eye betrayed some emotion. "What do you want from us?"

''You know she had a child?''

Mrs. Lange stared wildly. ''She's dead? Not her, too?''

''No. Your granddaughter is alive and well. Thanks to Shelly.'' Of course, Meg knew nothing of the kind, but it was a reasonable assumption, and as much comfort as she could give. ''She's in a foster home.''

''We have no granddaughter.''

His wife gave a small gasp through her silent tears.

Meg faced him. ''She's a baby. Six months old at the most. She didn't shame you.''

''She's the wages of sin. A bastard.'' He seemed to savor the word.

Meg looked at Alice Lange. Grief and hot tears filled her eyes, but she said nothing. Didn't dare say anything, Meg guessed. Perhaps it didn't even occur to her to protest.

Meg took another step forward. ''Mr. Lange, I have to ask you where you were yesterday evening.''

He stared at her, uncomprehending for five seconds, ten. Then he got it. Rage twisted his face. ''You may be a police officer, but you have no right to come to my house and accuse me of something like that! I won't have it! Do you hear me?''

''We both hear you,'' Ben said. He stepped to her side, dropping the pretense of being her shadow. With his size, he wordlessly expressed an implicit threat of force in a way she couldn't. ''But, given the conflict between your daughter and yourself, we must insist that you answer.''

A different time, a different place, Meg would

have called him to heel, like a good dog. This was her interview. She would never have interfered if Ben had been in her place. Every new partner, she had to start over again. Why did they all assume that she, a mere woman, couldn't stand up to an angry man?

Quelling her irritation, Meg told herself he'd learn. He was trying to be helpful. She'd proved herself too many times to get her feelings hurt.

Ben and Kenneth Lange were glaring at each other in a typically masculine game of chicken. Meg put her money on her new partner. He did that narrow-eyed, cold stare so well. And he carried a gun and the law on his side.

"Ken," Mrs. Lange whispered, her frightened gaze going from one man to the other. "Just tell him."

He looked away first. His face soured, and his voice was bitter with humiliation. "Home. My wife can tell you."

"That's right. He came right home from work," she said quickly. Too quickly, given the tears she was wiping from her face with the back of her hand? "We had dinner and prayed. The bishop called, didn't he? You spoke to him while I cleaned the kitchen and did laundry. I got the ink stains out of Kenneth's shirt…" She stopped, finished lamely, "That's all. And then we went to bed."

Meg switched gears. "What is the baby's name?"

"We have had no contact with our daughter."

At least he admitted he had one.

"She did write." The whites of Alice Lange's eyes showed as she realized that she was contradicting her husband. "Kenneth didn't read them."

"But you did." Meg was immediately sorry she'd spoken; Kenneth Lange's wife would pay for any disobedience, just as his daughter had. Just as Meg's mother had; as she herself had.

"Oh, no," Mrs. Lange whispered. "I wouldn't... Not when Kenneth said..." Her eyes filled with fresh tears. "How was she killed?"

"She was shot," Ben said.

Mrs. Lange put a hand to her mouth and backed up blindly. Suddenly a strangled sound came from her. She whirled and ran from the room. Meg made a move, then stopped. Her comfort wouldn't be welcome. Alice Lange wanted what she was unlikely to get: her husband's.

Another assumption. Irritated at herself now, Meg turned back to the man she had just realized she acutely disliked because he reminded her of her father. Okay, Kenneth Lange was a sanctimonious jerk who had disowned his daughter—*and* his infant granddaughter. He wasn't showing any sign of regret or grief at the news of Shelly's murder.

On the other hand, Meg didn't yet know what Shelly had done to anger him. And plenty of men hid pain because they thought they were supposed to.

Wait, she told herself. *Be sure. Then I can hate the SOB.*

"Your wife needs you," she said flatly. "We'll undoubtedly have questions another time. Good night, Mr. Lange."

He said nothing, only followed the police officers to the door.

On the porch, Meg turned. "One last question. Who is the father of Shelly's baby?"

For the first time, she saw pain on his face—pain and bitterness. "I doubt she knew herself. She was a whore." He closed the door; the porch light went out.

"Nice guy," Ben muttered.

"I wonder," Meg mused, turning up her collar against the snow and starting down the steps, "if anything she did ever pleased him."

Ben, just ahead of her, shook his head. "All I know is, she sure did figure out how to tick him off royally."

As, Meg thought suddenly, she had done with her own father. She sometimes speculated that she had wanted him to walk in on her that day with Johnny. She had wanted to hurt him, and what better way?

It was sad—no, pathetic—that young women had to feel so powerless. Sex seemed the only way for them to deal mortal wounds. What they didn't understand was that they, too, would be hurt.

Meg stopped beside her car. "Question is," she said, dealing with the present, "whether he was ticked off enough to kill her."

"Yep," Ben agreed. "That is definitely the question."

CHAPTER SIX

WHETHER KENNETH LANGE had hated his daughter enough to kill her was not the only question worth asking, of course. It might be interesting to know, for example, whether in his opinion real promiscuity was required to make a woman a "whore"—or whether any premarital sex at all was enough to qualify poor Shelly.

Also high on Meg's "to learn" list was discovering the identity of the father of Shelly Lange's baby.

At first sight, her studio apartment offered no clue.

It was above a detached garage, facing an alley. The older couple who had rented out the apartment to Shelly admitted to knowing little about her. She could come and go without their seeing her, the husband told Ben apologetically. She *seemed* nice. She paid her rent on time. The baby was always well-dressed and appeared happy. They did know that Shelly attended the junior college and worked part-time in the library there. She'd told them that she was enrolled in a program for young women on welfare, and that daycare for Emily was free. Is she all right? they asked, and cried when Ben told them.

Emily. Meg savored the name, picturing the little girl with soft brown hair and round cheeks. It was a lovely name, just right. Had Shelly chosen it her-self, or with Emily's father?

Ben and Meg briefly looked over Shelly's car, a ten-year-old Honda Civic with duct tape holding to-gether the upholstery, but otherwise scrupulously tidy inside. A back pack on the passenger seat held text books and school notes. In the trunk was a jack and spare tire, as well as tire chains for heavy snow. A red plastic rattle lay on the floor in front of the back seat. She'd been careful, Meg thought, and buckled her daughter in the back, even though it would have been easier to put her in the front, since the Civic was a two-door.

The one-room apartment had come furnished. Shelly had added a crib, painted white, and a plastic folding playpen. Ben and Meg looked around with-out opening drawers or the medicine cabinet. To-morrow the apartment would have to be dusted for fingerprints. Tonight was merely a reconnaissance, but not a successful one. No silver-framed photo-graph of a handsome man sat on the end table; no uncashed check for child support lay on the kitchen counter.

"Done?" Ben asked.

Meg took another lingering look around and felt a stab of pity for the girl, so young, who had done everything she could to make a cheerful home for her baby.

No assumptions, she reminded herself. It would be all too easy to see herself in Shelly. If she looked in the mirror, she'd see a reflection, not the true picture.

"Yeah," she agreed. "I'm done."

They sealed the apartment with police tape and

parted ways. Midnight, and Meg was finally able to go home.

Will was long since—she hoped—asleep. No matter how late she got home, Meg always slipped into his bedroom and kissed him good-night. How lucky she'd been, she thought, from such a hard start to end up with such a neat kid. Even if Jack chose not to play a role in his son's life, Will would do fine.

Why hadn't Shelly been as lucky?

The question hung in Meg's mind like a foul-smelling wisp of air, but she ignored it. Tomorrow was soon enough to investigate its origin—to track down the garbage that needed taking out. Tonight she would kiss her son's cheek, close her eyes and breathe in his essence.

And go to bed herself, to dream of something besides blood-red snow.

"COFFEE?" Scott asked, jiggling baby Emily against his shoulder as he stepped aside to let the two police officers into his house. He patted Emily's back and she let out an unladylike belch.

"No, thank you," Meg Patton said. She avoided meeting his eyes.

The other cop echoed her refusal. Both were being straight-faced and formal, even stiff. With a flash of anger, Scott wondered whether, if it weren't for Emily, he'd have been slapped in handcuffs and read his rights. Only once had Meg softened, and that was earlier when she'd phoned to warn him they were coming and to tell him Emily's name.

"Isn't it pretty?" she had said. Even over the

phone, he could hear the sweetness as she sampled it again. "Emily."

The name had been on the list Penny and he had made when she was pregnant. If the baby had been a girl, she would have been Emily, Sarah or Elizabeth. He wondered if Shelly knew that, if his wife, chattering, had shared every possibility as the neighbor teenager helped her refinish the chest of drawers for the nursery or paint the walls. Could her choice of name be coincidence?

Shelly Lange. God. Pretty, bright-faced Shelly, dead with a bullet in her head. He shied away from the too vivid picture he had from yesterday of the blood and the corpse frozen like meat in a locker.

When he made himself remember Shelly alive, it was the thirteen-year-old girl he saw, not the young woman he'd known more recently. Emily's influence, he thought again; he had this vision from his other life, of turning back just as he and Penny were going out the door, seeing Shelly cuddling Nate, making faces until he gurgled in delight.

A little girl herself, brutally murdered.

He gave his head a baffled shake, then realized both police officers were looking at him as if waiting for a response. "What?" Scott asked.

"Mr. McNeil," Detective Shea said woodenly, "I believe your doorbell rang."

"Doorbell?" Good God, he was losing it. "I'm sorry. I'm..." What? Lost in the past? Too tired to function normally? Busy burping a baby? "Excuse me," he said just as unemotionally. "That must be my housekeeper."

Marjorie bustled in, freed herself from her winter trappings, and delightedly took charge of little Emily. Leaving Scott, unfortunately, to face the police officers without her leavening presence.

"You're sure you don't want coffee?" he repeated, going back to the entry. Damn it, he sounded as if he were begging. The concept was so primitive *Accept my hospitality; prove that you trust me.*

"No, Mr. McNeil," Meg said, gaze expressionless. "We'd prefer to get right to our questions."

He didn't like having Meg Patton look at him as if he were bacteria growing in a petri dish. He knew her; they'd spent hours together. For God's sake, he'd helped find Shelly Lange's body! And for that he was being treated like a suspect.

Hell, why beat around the bush? He *was* a suspect, clearly.

"Fine," Scott said, as if unaware of the undercurrents. He nodded toward the arched opening into the living room. "Let's sit down. You're sure Emily is Shelly's daughter?"

Stupid question. Or phrased stupidly. Emily wouldn't be Emily if she weren't Shelly's baby girl. She'd be…who knows. Susan. Samantha. Lisa.

"Ms. Lange did have a photo, taken at Christmas, in her wallet," Meg said. "I have no doubt this is the same child."

"Good." He heard himself and thought, *Good? Why good?*

They all sat, Scott in the leather chair where he often read, Meg at one of the couch and Detective Shea in the other chair. Scott had been flanked, which made him edgy.

"Mr. McNeil," Meg said, "please tell us what you know of Shelly Lange."

"Uh…" He wanted to leap up and pace. He

moved his shoulders restlessly, but made himself stay sitting. "As I told you, she lived two doors down from the house my then wife and I bought when we came to Elk Springs. I was involved with developing the ski area from the beginning," he added as an aside. "Shelly was…just a kid. Twelve, thirteen. The moving truck had barely parked at the curb and she was over knocking at our door. She was always friendly, bubbly, liked being around people."

They were making notes, both of them. Scott felt more than ever like a lab subject.

"And so you established a…friendship with this girl?" The faint pause mid sentence made it clear where Detective Shea was going.

Scott's jaw muscles locked and his fingers tightened on the arms of the chair, but he was familiar enough with adversarial tactics to keep his voice civil. "No. My wife, who was home days, enjoyed Shelly's company. The girl seemed to like to hang out at our house, but mainly after school. I actually saw very little of her. Until…" His throat tightened.

"Until?" Meg prodded.

"We had a baby." His voice was as raw as bare skin scraping gravel. He was careful not to look at Meg. "Shelly baby-sat for us. Probably a dozen times. She was…really good with my son."

"Did you fire her?" Shea asked.

Scott didn't rise to the bait. "My wife and I got a divorce. We sold the house. I bought this one, she went back to Seattle to be near her parents." The truth, but not the whole truth. "I didn't see Shelly again until she applied for a job at Juanita Butte. I recognized her. Barely."

"Was she qualified for the job, or did you offer it to her because of your...past?"

Another one of those goddamn pauses raised Scott's hackles. "She knew how to work a cash register. She dressed with style and she was friendly. That made her plenty qualified to work in the ski shop."

"Did you see much of her after she hired on?" Meg asked, tone neutral.

"No," he said shortly. "I glanced in the shop now and again. That's all."

"What did she say when she quit?"

"She gave notice to her supervisor. I didn't know anything about it until later. She told Carol she was going back to school. It was about the time when winter quarter started. I don't know whether she really did."

"And did you call her later?" Every damn word Shea said held an undertone of doubt, even sarcasm.

Scott had too much self-control to show how irritated he was. "No. Why would I?"

One dark eyebrow slid up in unspoken answer *Because you had something going with her.*

Meg gave her partner a warning glance, then focused on Scott. "Did she have a boyfriend that you were aware of? Did you see her with anyone? Did her supervisor mention a relationship?"

He rarely paid much attention to that kind of thing. People talked, which meant he knew more than he usually acknowledged. But in this case...

"I saw her with someone. Surprised them once in an empty part of the lodge."

The passionate embrace might not have stuck in his memory if the two participants hadn't looked so startled and fearful. *Not fearful, embarrassed,* he'd told himself at the time, unable to understand why they'd be anything more. Surely they hadn't believed they'd lose their jobs because they were necking in an out-of-the-way part of the lodge.

"I presume," Detective Shea said with that heavy note of irony, "you recall who that 'someone' was."

Was this a good cop/bad cop game? Scott was getting seriously annoyed. What's more, he felt like a crud, throwing this poor kid to the wolves. But did he have a choice?

"One of the young guys who works in Mechanical." He frowned. "Tony. Uh... Tony Rieger."

"Mechanical," Meg repeated, making a note. When she looked up, her eyes met Scott's. "You understand that we'll need to interview a number of your employees. Anybody who knew Shelly."

"Yes, I understand."

"Then I believe that's all we'll need from you for now." She rose, closing her notebook.

Detective Shea followed suit.

They were going to walk out, just like that? Without telling him anything about what was going on?

"Wait just a minute." The crack of authority brought startled expressions to both their faces. Good. "Did you talk to Shelly's parents?"

"Yes, we did." Comprehension showed in Meg's eyes and she sank back to the couch. "I'm sorry. You want to know about Emily's status. Yes, we did see her parents. Mr. Lange apparently disowned Shelly—a year ago, he says. Since her baby was born out of wedlock, he considers her the 'wages of sin.' Quote unquote. He has no interest in custody. I didn't get the impression his wife is willing to defy him, even if she feels differently. So at the moment, if you're doing okay with Emily...''

Bad sign that he was so relieved. Emily wasn't his. She was a guest. He couldn't let himself get attached.

''She's fine.'' A reluctant smile caught the corner of his mouth when a happy squeal drifted from the bedroom wing. ''Obviously.''

Ben Shea almost smiled. Meg did. Forming dimples, the flash of merriment transformed the grim-faced law enforcement officer into a woman he could imagine kissing.

About the furthest thing from her mind, Scott thought ruefully, considering he was currently a murder suspect. The devil of it was, he had no easy way of taking himself off her short list. Scott had been alone in the lodge for the couple hours before Emily was abandoned. The security officers wouldn't be able to swear he hadn't left for an hour.

Unless Shelly had been killed substantially earlier, he wasn't off the hook.

And how could he prove that he'd never had a sexual relationship with Shelly? All he could do was hope like hell that Meg believed him. He was in his mid-thirties; to him, Shelly had been a kid. He didn't go to bed with teenagers.

Meg started to rise again, then sat back. ''Any chance you have a list of ski area personnel here at home? Names, jobs, phone numbers?''

''You seriously think somebody at Juanita Butte did this?'' He looked from her to Ben and back. ''Most of Shelly's life had nothing to do with the ski area! She only worked there for five months, and that was a year ago.''

"It's just a starting point. Emily was left in the area parking lot. Why were they there? And the murderer almost had to know that country. Unless he'd killed and dumped Shelly hours earlier while it was still daylight—and then why abandon Emily when and where he did?—he'd have been turning into the Puma Lake road in the dark. Would he have dared if he hadn't driven it in winter conditions before? If he didn't know it was used regularly by cross-country skiers and snowmobilers? He sure as heck couldn't afford to get stuck."

"Patton…" her partner growled in clear warning.

Meg waved him off. "It's just common sense. Mr. McNeil can figure this much out himself."

Shea still didn't like it. Standing, he said stiffly, "We'd better be on our way. We need to talk to Forest Service people. And reporters."

"Why don't you do that while I get the information from Mr. McNeil?" she suggested. "I can meet you at the office in…say, an hour and a half?"

He scowled at Scott and conceded grudgingly, "Yeah, okay."

Scott let her walk her partner to the door. He heard the murmur of their voices for several minutes before she returned.

The other man gone, Scott offered coffee again. This time she took him up on it. Perching on one of the bar stools in the kitchen, she watched him pour.

"You don't want to think anyone who works for you could commit murder," she observed.

Glass damn near cracked as he whacked the coffeepot back down. "Would you? No. I don't. If I hired somebody who could do this, that makes me responsible. And a bad judge of character."

She tilted her head to one side and regarded him gravely. "You've heard the saying that anybody could commit murder in the right circumstances."

"Yeah." His mouth twisted. "The right circumstances for most of us involve protecting our wives or children. Or self-defense. That I could understand."

"How do you know this murderer *didn't* have one of those motives?"

"What?" He looked incredulously at her, sitting so calmly in his kitchen, gun on her hip, talking about rational reasons for killing.

"Shelly's father implied that she was promiscuous. What if one of those affairs was with a married man? What if she was blackmailing him? Isn't that a threat to the security of his family?"

"Not the same kind of thing," Scott argued.

"Not to you or me." Meg stirred cream into her coffee. "But to the man who murdered her, it might have seemed that way."

"And maybe he just enjoys killing."

"Maybe," she agreed. "But we haven't had a serial killer working around here. And someone wandering through Butte County wouldn't have known about the Puma Lake road."

"He might have stumbled on it," Scott said stubbornly. "Taken a chance."

"Why would he? Why not kill her and dump her body out between here and Medford somewhere? Lower elevation, lots of deserted roads, not much snow…" She shrugged. "Which is not to say we won't consider every possibility."

"Did you find any fingerprints on the car seat?"

"Only glove prints."

He grunted, disappointed.

She sipped coffee, watching him over the rim. Speaking abruptly, she asked, "Why did you tell me you didn't have any children?"

He'd been waiting for the question. Scott looked around the kitchen, done in pale natural maple with a rust-brown tile countertop, and tried to ground himself. This was a long way from the past; he could recite the bare facts without tapping into the emotion.

"It's not something I like to talk about." Even to his own ears, his voice was robotic, mechanization without soul. "My wife and I had a son. Nathaniel. Nate. He died of Sudden Infant Death Syndrome when he was five and a half months old."

"Ohh," came out on a soft, pitying breath. Startling Scott, Meg laid a hand over his and gripped with fierce strength. "I'm sorry. Sorry for your loss, and sorry I asked."

He turned his hand; palm met palm. "You had to," he said roughly, telling himself the burning in his sinuses wasn't tears. "Now you know."

"Is that what happened to your marriage?"

"Yeah." He cleared his throat, swallowed hard, blinked a couple of times. "We couldn't get past the grief. And the blame."

"Blame?"

She had kind eyes, soft and blue like a summer sky. Now, after that first moment, he didn't sense pity coming from her so much as compassion. Scott still didn't want to lay bare his pain, but somewhat to his surprise he did feel a compulsion to finish the story.

"I put Nate to bed that night. Penny believed I'd

done something wrong. She could never decide what, but something." He swallowed. "She was right, as things have turned out. If I'd laid him on his back…"

Meg's fingernails bit into his hand. "You didn't know. You *couldn't* know. Not even the doctors did."

Now his eyes burned. "But I still can't help thinking. That one night, if I'd just put him down on his back…"

"You couldn't know," she repeated.

She might as well not have spoken.

The present had vanished but for the anchor of her hand on his. He was seeing the past, the soft darkness of the nursery, the golden glow from the Pooh night-light. Hearing the swish, swish as the rocker slowed and stopped when he rose to gently lay his sleeping son in his crib.

Nate sighed and pulled his knees up under him so that his diapered bottom stuck up. Scott was once again tucking the blankets over the small figure, his hands lingering, feeling the warmth. Slowly backing away from the crib, trying not to wake the sleeping baby.

He was trying to remember if, after that sigh, he'd heard his son take another breath.

"Scott."

He tasted blood, his jaw clenched so hard.

"Scott, you couldn't know." She took his coffee mug from him, held both of his hands, looked deep into his eyes. "It happened. It might have happened no matter what."

He bowed his head and fought for control. "That's not the worst part," he said rawly.

"What is?" Meg's voice was aloe on a burn, soothing, liquid.

"I blamed Penny, too. I told her so. I couldn't have hurt her more if I'd tried. Hell, I probably was trying! I could see in her eyes that she thought I was right. She'll live with that forever."

"Why did you blame her?"

He freed one of his hands to rub it across his face. Usually he'd have been embarrassed by the dampness. Today the fact that he'd cried seemed... unimportant. Natural. How long had it been since he'd had a woman's comfort?

"She smoked when she was pregnant. Just couldn't quit. Nate was born two weeks early, a couple ounces under six pounds. The doctors had warned her."

"And birth weight seems to have a connection to SIDS."

"Yeah." He scrubbed his face again.

"But most babies born to mothers who smoke don't die."

"No." Now his eyes were so dry they felt windburned. "Penny tried. She cut down. She did her best. If only I'd kept my mouth shut..."

"But she must have been thinking the same thing. That's why she wanted to blame you."

"Yeah, and I wanted to blame her." He uttered a short, gruff laugh that held absolutely no humor. "Hell of a note. Feel guilty? Must be someone else's fault. Make sure they know it."

"And it wasn't anyone's fault."

His eyes met hers. "Maybe. But I'm not sure I'll ever believe that."

"I think," she said softly, not looking away from

his pain, "that someday you will. Or at least that you'll find peace."

Enough self-pity. Scott let go of her hand and stepped back, physically as well as emotionally. "I've learned to live with it. That'll do."

Her blue eyes seemed suddenly clear rather than soft, and disconcertingly perceptive. "Most of the time, it has to," she said.

"I'll go get my company directory."

Nodding, she accepted his retreat. "Thank you."

Twenty minutes later she was gone and Scott prepared himself to head up the mountain to break the bad news to people who'd known and worked with Shelly Lange.

He only hoped they were more upset by her death than by the fact that every one of them was now a murder suspect.

CHAPTER SEVEN

THE DESK OFFICER on duty at the Elk Springs P.D. told her Chief Murray was in. "I'll take you on back," she said, eyes full of curiosity.

Meg had hoped that this time she'd be just another county sheriff's deputy here to see the police chief. Yeah, right. People had been talking. The unexpected reappearance of Renee's sister had been worth a good gossip or two.

"Is Renee here?" Meg asked.

That question earned a more probing glance. "I think she's on a call. Shall I check?"

"No, thanks. I'll catch her at home." Meg waited a few steps down the hall while the young woman officer stopped in an open doorway.

"Chief, Deputy Patton's here to see you."

Apparently he agreed to see her—Meg didn't hear his voice—but the officer waved her in.

Oh, God—oh, God—oh, God. Fifteen years and one big secret later, she was about to see Johnny Murray again. Her heart was trying to bounce out of her chest.

She had a horrible feeling that Renee was right; however much she'd dreaded telling Johnny—Jack—about Will, it was worse facing him now that he'd already discovered the secret.

Taking a good firm grip on her pride, Meg sauntered into that office as if she'd been here a million times. She wasn't about to give away the fact that she was pumping out adrenaline as if she were entering a deserted building after an armed felon.

Meg looked everywhere but at Jack, but he might as well have been strung with blinking lights. She saw him through her pores, even though she made herself take her time and glance around.

The office was modern and spacious but institutional, with pale gray linoleum tile, cream-colored walls and gray blinds at the window. He hadn't bothered to personalize it with artwork, but had managed to make it his own all the same with the heaps of files that sat on every surface, the file cabinet drawers that were open, the uniform coat hung haphazardly over a chair back.

"Well," Meg said brazenly, "your mother tried."

Jack's eyes narrowed. "You want to explain that?"

"You haven't gotten any neater."

He shook his head. "And you're as mouthy as ever."

"That's what you liked about me." She turned a chair around and straddled it with her arms crossed on the back. And she looked, finally and thoroughly.

He'd changed so much he wasn't Johnny anymore. And yet he was. Oh, she knew that face, lean and stubborn. Those eyes, the color of melting chocolate. That straight dark hair, which had once grazed his collar and fallen over his forehead. As if it was yesterday, she saw him pushing it impatiently back before making a point with some emphatic gesture.

Only then...then he'd been skinnier, not so muscular. His feet and hands had been too big even for his lanky body. His walk had been gawky. He'd tended to hunch his shoulders and slump in his seat, not hold himself with pride and patience. His face had been more open, too, happier, she thought.

He'd been a boy, not a man.

He'd looked like her son.

He still did.

He waited out her scrutiny, or didn't notice it because he was busy looking her over, too.

"Actually," he said at last, his gaze flicking lower, "I'm not so sure that is why I liked you. You had other qualities that attracted me."

She made a face, conceding the point. "We were young, weren't we?"

Did his eyes soften? "Yeah. Kids."

Meg looked around again. "Was this my father's office?"

"Yep." Jack leaned back in his desk chair and clasped his hands behind his head. The uniform fabric pulled tight over impressive muscles.

Meg didn't feel a twitch of interest.

She looked pointedly at the file spilling its contents onto the floor. "He must be rolling over in his grave."

Jack raised an eyebrow. "Maybe I hope so. Could be that's why I'm tossing files all over the place."

"Hoo boy." She congratulated him. "Quite a revenge."

Anger flickered in his eyes and he sat up abruptly enough to make his chair squeal. "Your father and I made our peace. I can't help it if you didn't do the same with him."

"He never would have given me any peace." Meg held up a hand. "Let's drop it. There's no point in our quarreling. Too many years under the bridge. You said it. We were kids. How about if we leave it at that?''

His mouth thinned. "How can we, considering?''

"You mean Will.''

"How could you not tell me?''

"I didn't dare.''

His jaw muscles spasmed. "If I'd known you were pregnant, I wouldn't have left that day.''

He looked as if he believed it. Who was she to disillusion him?

"I'm here today for official reasons,'' she said.

His face went stony, expressionless. "All right.''

"You've heard about the body we found at the Puma Lake trailhead?''

Jack inclined his head.

"The victim lived in Elk Springs. So do her parents. She attended the junior college. Just wanted you to know we'll be conducting interviews.''

He didn't blink. "As always, we'll be happy to cooperate in any way.''

"And we'll keep you informed.''

"Finc,'' he said curtly.

Oh, good. They were off on the right foot. Suddenly ashamed, Meg was glad Will couldn't know how she'd set about this interview.

She hesitated. "Will told me about coming here.''

"Apparently your edicts didn't cover visiting Aunt Renee. He looked pretty shocked when he saw that I recognized him.''

She found herself smiling ruefully. "It's hard to be specific enough to cover everything. He thinks creatively.''

"Like his mom.'' Jack wasn't exactly smiling,

but his mouth had definitely relaxed. "You always were too smart for your own good."

"That depends on your point of view." She went solemn again. "He's your son, Jack."

"I can't deny it. He's the spitting image of me in that high school graduation picture my mom keeps on the mantel at home."

"Will wants to know you."

His face hardened again. "Then why didn't you give him that chance fourteen years ago?"

"You know why."

His gaze didn't waver. "No, I don't."

"You saw my father."

"If I had a daughter and I walked in on some guy on top of her with his pants down, I don't know how I'd react."

"Do you remember when I had a black eye?"

A nerve spasmed below his eye. "The time you said you'd poked it with the handle of the mop?"

"I lied." She swallowed. "The broken jaw?"

Jack closed his eyes. "Why didn't you tell me?"

"I was ashamed." She studied him. "Why don't *you* sound surprised?"

"A couple months ago Renee told me your father was abusive. I think maybe I wasn't surprised even then, but I wanted to be."

With genuine curiosity, Meg asked, "Why would you want to think well of Ed Patton?"

Jack swore and ran a hand over his face. "He was good to me. After I came on the force. Sometimes I wondered if he recognized me. I never reminded him and he never said."

"I don't remember you having any interest in being a cop." That was phrasing it tactfully, Meg congratulated herself; actually, he'd talked about medical school or biology or becoming an astronaut, none of which she'd figured would amount to anything, Jack being Jack. Probably, she had thought, he would drift into taking over his father's appliance store.

He met her eyes as if with difficulty and said, "You're not the only one who was ashamed."

Meg blinked. "What are you saying? You had to prove something to Dad? You decided to make a man of yourself?"

His mouth thinned. "Is that so bad?"

She made a sound. "The bad part is that your idea of a man was anything like my father's."

"You're a funny one to talk." He nodded toward the badge pinned to her uniform. "You seem to have walked in his footprints, too."

Was that shame or anger heating her cheeks? "It was all I knew. College wasn't an option."

His lip curled. "Come on. You must have had other choices in the military. Why aren't you an electrician? A computer programmer? A journalist?"

She didn't like being sneered at. Her instant, hot defensiveness was, ironically, the answer to his question.

"I needed to feel strong."

Jack didn't say anything. Didn't have to. He just lifted one dark brow in that speaking way he had.

Meg made a face. "Yeah, okay. So maybe it makes sense you went the same route. That means you do understand that I was scared of my father."

"So scared you had to disappear for fifteen years?"

"He'd have taken Will away from me if he'd known he existed. He always wanted a son. And he'd have done anything to hurt me."

"You could have told me," he said stubbornly. "When I took off, didn't he come looking for you?"

"Yeah…" He swore. "I wouldn't have told him."

"Are you sure?"

"Of course I'm sure!" he snapped, but she saw in his eyes the truth: he didn't know.

"He was a bad man," she said. "So full of anger he couldn't hold it in. I don't think he ever loved anybody, or ever thought about anybody else's feelings."

"Renee tells me you found your mother. Why did she marry him in the first place?"

Meg sighed and rested her chin on her forearm, squeezing her eyes shut for a moment. She saw her mother in the hospital bed where she died, wan and thin and attached to life by needles and tubes.

"He said the right things. And when he told her what crap she was, she believed him. Why not? Her father had told her the same things."

Jack shook his head. "But you never believed your father. Why's that?"

"Are you so sure I didn't?" Voice flat, Meg pushed herself to her feet. "I'm not in the mood to be psychoanalyzed. I shouldn't have started this. I just wanted you to know that I'll be glad for whatever you can give Will. And I wanted to say I'm sorry for not sharing him. I was afraid. I don't know if that's enough excuse or not."

"Too late to improve on it." Jack clearly wasn't

in the mood to say, "Sure it is. You're forgiven."
She couldn't blame him.

Meg sighed. "Don't take out your anger at me on
Will."

He swore. "Goddamn it, Meg! Do you really
think I'd do that?"

She bowed her head and swallowed the lump in
her throat. "No," she said inaudibly. "The other
day…it sounds like you were nice to him. He was
excited. It must have been a shock. I *am* sorry about
that."

"Were you planning to keep him hidden for the
next four years?" Jack studied her with genuine curiosity.

"No." She grimaced. "I kept chickening out.
Some things I'm brave about, but I guess telling you
the truth wasn't one of them. I really am…"

"Sorry. Yeah, yeah." Jack frowned. "I won't
make any promises."

"No." She met his eyes with naked hope. "Just
give him…"

"What I can." He finished her sentence again. "I
heard you the first time."

Meg pushed herself to her feet and held herself
straight. "I love my son. Don't hurt him."

Another flicker of anger narrowed his eyes.
"Some things can't be helped. But I won't on purpose. That's the best I can do."

Meg hesitated, gave an abrupt nod and left. She
couldn't ask any more of him. If Will got hurt, it
was her doing, not Jack's. She had made the decisions that counted, long ago.

She refused to regret them.

SHELLY LANGE'S APARTMENT had little to tell Ben and Meg, though poignancy aplenty lurked to tap them on the shoulders.

Textbooks and a binder full of notes testified that she was, indeed, a community college student. Meg thumbed through the binder. Math 103—pretty basic, it must not have been one of her strengths. English 202—report writing. Child Development. That one made Meg shiver. Shelly's reason for taking it was likely personal. Ceramics. Aerobics. A reasonably full schedule. No hint at her major, if she'd settled on one yet.

No computer; she must have used the computer lab on campus. Both her wardrobe and Emily's were fairly extensive, which surprised Meg given Shelly's limited income. Without any real hope of finding anything interesting, Meg flipped through the miniature corduroy overalls and cute printed turtlenecks in the dresser drawers stenciled with bunnies. In the bottom, she found a grocery sack. Interested, Meg sank back on her heels.

These were larger sizes—eighteen months, two years. Cute stuff, but used. She found the receipt from the Salvation Army store. All these clothes had cost $13.78. A flyer mentioned a red tag sale.

Shelly had been a careful shopper.

"Damn it, no address book," Ben said behind her.

"Figures," Meg muttered. "Did you look in the phone book?"

He grunted. "The only numbers she'd noted were for the Pizza Palace and the women's center at the community college."

"Any reason Scott McNeil can't come get the crib and Emily's clothes?"

Ben sent her a sharp glance. "You've talked to him?"

"He called this morning to ask." Meg made a point of turning away so her partner didn't see the blush she feared might belie her casual tone. She wasn't about to tell Ben about the fifteen-minute conversation covering a little bit of this and some of that—the kind you had with someone when words came easily, when you both wanted to share the small happenings of your day. Scott hadn't asked questions about the investigation; she hadn't asked any more about his wife and baby. They'd just... talked.

She'd hung up the phone reluctantly. And blocked out the voice of conscience that whispered, *He could have been sleeping with Shelly. He could have killed her and then called 9-1-1.*

Brushing aside that particular wisp of memory, Meg continued, "He's rented a crib and bought a couple of outfits for her, but he's going to have to do some major shopping if we don't free this stuff up."

"It's all a mess."

Meg followed his gaze. The fingerprint techs had already been in. Powder dusted the rails of the crib and grayed the cheerful yellow ducks printed on the sheet. The handles of the white-painted dresser that held Emily's clothes were smudged. The clothes themselves would all have to be washed.

"He has a housekeeper," she said dryly.

"True." Ben shrugged. "I don't see why he can't take the kid's things once we've looked 'em over."

Looking Shelly's possessions over didn't take long. She had so little. No photo albums. The only picture was a framed eight-by-ten version of the one in Shelly's wallet, sitting atop Emily's dresser.

The couch pulled out into a bed. Dishes and utensils were minimal, food sparse in the tiny kitchenette. Shelly had apparently eaten fruit and microwave dinners; her beverage of choice was Pepsi. A twelve-pack was unopened on top of the small refrigerator; four were cold in the fridge. One cupboard held rows of baby-food jars, a box of Gerber's oatmeal, and several cans of formula.

The lack of possessions suggested she'd left home in the clothes she stood up in. No chance to pack stuffed animals or photos of friends or high school yearbooks. She'd started from scratch, which for a pregnant nineteen-year-old girl meant she'd begged, borrowed and stolen food and shelter. Meg knew.

It looked to her as if Shelly had done darn well for herself—and for Emily—under the circumstances. She was lucky or smart. Maybe both.

But however smart, she'd gotten into a car with a man who'd intended to murder her. Meg's job was to figure out why Shelly had gone. If he'd forced her, how? If she'd gone willingly, why did she think she could trust this man?

Or woman, Meg amended silently, although she was reasonably sure the perp was a man on two counts: first, the crime didn't have the stamp of a woman; and second, the footprints returning alone to the parking lot were way bigger than Shelly's.

"We need to take a look at Shelly's bedroom at her parents' house," she said aloud.

"Her father's the kind I can see burning everything she owned after he booted her out," Ben said.

"Maybe," Meg agreed doubtfully. Her own father had shut her bedroom door, shrugged and not bothered. She knew; she'd asked Renee. But then, he hadn't cared, not really. What Meg hadn't figured out yet was whether Kenneth Lange did care underneath the bluster.

They went by the Lange's quiet brick house, but no one came in answer to the doorbell.

"The college?" Ben suggested.

Meg glanced at her watch and nodded. "Students should still be around."

They picked up Shelly's schedule at the Admin office after listening to expressions of regret from staff who obviously hadn't known her well enough to be of any use to the investigation.

The Child Development class would be letting out in ten minutes. Shelly would normally have taken math that morning at nine and aerobics at three. English and ceramics were Monday/Wednesday classes, but the secretary marked a map of the campus so Meg and Ben could find the professors' offices.

The Child Development instructor was a woman, fortyish, who stopped midsentence when Meg eased open the classroom door and she and Ben slipped into the back.

Behind the podium, Clara Simpson said, "Yes? May I help you?"

Students turned in their seats, pulled into a semicircle.

Meg hesitated, then stepped forward. "I apologize for interrupting. I'm Deputy Margaret Patton. This is Detective Ben Shea." She looked from face to face. "I imagine you've all heard that one of your fellow students, Shelley Lange, was murdered three days ago. We're the investigating officers. We'd like to talk to each of you privately for a moment before you go to your next class."

The instructor said briskly, "Why don't you get started now? We discussed the tragedy earlier and would like to do everything we can to help."

Meg nodded her thanks. "Would you mind waiting, too, Professor Simpson?"

Clara Simpson wore Birkenstocks and a flowery broomstick skirt, her graying blond hair in a loose knot on her head. She had a no-nonsense air and kind eyes.

"Certainly," she agreed. "Class, let's continue our discussion while the officers take you aside one at a time. Jennifer, we were discussing separation anxiety in the eight-month-old child. You had a comment?"

"Yeah," the young woman said. "My older sister, see, she has a baby, and he's always crawling after her and crying if she shuts, like, even the bathroom door. He's like, like some kind of *leech. She* doesn't mind, but...eww." She gave a delicate shiver.

Meg tuned her out. She and Ben each chose a student and summoned them out into the hall.

Twenty minutes later they'd released the last of them. Some of the girls weren't even sure who Shelly Lange was. The guys did; Shelly had been really hot, as one put it. Several had known her from high school, and talked about a party girl who got okay grades but didn't try very hard.

"She really liked..." That boy flushed.

"Drugs?" Meg supplied. "Sex?"

"Um..." He shifted. "I don't know about sex. But boys, yeah. She always had...kind of a crowd around her. You know?"

Neither he nor any of the others knew who Shelly had dated her senior year of high school or the summer and fall after graduation.

Clara Simpson didn't have much to contribute, either. "I'm sorry," she said. "This is the first time I've had her in a class. She was doing very well— she contributed to discussions, turned her work in on time, and seemed quite involved. I'm told she's a young mother, however, so her interest is understandable."

Meg left a card, just in case Professor Simpson heard anything or thought of any insight into Shelly's behavior. "We're trying to get to know her, of course," Meg said, "but I'm also very interested in finding out about any men she might have been involved with. We have no idea who the father of her baby is."

"I'm afraid we had no personal interaction," Clara Simpson said apologetically, "but I'll certainly keep an ear out."

The aerobics class was even less helpful, not surprisingly. Ninety percent of the students were female. A few knew Shelly had had a baby, and they were awed that she had gone through pregnancy so recently but still had such a great bod.

"I mean, she didn't even have any stretch marks," one named Liza said in awe.

"Yeah, she was really fit," chimed in a second.

A quiet, thin girl said, "It's so sad. What's going

to happen to her baby? Does she have, like, parents or something?"

"Yes, she does." Meg chose to leave it at that.

Her pager beeped, and Meg glanced down at the read-out. "Coroner," she told Ben.

The aerobics instructor took them to her office where Meg used the phone. The autopsy was over, Bobby Sanchez told her. He'd assisted Dr. Myron Bart, a pathologist at St. Anne's Hospital. No surprises. The bullet wound had killed Shelly Lange instantly. She wasn't pregnant, and apparently hadn't had sexual relations in the twenty-four hours preceding her death.

"Toxicology screen is back," he continued. "No drugs or alcohol. She was a good girl."

"According to one of the students here at the college, Shelly was still nursing."

"Yeah, that's in the report."

"Emily seems to have come first," Meg commented to Ben as they returned to their car. "The party girl did nothing that would endanger her child. Which makes the timing of the murder odd. Did she start a new relationship? Her landlord and his wife didn't think so. She doesn't seem to have done anything lately that would have set her father off."

"We don't know that," Ben reminded her.

"No," she admitted. "Shelly must have some real friends. Somebody who can tell us what was happening in her life. Whether she'd approached her father. Was seeing a man."

"What I'd like to know is what she lived on." Ben unlocked the passenger side door. "Whether she was paying her bills."

They decided to split up for the rest of the day.

Ben would go to the Women's Center to find out
what help they'd given Shelly. From there he'd stop
by the bank, see what a credit check turned up, and
again interview the elderly couple who owned
Shelly's apartment.

Meg would drive up to Juanita Butte.

Cars with skis in racks on top streamed down
from the mountain. A few wended upward, but the
smaller crowd that would take advantage of the
night skiing would show later. By the time Meg
parked behind the lodge, the lots were two-thirds
empty.

The perfect time, she figured, to catch some of
the employees.

Upstairs in the lodge, she poked her head into the
office where Scott's secretary reigned. Trish Lord
was thirty-one years old and pregnant. After racing
at Mt. Hood as a kid, she'd started at Juanita Butte
operating a lift, eventually taking secretarial and
computer classes during the off season at the college. All she'd wanted to do was ski, she'd confessed to Meg the other day. And now the obstetri-
cian said not while she was pregnant.

"As if I have time, anyway," she added, making
a face. "My husband's started his own contracting
business, and I do the bookkeeping at night. And,
you know—" she'd gently touched her swelling
belly "—I don't especially miss it."

"To everything, there is a season," Meg had said
softly, and seen the agreement in the other woman's
eyes. Trish was comforting proof that even ski bums
did grow up eventually.

Today, when Trish saw Meg, she said, "Scott told
me about Shelly Lange. How horrible! Are you

looking for him? He's out taking a few runs, but I can page him if you need him.''

''Heavens, no! I wouldn't want to ruin his fun.''

''Work,'' the secretary corrected her, going stiff. ''He's General Manager. How can he know whether the lift attendants are doing their job, or how long lines are, or whether complaints about grooming on Sunset are right on, if he doesn't get out there?''

Meg held up her hands. ''You're right. He couldn't, any more than cops can do their job from the station. Conditions look good today, though. Unless you groomed away all the fresh snow...''

Trish's quick grin lit her face. ''Are you kidding? That's not just snow, it's powder! Light as air. People come here for it. I'd rather be out on the hill, too.'' She glanced ruefully down at her stomach, bumped up against the desk.

They discussed how hard it would be to ski pregnant, given the different center of gravity. Then Meg said, ''I want to talk to the security guys when they come on. But I wonder... Did you know Shelly Lange?''

Trish tapped a few keys and her screen went dark. ''To talk to,'' she said willingly. ''She didn't work here that long. And somehow she wasn't...a woman's woman. Know what I mean?''

''Just because she was so pretty?''

''No. I mean, she was, but...'' Trish thought. ''It was like other women were invisible. The only people she saw were men. She wasn't exactly rude—I even kind of liked her—but I had the feeling that...oh, she *needed* to be noticed by men. You know?'' Trish appealed again.

''Mmm-hmm.'' In basic training, Meg had known

a woman just like that. She was cordially disliked by anyone not male, but Meg had finally decided that Shannon Colter's problem wasn't so much that she loved men as that she needed them. She was an extension of whatever man she was with. Maybe she was invisible to herself without a man around, as if she could see herself only as the shadow cast by his sun. Meg outlined her theory to Trish, who nodded immediately.

"Yeah, she was like that. Not rude on purpose, but always looking over your shoulder at some guy coming into the room. Even if she didn't move a muscle, you could feel her quivering to attention. Like my science teacher said, everything magnetic in the earth points toward the pole."

"Did she like, uh…all men equally?"

Trish blinked, hesitated, then said candidly, "Nope. She had a boyfriend, but *he* became invisible when someone more important came in. And older. I'm not sure which part attracted her."

"Like Scott," Meg said thoughtfully.

"Yeah, but he would never have looked twice at her. So I think she, well, *settled*."

Meg snapped to attention. "As in, she had an affair with someone here? Besides the boyfriend?"

Trish physically shrank back in her chair, her expression becoming wary for the first time. "I didn't say that. I don't *know*." She drew out that last word.

Meg pounced on it. "But you suspect."

"Once, I saw…" She stopped. "But I probably misunderstood totally. He's…well, not that kind of guy."

"Trish," Meg said quietly, "I'm not heading up a lynch mob. I can be discreet. So long as this man had nothing to do with her death, I'll keep my mouth shut.''

Trish gazed into space without focus. ''I'll think about it,'' she said finally, and after that she clammed up.

Meg conceded temporary defeat and headed down the stairs to the security office. It was bare bones, reminding her of her home-away-from-home, the police station. Here, on the mountain, the public generally turned to the ski patrol for help, although they'd send for a security officer if a crime had been committed.

Her timing was perfect. Len Howard and Jerome Baker, the two security men who'd been on duty Monday night, had just arrived and were having coffee and doughnuts before beginning their shift.

Len spread a map of the ski area on the gray steel desk and outlined their movements from five o'clock—nightfall—until Scott had left the lodge at eight-thirty and discovered the baby.

They were confident, within narrow windows of time, about when other employees had left. They claimed that one or the other had seen the employee parking lot every half hour at least.

''We have a dozen vehicles parked there,'' Jerome explained. ''Unless they're in the shop for repairs, that's where we keep the dozers we use on the parking lots, see. And the half-pipe grinder. That kind of equipment doesn't come cheap.''

The half-pipe grinder was a grooming machine, she knew, to create the chutes for snowboarders. From what Scott said, definitely a big expense.

''No,'' Meg agreed, weighing how she could ask her next question. She couldn't see any way of disguising what she really wanted to know. Would they be outraged?

"Okay," she said, pretending to think. "From seven on, the general manager's Jeep was the only employee vehicle left in the parking lot."

"Except for Jerome's Bronco," Len contributed. "He gave me a lift."

"Right." She took a breath. "Would you have noticed if Mr. McNeil's Jeep was gone?"

"Yeah, sure." He frowned. "But he was there. I mean, he was the one who found the kid."

"Yes, but could he have left for a while and come back?"

His eyes met hers. Len Howard was no dummy. "Maybe for twenty minutes," he said. "I guess twenty-five, if he timed it perfectly."

"You're positive you'd have noticed if his Jeep was gone." She looked from one man to the other.

"I'd have noticed," Len said.

"I did." Jerome had been twirling a toothpick in his mouth. Now he plucked it out. "He never left. I remember thinking how he was probably going to bunk down up here. And how he oughta have somebody to go home to. All he does is work."

She couldn't shake them. Scott McNeil couldn't have been gone for long enough to take Shelly Lange to the Puma Lake trailhead, murder her and come back to park in exactly the same spot. Even assuming Meg could figure how Shelly and Emily had been magically transported to the Juanita Butte parking lot where he would have had to meet up with them.

Nope. Scott McNeil was definitely, officially, off

the hook. Which didn't surprise Meg, but did relieve her.

Maybe a cop here and there had been careless enough to fall for a murder suspect. For the first time, she understood how it could happen. Had even felt it happening.

Which meant Scott McNeil wasn't the only one off the hook.

She was, too.

CHAPTER EIGHT

MEG WAS IGNORING traffic outside the glass front of the ski shop where she'd been asking questions until a sixth sense made her turn her head. There was Scott. Sunglasses pushed atop his black ski hat, he was unzipping his parka as he stopped to talk to someone she couldn't see. Which didn't matter, because for those seconds while she stared, no one else existed. Only him.

The salesclerk kept talking, but Meg didn't hear. She'd tried very hard not to let herself notice how damned sexy Scott was, which left her staggered now that she did. Now that she *could.*

Above the bulky ski boots, unbuckled, plain black ski pants made the most of long, powerful legs. A red sweater under the black parka stretched across his broad chest. His face was lean, craggy, intense; his mouth interesting, crooked, sensuous without being full. His chin bristled with pinpricks of a red more fiery than the thick tousled auburn color of his hair.

She felt a quick, tender squeeze of amusement. He hadn't had time to shave this morning. Emily must have been cranky.

He yanked his gloves off as he talked, then slapped them against his thigh. A moment later he lifted a hand in farewell and started to walk away.

But his head turned as he went, his sweeping gaze taking in everything around him.

Including, through the glass, Meg.

His stride checked. Without looking away, he pushed open the door and came into the shop. From behind the counter, one of the two clerks said, "Mr. McNeil. Is there a problem?"

"No problem." His eyes never wavered from Meg's. "Are you done in here?"

"For now." She did manage to bestow a vague smile toward the two young women. "Thanks. If you think of anything…"

"Sure. I didn't know her, but I wish I could help," the one assured her naively, eyes wide.

As the glass door closed behind her and Scott, Meg muttered, "You hiring 'em before they even graduate from high school?"

He was behind her, but she heard the faint smile in his voice. "That's…uh, Melody something. She did graduate. Last May. She's smarter than she looks, or so I'm told."

"Wouldn't be hard," Meg muttered, before guilt stabbed her. "I'm not being nice. There's nothing wrong with being young and innocent."

He was kind enough not to ask, as she had the other day, whether she ever had been.

Instead he asked tactfully, "Learn anything useful?"

They'd reached the hallway outside his office. "Just that you couldn't have killed Shelly," Meg said, blunt to the end.

Only in his eyes did she see his anger. "And you thought I did?"

"Nope." Since he wasn't moving, she walked

past him into his office. "Just thought I should be sure."

"Well, good." Irony hung like icicles from his tone. "And how did you satisfy yourself that I couldn't have pulled it off?"

She told him and watched as he mulled it over.

"I'd rather," he said, "that you'd just had faith in my character."

She made a production out of inspecting the painted mask that hung on the wall. "I don't know you that well."

Scott stayed by the door. "Did you seriously think I might have done it?"

"No." Meg pressed her lips together, then faced him. "No. But I've been wrong. Every cop has. The worst serial murderers can be charming. The kind you want to trust."

Emotion flickered in his eyes, the gray of a California fog. "Am I charming?"

To heck with the social niceties. "No," Meg said again. "I don't like charming men. You're… forceful. Straight with people."

His mouth had a wry look. "You make me sound irresistible."

"You're also kind underneath that occasional gruffness. Otherwise you would have shaved this morning."

"Shaved?" His hand went to his chin, and he grimaced. "What if I said I'd forgotten?"

"I'd know you were lying. You're not a man who forgets anything."

A muscle twitched in his cheek. "Even when I wish I could."

"I'm sorry…"

"No." He pushed himself away from the door frame. "You're right. Emily was fussy this morning. I figured—" ruefully he scraped a palm across his jaw again "—nobody would notice."

"Ah," Meg said softly, "but I notice everything."

"So I see." Now his eyes held a smile. "About me, anyway."

"Gave myself away." She tried to sound light, to make a joke out of it, but her mocking smile trembled around the edges.

"Will you have dinner with me tonight?" Scott asked.

"Dinner?" How had they gotten here?

"Yeah. As in a date." His voice changed subtly. "Or am I misreading you?"

Crunch time. The coward in her wanted to begin evasive maneuvers; the woman wanted to charge into the barrage of fire, the certainty of pain be-damned. It had been a long time since she'd let her-self be a woman, not a cop, a military officer, a mother.

"No," she said quietly. "You're not."

Light flared in his eyes. "Then?"

"I can't tonight." Was that regret or relief she felt? At her age, she was discovering, it was scary to think about falling in love. What had once been joy, whispers to her friends, notes and corsages was now a serious business. "I need to talk to Will— my son," she explained. "Besides, I'm in the mid-dle of a murder investigation. I can't just…just drop it so I can get dressed up and go out to dinner."

He lifted his hand and touched her cheek, just a

brush of his knuckles that raised goose bumps down to her toes.

"All right. What about tomorrow night?"

"The investigation…"

"You must eat."

"Actually, I forget a lot of the time."

"We can make it quick." His eyes were grave, intent. He knew this was serious business, too. "But…let's make a start."

"A start." Meg swallowed. "I…" There was the battle line again, the temptation to retreat. She wouldn't let fear rule her life. She never had, and she wouldn't start now. "Fine," she said, voice completely steady. "Why don't I come by your place. Seven o'clock?"

The faintest of smiles softened his mouth. "Deal."

"Now, tell me where to find Tony Rieger."

"I'll take you."

"No," she said quickly. "I don't want to be associated in his mind with you. You're his boss, with a capital B. He might tell me things he wouldn't want you to know."

Scott frowned, mulled it over, then agreed and gave her directions.

Outside, the sun had sunk behind the mountain, leaving the ski area in the shadow of oncoming dusk. The air was noticeably colder. She shivered, thought again about going shopping for warmer clothes, and hurried past a copse of trees screening the guts of the area from the public. Big metal buildings housed the mechanical department, whose job was to keep grooming equipment, dozers, 4x4s and snowmobiles running.

Tony Rieger was taking a break in a small office with a computer and a space heater. It wasn't all that different from one in a gas station: the only window looked out at the shop and greasy finger-prints discolored the computer keyboard and the corners of paperwork stacked on the desk. Nothing fancy here.

Tall, with curly dark hair, brown eyes and cleft chin, Tony was not happy to see a uniformed officer. He was young and inexperienced enough to show it.

"Yeah," he agreed sulkily. "That's my name."

"You've heard about Shelly Lange's death."

A spasm of emotion twisted his face. "Yeah. I heard."

"I understand the two of you dated."

His dark eyes flashed up. "Who told you that?"

"Does it matter?"

"Yeah, it matters!" He sounded belligerent. "Like, somebody's trying to get me in trouble, and I'm not supposed to care?"

"Why would the fact that you dated Shelly mean you're in trouble?" Meg asked.

"She was murdered, wasn't she?" He moved jerkily around the office, finally ending at the door. His back to Meg, he splayed both hands on the metal door and bowed his head. His mechanics' jumpsuit badly needed a wash. "Jeez, I can't believe... I mean, Shelly! Of all people..."

"Why 'of all people'?"

"She was so...pretty. Everyone liked her."

Everyone male, Meg thought, unsurprised that he hadn't noticed Shelly's admirers didn't include any female friends.

Meg perched on a stool and flipped open the notebook that sometimes felt like an extension of her arm. "Tell me about your relationship."

He turned, his eyes baffled and red-rimmed. "We just…saw each other for…I don't know. A couple of months."

"Who broke it off?"

"She did… Well, I guess I did, because I didn't like sharing her."

"Sharing?" Meg repeated. She pretended to make a note, watching him.

"Before me, she'd been seeing some other guy. Someone here. I don't know who. She was scared of him. He was, like, possessive. You know? We had to be really careful that nobody saw us together. You see? That's why I wanted to know who told you."

"Let me get this straight. She'd broken up with this other guy, but she was still scared enough of him that she didn't want to be seen with you in public."

"Yeah." His Adam's apple bobbed. "At least, that's what I thought. But then after a while I figured out that she was still seeing him, too. I was, like, backup. She admitted he was married, so I guess he was busy a lot of the time, and that's what she wanted me for."

His pride, if not his heart, had been hurt. Meg wondered why he'd admitted so readily to something so humiliating. He hadn't even made her prod.

Heck, maybe he was just a good citizen. Believed in law and order. Cared enough about Shelly to want her murderer brought to justice.

Or was scared of the man who might have killed her.

"What else did she tell you about this guy? You're sure he worked here?"

"Yeah. I think he was older, had more money. I tried to get her to tell me who he was. I was going to make him back off. I guess she knew that. Maybe that's why she never said who he was."

"Okay." Meg doodled in her notebook. "Please tell me where you were Monday."

"This guy who works with me—Jeff Drake—he got married Sunday. Over in Eugene." Tony was eager to tell her. "A bunch of us went. We stayed over until Monday, since that's the slow day here. We got home maybe eleven? I just crashed the minute I walked in the door."

He directed her to two of the guys with whom he'd driven to Eugene and back. When they clambered out of the engine of one of the huge grooming machines, they confirmed his story. Unless the three had colluded to murder Shelly Lange—very unlikely—Tony Rieger had had nothing to do with her death.

As Meg walked back past the office, Tony stopped her.

"You know she took classes at the community college?"

She agreed that she did.

"Well, see, I've been taking some evening classes, too." He talked fast. "Anyway, I know this girl who's taking English 202 with Shelly. Kari says Shelly had something going with the prof. They were really obvious, Kari says. And Shelly got an A, but she didn't deserve one. I just thought you should know."

The English professor was the only one Meg and

Ben hadn't yet talked to. Meg scribbled down the full name and phone number of Tony's friend and thanked him for the additional information. She wasn't quite sure what had prompted it: resentment, a genuine desire to be helpful, or fear that she still suspected him. But a chat with this Kari would be interesting indeed.

Meg went straight to her squad car, radioed in and headed down the mountain.

"TOMORROW NIGHT? Uh, yeah. Thanks. That would be cool. Um…" Will hesitated, his hand feeling sweaty on the phone. "Who'll be there?"

"Just my parents." His father paused. "Your grandparents."

Oh, wow. Grandparents. Unreal.

"They know about me?"

"I told them today. They're eager to meet you."

His heart was beating like crazy. Will swallowed. "I'll have to ask Mom. About dinner, I mean."

"She's not home?" his father asked.

"No…" Will heard the garage door. "Wait a minute. I think that's her now."

"Well, you just call me back. Okay?"

"Yeah. Sure." Will hung up before he realized he didn't know his father's phone number. This was all too strange for him.

Mom came in the door from the garage.

"What's for dinner?" Will asked.

She groaned.

He looked in the cupboard. Bare. "We could order a pizza."

"What did you have last night?"

"Pizza. Hey." He brightened. "I have some left. You want me to put it in the microwave?"

"I can do better than that." Mom kissed him on the cheek and headed for her bedroom.

Will trailed her, stopping out in the hall where he couldn't see her shedding her gun and uniform. He raised his voice. "Dad called."

"Did he tell you I talked to him today?"

"Yeah." Will stared at the framed photo of his mom and her two sisters together as little girls that hung on the wall. They all looked back at him, their faces so solemn, he'd asked Mom once if they'd been unhappy when it was taken and she'd said, Yes, that day their dad had yelled at them right before the picture was snapped. That's why they weren't smiling. Why didn't she hang up one where they looked happy? he'd asked. Because we weren't, she'd answered, never really totally, but see—she'd touched the little girls in the picture—see how close they'd stood, their arms around each other? See how much they trusted each other? How they were one against the world? Will didn't say, *But you left.* He could tell Mom was thinking it. That her sisters shouldn't have trusted her.

"What did Jack say?" his mom called from the bedroom, her voice more distant, muffled. She was either in the bathroom or had her head stuck in the closet.

"He asked me to dinner tomorrow night. To meet his parents." *My grandparents.* "Can I go?"

He worried she'd ask if she had been invited. Because she hadn't been. Will guessed that his father's parents remembered her from when she was their son's girlfriend. But they hadn't wanted her to come to dinner.

She appeared in her bedroom doorway wearing jeans and a long baggy sweater. "Don't be silly." Her smile was wavery, like it had been when she let him go to Oregon for two weeks with a buddy when he was eight. As if she knew she had to say goodbye but didn't want to. "Of course you can go," Mom said. "Isn't that what we're here for?"

"What if they don't like me?" Will blurted. That shaky smile of hers had made him feel like crying. Not that he would, but suddenly he was scared. What if these grandparents hated him? What if his dad didn't like him that much?

What if Mom was letting him get to know his father because she didn't want him anymore?

Will knew immediately that wasn't right.

Okay, what if she knew she was dying, like his other grandma had, and she wanted to be sure he had family before she was gone?

But she looked awfully healthy.

Mom had always said they should be honest. So he asked, almost nonchalantly, "You wouldn't want me to live with Dad, would you?"

Fire entered her eyes. "Did he ask you?"

"No..."

"You've got it right. No. Not on your life!"

"Dad didn't ask," Will said in a rush. "I just...well, wondered. If you were hoping maybe he would. I mean, I know it's hard having me all the time when it's just you..."

His mother framed his face with her hands and lifted his chin so he couldn't look away. "It is *not* hard having you. I love you. Period. You're stuck with me until you leave for college, okay? Maybe you won't even get rid of me then. I might come along. They hire housemothers for the dorms, you know. My police experience should be a plus.''

"Yeah, right.'' He wriggled free of her hands, although he wouldn't have minded a hug if she'd insisted.

She didn't. Instead she tucked her hand in the crook of his arm and pulled him into the kitchen.

"Actually,'' she said, "I'm glad Jack asked you tomorrow night. I have plans, too.''

"Plans?'' He watched her open the refrigerator.

She gave him a grin. "Unbelievable as it may be, your very own mother has been asked out by a man.''

"Asked out?'' Will repeated in shock. His mother hardly ever dated. She said she didn't have time. Why did she suddenly have time, when she was never home?

"Scott McNeil. He's the general manager of the ski area.''

"The guy who found the baby.''

"That's right. I forgot I told you. He's... interesting.''

He stared at her incredulously. What did she mean? Did "interesting'' mean she had the hots for this guy? His *mother?*

Besides, he'd had this secret dream ever since Mom announced they were moving back to Elk Springs. In the dream, his mother and his father realized they still loved each other. They got married, and his dad was there to take Will fishing and let Will whup his butt on the basketball hoop he'd install at their home. Maybe he'd even put a small one-on-one asphalt court beside the garage, like Silas Norden's dad had. They'd be a family, Mom and Will and his then faceless father.

Okay, it was probably a dumb dream—he'd recognized that from the start. But now he thought it might not be impossible. Jack Murray wasn't married. He seemed like an okay guy, and he looked like the jock type women would go for. So why not Mom? And Mom was still pretty, for her age. Think how perfect it would be!

"Are you, like, interrogating him?" Will asked hopefully.

"Scott?" She set a head of lettuce on the counter. "If I had to interrogate him, I wouldn't date him. No. He's definitely in the clear on this case."

Will slouched against the island. "But you don't know him that well. What if you don't like him?"

"Then I won't go out with him again." She produced a green pepper, cauliflower and two carrots from the vegetable drawer. "That's why you date. So you can get to know each other."

She wouldn't like him, Will decided. She was just flattered, because she didn't get asked often. And she always said the guys her age who were single were creeps. This one wasn't that bad, so she'd figured, what the hey.

But she must be thinking about Will's dad a lot. Here they'd had *sex,* and now they were seeing each other for the first time in all those years. How could she not be thinking about him?

In fact, it might not be a bad thing that tomorrow night Will could say, just casually, "Mom went out to dinner with some guy." Dad might not like the idea. He might be spurred to making a move faster than he would have otherwise.

Yeah, Will decided, his dream might not be as dumb as he'd originally thought. Now that he'd met his father, Will could see it coming true. He wasn't going to worry about this McNeil guy. How could he compete with Jack Murray?

"Have fun," Will said with a shrug, and grabbed the carrot stick she tossed him.

WEARING A HOUSEDRESS, Alice Lange blocked the doorway, just as her husband had the other time. The hand that gripped the door was dry and flaky; the fingernails were short and unpainted. In the light of day, her face looked colorless.

"Why would you want to see Shelly's bedroom?"

"I'm really just hoping to get to know her," Meg explained. "We can get a warrant if you insist, Mrs. Lange. But your cooperation would be preferable."

Anxiety hung around her like a cloud of gnats. "My husband…"

"I'll wait while you call him, if you'd like."

She agonized, the indecision deepening every line on her face. "I'm not supposed to bother him at work."

"Why would he object to my looking at Shelly's bedroom?" Meg asked reasonably.

"He won't like you being here," Mrs. Lange worried aloud.

Once she must have been as pretty as her daughter, Meg thought again. Had she ever had Shelly's spirit? It was hard to imagine in this woman who didn't care for herself physically, who deferred to her husband even to the point of rejecting her own child.

"Why?" Meg asked again, though she knew. Or thought she did.

"He says we don't have anything to do with whatever Shelly got herself mixed up in. Maybe drugs or organized crime or whatever." The words came out by rote, clearly not hers. "It upset him, you asking where he was that night, like he might hurt his own daughter."

"He said he didn't have a daughter. He'd disowned her."

"That was hard, but she had it coming. A father should be obeyed, don't you think?" Alice Lange looked at Meg as if she expected understanding.

"It depends what the father asks of his children," Meg said flatly. "He's there to love and guide, not rule."

"The Bible says a man should be the master in his own home." It was a fact, no argument. But grief…oh, yes, she could wish it might be otherwise.

"Mrs. Lange," Meg said gently, "can you tell me why your husband and daughter clashed?"

She clutched the door frame, her knuckles white. "It was men. Shelly really liked the boys, even when she was twelve or thirteen. She always wanted her daddy to spend more time with her—she just couldn't understand that he had to work and that the Lord had called him to counsel others. Well, after she discovered boys, she didn't care any more whether her daddy was there or not. They fought all the time. He wanted what was best for her. That's all. Sometimes I thought maybe she had a disease. You know, that one where a woman wants…" She swallowed convulsively. "Men. That way. You know."

Meg was glad Ben wasn't with her. Mrs. Lange wouldn't have been even this forthcoming if it hadn't been between two women.

"May I come in?" she asked. "So you're not letting the heat out?"

"Oh!" She blinked several times. "Oh. Yes. Please do come in, Officer. I'm afraid I don't remember your name."

Meg introduced herself again. They sat in the living room, Meg on a couch that might have been there when Shelly was a little girl. She could see it, the doilies protecting the arms, Shelly forbidden to put her feet on the olive-green fabric.

Alice Lange faced her, sitting on the recliner but with her spine so straight it didn't touch the back of the chair.

In answer to Meg's question about whether she knew the names of any of the men with whom Shelly had been involved, Mrs. Lange said, "Oh, there were always boys from school. Why, she'd sneak out her bedroom window at night to meet them! But at school, she had such a crush on a teacher, he called us in to ask us to talk to her. She was following him around and making excuses to hug him and such."

"Was that in high school?" Meg asked, making notes.

"No, seventh grade, I think. Or was it eighth?" Mrs. Lange closed her eyes, squeezing out tears that made damp tracks on her cheeks. "Shelly was such a sweet little girl. That's why I think it might have been a disease. She was still sweet. It was just men. Always men.''

Meg couldn't help thinking that if Kenneth Lange had given his daughter the attention she craved, Shelly might never have been so desperate for a different kind of attention from any and all men.

Or was that too easy an answer, one seen through Meg's experience, not Shelly's at all?

''Mrs. Lange.'' Meg waited until the other woman opened her eyes, sniffed, wiped away the tears. ''I have to ask this. Is there any possibility your husband made sexual advances on your daughter?''

''My husband?'' Astonishing for this day and age, it took a minute for Alice Lange to understand. When she did, she sucked in a breath. ''How can you even ask…''

''Because it happens,'' Meg said bluntly. ''More often than you'd think. As I said, I have to ask.''

''My husband lives in a godly way, Officer.'' Her cheeks flushed with outrage. ''He has even suffered doubts over whether a man should have such relations with his wife when procreation is not the goal. He would never think of his own daughter in such an obscene way.''

''I'm sorry I had to suggest it.''

''You've met my husband.'' Alice Lange quivered with such emotion, the recliner creaked. ''Surely you could see what kind of man he is!''

Too tactful to say, *Yep, sure could,* Meg only repeated, ''I'm sorry. I had to ask.''

''Look at her room.'' Mrs. Lange stood. ''And then leave, please.''

Behind the closed door, Shelly's bedroom had

been sterilized. It was perfect, the room of a preteen. Stuffed animals slumped in too tidy a row against the pillow on her twin bed. The spread was ruffly, as were the curtains; the books on the one shelf were titles like *Alice in Wonderland* and *The Secret Garden,* worn and well-loved, but surely not by the eighteen-year-old Shelly. Porcelain dolls stood stiffly behind glass in a case. The only thing of interest Meg found were the high school yearbooks, in which Shelly was pictured as a bubbly, glamorous, popular girl—a homecoming princess, cheerleader, and "Most likely to marry well," according to her peers.

Shelly's parents hadn't preserved their daughter in this room. Nor had they stripped it to wipe out any evidence of her existence. Instead, they had selectively discarded what they didn't like, as if they could create a different reality.

The disturbing part was that, along with posters of rock stars, her parents had discarded Shelly herself, the living, breathing young woman their daughter had grown into.

Meg had thought Shelly's mother might feel differently than her husband. She'd been wrong. He'd spoken for both of them: they had already said their goodbyes. The real Shelly's death didn't touch them; they didn't know her. Didn't want to know her.

Meg drove back to the station feeling grateful, most of all, that the Langes weren't seeking custody of little Emily.

The Harlequin Reader Service® — Here's how it works:

Accepting your 2 free books and mystery gift places you under no obligation to buy anything. You may keep the books and gift and return the shipping statement marked "cancel." If you do not cancel, about a month later we'll send you 6 additional novels and bill you just $3.57 each in the U.S., or $3.96 each in Canada, plus 25¢ delivery per book and applicable taxes if any.* That's the complete price and — compared to the cover price of $4.25 in the U.S. and $4.75 in Canada — it's quite a bargain! You may cancel at any time, but if you choose to continue, every month we'll send you 6 more books, which you may either purchase at the discount price or return to us and cancel your subscription.

*Terms and prices subject to change without notice. Sales tax applicable in N.Y. Canadian residents will be charged applicable provincial taxes and GST.

If offer card is missing write to: Harlequin Reader Service, 3010 Walden Ave., P.O. Box 1867, Buffalo NY 14240-1867

NO POSTAGE
NECESSARY
IF MAILED
IN THE
UNITED STATES

BUSINESS REPLY MAIL
FIRST-CLASS MAIL   PERMIT NO. 717   BUFFALO, NY

POSTAGE WILL BE PAID BY ADDRESSEE

HARLEQUIN READER SERVICE
3010 WALDEN AVE
PO BOX 1867
BUFFALO NY 14240-9952

Play The Lucky Hearts Game

and get... FREE BOOKS, a FREE GIFT... and MUCH more!

yes! I have scratched off the silver card. Please send me my **2 FREE BOOKS** and **FREE MYSTERY GIFT**. I understand that I am under no obligation to purchase any books as explained on the back of this card.

Scratch Here!
then look below to see what your cards get you...

DETACH AND MAIL CARD TODAY! (H-SR-09/99)

© 1998 HARLEQUIN ENTERPRISES LTD. ® and TM are trademarks owned by Harlequin Enterprises Limited.

336 HDL CTH2   **135 HDL CTHQ**

Name
_____
(PLEASE PRINT)

Address _____ Apt.#_____

City _____ State/Prov. _____ Zip/Postal Code_____

Twenty-one gets you **2 FREE BOOKS** and a **FREE MYSTERY GIFT!**

Twenty gets you **2 FREE BOOKS!**

Nineteen gets you **1 FREE BOOK!**

TRY AGAIN!

Offer limited to one per household and not valid to current Harlequin Superromance® subscribers. All orders subject to approval.

PRINTED IN U.S.A.

FINGERING THE PINK SLIP of paper with the message—Renee called—Meg dialed her sister's phone number.

"Patton, here." The voice was brisk, businesslike, a cop.

Two peas out of the same pod, Meg thought wryly. She put her feet up on her desk. "Hey. Meg, here."

"Meg." Her sister's voice changed. "At last. Do you know how tough you are to catch? Anyway, is everything okay with Jack and Will? I, uh, wanted to say I'm sorry for my part. I was trying to hustle him out…"

"Hustle?" Meg got it. "You mean, when Will came to see you? Oh, I know my son too well to blame you. And, yeah, things are fine. I should have listened to you and not procrastinated. My fault. But Jack took it better than I deserved. Will's going there for dinner night."

Renee expressed pleasure; they chatted idly. Ben knocked on the glass insert in Meg's door and jerked his thumb toward the parking lot. She waved him off, but opened her mouth to say, *I've got to go.*

What came out instead took her by surprise. "Have you ever had an investigation that got really personal for you? I mean, either the crime hit too close to home, or the people involved made you think about stuff in your own life?"

Renee was quiet for a moment. "Yeah," she said at last. "I had one like that."

"What was it?"

"Daniel's dog brought home a human skull. I spent a few weeks following up on missing people. I'd lay awake nights thinking about you and Mom."

I'm sorry. Meg didn't say it, not again. Apologetic words were like table manners, something your upbringing made easy or hard, but good or bad they said nothing deep about your true state of regret or repentance.

"How did you handle the investigation?" Meg asked. "I mean, how did you keep your feelings out of it?"

Again there was a small pause before Renee said brusquely, "My feelings weren't a problem. I did my job. That's all."

Subject closed. Or maybe Renee had chosen a simple way of saying, *I decided I could do fine without the mom and sister who chose to go missing. And I'm still doing fine without them. Without you.*

Whatever, she didn't want to talk. It hurt, but Meg had to respect that. Choices made couldn't be unmade. Love and trust once lost couldn't be restored.

Right this minute, Meg was glad Jack was holding out welcoming arms to Will, because otherwise she'd think she had made a big mistake.

"Okay," she said to her sister, her voice as uncaring as she could make it. "Listen, I've got to go. I'll see you later." She hung up without listening to Renee's polite promise to call.

A big mistake, Meg thought again, pressing a fist to her left breast as if she could stifle the heartache. Or maybe she should think of it as a lesson.

You can't go home again.

CHAPTER NINE

A SEXY WOMAN was on his doorstep, and Scott had to say sheepishly, "I, uh, couldn't find a baby-sitter. Do you mind if I bring Emily?"

Meg Patton smiled, making him immediately regret the loss of the evening he'd planned. Did you kiss a woman for the first time in front of a baby?

"Oh, yeah," she said, "entertaining a baby in a restaurant is so much fun. How about if I go pick up some take-out?"

She'd changed out of her uniform, which he took as a good sign—maybe she planned to do more than eat and run. Or should he say, *had* planned, before she discovered her date had become a threesome?

Below the parka, her pants were black, the fabric something plushy. Corduroy? Velvet? He didn't know, only that it was softer and dressier than denim. On the other hand, the black boots beneath them didn't make it look as though she expected to be taken to Chez Marie, which was a relief.

"Can I admit something?" he asked.

"If you invite me in."

Feeling like an idiot, Scott stood back. Busy imagining her without so many clothes on, he hadn't even noticed the freezing air rushing in.

"Just my way of making you welcome."

"Ah." Inside, she didn't unzip her parka. "Confession?" she nudged.

"My housekeeper couldn't stay tonight, but I asked her to make dinner. A lasagna is ready to go in the oven. Unless you'd be uncomfortable here," he added scrupulously.

Her smile deepened. "Let me get this straight. You've been scheming to keep me locked in your house."

"Uh…" He hadn't actually tried very hard to find a baby-sitter once Marjorie had turned him down. "I guess you could look at it that way. The truth is, I didn't like the idea of leaving Emily with some fourteen-year-old who'd spend the whole evening on the phone with her bosom friends giggling about boys."

"Is that what Shelly did?"

The question was a zinger, pulling a double punch: he had a sudden memory of coming home with Penny and finding Shelly curled up on the couch asleep, looking almost as young as Nate; superimposed was the image of Shelly's crumpled body.

"Is that why you came tonight? To ask more questions?"

He saw a flash of hurt in her eyes. "No. You're right. I'm sorry."

Scott swore. "No. I'm the one who's sorry. I don't like to think about Shelly alive because she's all tied up with Nate in my mind, and I don't much like remembering her dead, either."

Meg gave a small nod, left it there. "Where *is* Emily?"

At a distant clang, his mouth tilted up. "Kitchen. She's emptying the pans out of a cupboard."

Meg shed her outer garments and followed him and the clatter of metal. They found Emily's pink corduroy rear end poking out of the cupboard. A delighted squeal was followed by a lid that came shooting out to roll across the kitchen floor. Scott winced.

"You might want to try keeping plastic storage dishes in the bottom instead," Meg suggested.

"Ah, she's not hurting anything." He bent over and patted that round, diapered bottom. "Right, Emily?"

Wham! A sauce pan crashed into his shins. Scott jumped back. "You've got a mean arm on you, kid."

Meg's chuckle was almost as delighted as Emily's. They were both easy to please, he thought in amusement.

"So," he said, "what's it going to be? Lasagna, or takeout?"

"Oh, there's a toughie." She gave him a look. "I'll bet your housekeeper can cook."

"Yep. Why do you think I hired her?"

"Pop it in." With the ease of a child, Meg sat cross-legged on the floor so she could peer in at Emily.

As he turned the oven on to preheat and got the foil-covered casserole dish out of the fridge, Scott listened to her talking to the baby.

"Hi, Emily. I'm Meg. You know, you're missing a good bet here." She rose to her knees and opened two drawers before she found what she wanted: a wooden spoon. Back down at baby level, she showed it to Emily, who sank back on her rear end on the floor. "See? You bang it on the pan. Like this."

Emily got the idea. A thunderous metal drumming vibrated Scott's eardrums.

"Thanks!" he called.

Meg gave him a wicked grin. "You're welcome."

Emily wasn't crawling yet, although she was learning to scoot along on her tummy like an eel wriggling through the water. Mostly she was content when he plopped her down in a sitting position, as long as she had something to entertain herself with.

"She eating solids yet?" Meg asked.

"Cereal. She likes to play with Cheerios and slices of banana. She's getting the hang of it."

Emily's soft dark hair stuck straight up, as if the ceiling called to it. Her brown eyes were wide and gleeful, her cheeks plump and pink. Meg was making faces at her, and Emily laughed until her belly quivered. All the while she banged pots and lids and finally the cupboard door with her spoon/drumstick.

Finally he couldn't take it any more. "All right, pip-squeak," Scott said. "Let's find something quiet for you to do."

Emily didn't want to do quiet. She screeched and then burst into tears when he scooped her up. Meg rose, too.

"Can I hold her? I haven't had an armful of baby in a long time." Immediately, she looked appalled. "I'm sorry. I know you…"

Scott shook his head and handed over the sobbing little girl. "Don't worry. It's hard not to talk about babies with her here."

They finally got her settled in the living room, where the softer dhurrie rug in front of the couch was strewn with her toys: stacking bright-colored rings, foam cloth-covered blocks and a plastic noise-maker that whinnied and mooed and baaed when she punched buttons or turned knobs or moved levers. The sight of Meg sitting on the floor playing with the baby tweaked a few uncomfortable emotions in his chest.

Since Emily had come, memories thinly disguised as dreams haunted his nights. They didn't bother with disguises during the day, just trooped around after him like ducklings who thought he was mama, pecking at his heels.

So far they'd mostly been of Nate, with Penny present only by necessity. One night he'd lived again seeing his son born: the vivid colors, Penny's grunts and wails, the slick head crowning, the rush with which he'd come out, his rasping cry and the sight of him suckling on his mother's breast. Scott had never known such euphoria, such awe.

He'd awakened—or had he ever been asleep?— and read for a while, some thriller that was supposed to be great but failed to grip him. Eventually he'd slept again, only to find himself in a movie theater, with Nate's funeral playing on the big screen.

Scott would have been the star if he'd displayed any emotion, but as it was he walked through the part looking blank, numb, a man in a dark suit with dry eyes and a sobbing wife on his arm. Jesus, the sound of the casket dropping the last inches into the ground, the clunk of dirt striking the shiny top, the minister's speech about God's will, the guilt clawing at him—was this somehow his fault? Had he done something wrong? Hurt his son laying him in the crib? committed a sin that demanded repayment?— all of it filled the screen and crashed over his head in Dolby sound.

But watching Meg sit there on the floor playing with Emily, apparently completely absorbed in the baby's chortles and wonder, brought back Penny, too.

In retrospect Scott realized they had married too young, that even then a silence had been growing between them, one they'd needed a child to fill. Nate had been fresh glue to their relationship. He'd allowed Scott to see his wife anew. She'd been a wonderful mother: soft, gentle, patient, content to wrap her life around their son. In a primitive, male way, Scott had found appealing the idea that he and their son were her whole world.

One morning, on a thin cry of terror and grief, her world was torn in two.

"Penny had other children," he said suddenly, earning a startled look from Meg. "Later, I mean. She remarried. A boy and a girl, according to my mother. The oldest must be almost ready for school now."

Understanding softened Meg's eyes. "Does it bother you that she had more?"

"No." He shook his head. "No, I was glad for her. After Nate...after he was gone, I had work, a life. Penny didn't have anything."

"Did you really have that much of a life?" Meg asked gently. "Or were you kidding yourself because you didn't want to admit how much you'd lost?"

A week ago he'd have scoffed at the idea. Now

he made a sound in his throat. "I was kidding myself, of course."

Her mouth curved. "Honesty."

"Emily coming along hasn't been a bad thing for me," Scott admitted.

"How like a man." A dimple flickered in her cheek. "Not 'she's been good for me,' but she 'hasn't been a bad thing.' For starters, she's not a *thing*."

Probably by accident, Emily had stacked blue and red rings onto the central rod. Not in the right order, of course, but they were both on there. She looked so damned cute, with her downy hair that refused to lie flat and small plump hands and a smile that lit a room. She made him think about Nate, but she wasn't Nate; he had no confusion there. Emily Lange was her own determined self.

And he was having a harder and harder time imagining the day when he handed her over to some eager adoptive parents.

When that day came, he wasn't so sure he'd still think she had been good for him.

Scott let out a gruff laugh. "This has been a hell of a dinner date. Now you know why I have women lining up."

Meg's smile was pure delight, too. "I have a suspicion you do."

Pleased despite himself, Scott countered, "Not so's I've ever noticed."

She gave him a long slow look that raised his blood pressure. "Come on, you're a sexy man. Maybe you just haven't been ready to start noticing."

"Oh, I'm ready," he said. He'd gone right on past

"noticing" to Step No. 2. He was already savoring the idea of kissing Deputy Margaret Patton. He had always liked tart better than sweet.

Scott didn't let himself contemplate the question of why, then, he'd married such a sweet woman.

Emily flung a ring away and let out a screech, then kicked the whole toy away in a fit of rage.

"Did it get the better of you?" Meg asked, scooting toward her. Meg's hair, loose tonight, streamed like a ribbon of moonlight over one shoulder and breast. It was all Scott could do to tear his attention from her slender, creamy neck and his fantasies of kissing his way down to her shoulder and breasts.

Emily helped by letting out a bellow and looked tearfully at Scott at the same time as she lifted her arms. Forget food or sex as a way to a man's heart. This little girl already knew the secret.

He stood and picked her up in one movement. "Hey, getting hungry, pip-squeak?"

Her lower lip trembled and tears shimmered on her lashes.

"Yep, I'd say so," Scott murmured. He looked apologetically at Meg. "Why don't you come pour us some wine while I warm Emily's formula? I can smell the lasagna. I'll throw a salad together as soon as I put her down for the night."

"A salad I can do," Meg said firmly.

Emily snuffled until the microwave beeped and he pulled out her yellow plastic bottle. Then she grabbed for it and began to suck furiously.

"Why don't you take her out into the living room?" Meg suggested. She was already hauling things out of the refrigerator. "I'll just putter here."

THE BABY NODDED OFF just as she finished her bottle. Scott had to wake her up to change her diaper and wriggle her out of the overalls and into a sleeper, but when he settled her on her back in the rented crib and gently pulled a flannel comforter over her, Emily closed her eyes and stuck her thumb in her mouth. Scott slipped out of the room, taking only one quick peek back in.

He was getting better at this.

He returned to the kitchen to find the table there set with quilted place mats and matching napkins folded into small fans.

"I rooted around," Meg said. "I hope you don't mind."

"Don't be ridiculous." He couldn't remember the last time he'd bothered to do more than hook a leg over a stool and shovel his microwaved food in his mouth while he read the newspaper. He guessed he'd needed a woman's company.

"Next time we'll go out," Scott promised.

Meg gave him a quick, absentminded smile as she shredded lettuce. "I like this better, anyway."

Emily wasn't the only one who knew her way to a man's heart. "Your son's a lucky kid. Does he know that?"

"Most of the time." Meg picked up the peeler and started in on the carrots. "Right now, Emily's lucky to have you."

Right now. Two innocent words reminded him of the ache ever-present under his breastbone.

"You'd have found some place for her."

Another quick glance made him wonder if she didn't see more than he'd like. "But not all places feel like home to a child."

He was a man generally suspicious of compliments. She had a way of slipping them under his guard. He said abruptly, "This place didn't feel much like home until she came along. I barely slept here."

"It's a beautiful house." Meg touched the leaf pattern in the tile backsplash. "Did you design it?"

"With the builder. Gave me something to think about."

"Did your wife ever live here?"

"No." He didn't want to talk about Penny, and could think of only one out. "You found Rieger okay yesterday?"

"Mmm." She set the salad bowl on the table and watched him take the lasagna from the oven. "Yum, garlic bread, too."

"Let's hope Emily doesn't wake up just as we sit down. It wouldn't be the first time."

Over dinner they talked about the investigation. He frowned at her recap of Tony Rieger's story. "He thinks Shelly was afraid of someone who works at Juanita Butte?"

"Well, he didn't make it sound as if she feared for life and limb. More that she was seeing someone who was possessive. Although…" Meg frowned, her fork halfway to her mouth. "I wondered if he wasn't so forthcoming because *he* was afraid. If this guy killed her because she was messing around with other men…"

"But Tony was old news, from what you say."

"Yeah, the guy'd have to become a serial murderer if he decides to knock off every man Shelly dated. She got around."

"She was a nice kid." And he sounded defensive, for no reason he could figure.

Meg didn't seem to notice.

"Her father's a jerk." Her voice held some indefinable tension. "If I can indulge in a little pop psychology, I'd say she was trying to find herself a new daddy. Hard to tell if sex was ever really the point with all these men."

"I barely met Lange." Scott chewed thoughtfully. "I'm trying to remember Shelly's mother and coming up short."

"That's because there's not much to notice. Her entire purpose in life seems to be keeping her husband happy. No, that sounds too active. Trying *not* to make him unhappy."

"She's afraid of him?"

"Yes, but also genuinely of the opinion that the man should be lord and master in his home. Her role in life is to smooth his way."

Scott growled a profanity.

Meg touched his hand, sending a shockwave up it. "I think we can assume Kenneth Lange never gave his daughter her bottle or changed her diaper or tucked her in."

"Then he's an idiot."

"That, too," she agreed serenely.

Something he'd been wondering. "Is your son home alone tonight?"

Her head was bent as she stripped the crust off a piece of garlic bread, but he felt her hesitation. "No," she said then, voice too even, too careful. "He's with his father. He lives here in Elk Springs."

Scott was uncomfortable to discover that he didn't like the idea of her seeing her ex—on a regular basis. Chatting about the good old days with him. Smiling. Sharing the boy they'd made together.

What in hell was wrong with him?

In the face of his silence, Meg continued. "I have family here in town, too, you know."

Scott asked about her sisters, but he felt restraint there, as well.

"You're not close to them?" he asked, and was stunned when she flinched.

"No, I guess you could say we're not." She continued shredding the bread. "My fault."

"Why?"

She told him a story then, about a pregnant, sixteen-year-old girl who ran away from home in terror of what her father would do to the child she carried.

"Did you ever meet my father?" At Scott's shake of the head, Meg continued. "He was cold. Except when he was angry, which was too much of the time. Abby and Renee and I were disappointments to him. He wanted a son. Well, look at us! In our own ways, we tried to meet his expectation. How else to explain two daughters who are cops and the third who's a firefighter? But, you see, whatever we did was never enough. He'd have punished me for getting pregnant, and the worst thing he could have done was sue me for custody. Once he found out I'd had a son..." She shuddered, this fearless woman.

"And if he'd raised your boy..."

"Will would either be a juvenile delinquent, or he'd be just like my father."

"Sounds as if you did the only thing you could do." Scott frowned. "So what's the problem with your sisters?"

"I should have found a way to rescue them, too. I should at least have called regularly and *listened* to them. Instead I just—" now she was stabbing her lasagna with her fork "—took the course of least resistance. I didn't do anything. I convinced myself they'd be fine. They didn't need me." Meg looked up at last, torment in her eyes. "You know what I had the gall to say to them just last week?" When he wordlessly shook his head, she said in a tone of self-loathing, "I told them, my own sisters, that for Will's sake I'd felt I had to think about the future, not the past. Well, they were in my past and I let them down."

"You can only do what you can do." Scott grimaced. "I'm sorry. That's pat. But also true. You were sixteen, not even an adult yourself. And it seems like Will's father wasn't helping you."

Her gaze shied away from his again; she didn't want to talk about Will's father. "Okay, I was sixteen." She poked that poor lasagna again, as if she were trying to maim it. "A kid. I'm excused. So why didn't I call when I was eighteen? Or twenty-one? Or whenever 'adulthood' struck?"

"Because it was too late," he said bluntly, "and you knew it."

She stared at him in shock, then gave a laugh that held not a grain of amusement. "You understand, don't you?"

Scott swore. "We're all cowards sometime. Why should you be any different?"

"Because I'm the big sister and I'm supposed to be perfect." Humor did light this smile. "Big sisters can never admit they're wrong. Didn't you know that?"

"Yeah, I had a pretty good idea," he agreed, cracking a smile of his own. "Big brothers hold to the same belief."

"You're one?"

"I have a little brother." Six two and two hundred pounds, but "little" forever more to Scott. "He's a park ranger at Bryce in Utah."

Meg asked, so he told her some about growing up with a father who worked nine-to-five Monday through Friday but packed the family up every weekend and vacation to head for the mountains.

"We backpacked, camped, skiied... The farther away from civilization, the happier he was."

"Past tense?"

"He died three years ago. Stroke." A late-night phone call from his mother had set Scott to frantic efforts to get plane reservations. His mother had called back ten minutes later. Dad was dead. Just like that. Scott rubbed the back of his neck. "It was sudden, at least. He'd have hated a long stay in a nursing home."

"And your mother?"

"Doing fine. Her idea of a vacation these days is a Caribbean cruise."

They talked about nothing and everything after that: family, childhood, movies and pets. He told her about the first few days with Emily, when she would cry and cry and nothing he did was right, because he wasn't her mother; about the gradual change, the sense that they were connecting, her increasing trust.

Emily didn't wake up, and Meg didn't rush off to interview a murder suspect. Just as she'd been content earlier to play with the baby, now she seemed happy to sit at his dining room table, sip wine and talk.

The further the evening wore on, the more Scott thought about the end of it. The idea of kissing her, now that was a spice to flavor any topic.

Funny thing, though. He wasn't sure their conversation needed any jazzing up. He thought of himself as someone who went straight to the point, not given to meaningless chitchat.

So maybe this wasn't meaningless.

Which meant he liked her. No more, no less. *Don't get carried away,* he told himself. *Remember the Emily factor.* Having a baby in the house was making him soft, too inclined to feel domestic.

The argumentative side of him countered, *Yeah, but if that's all you feel, a tart-tongued lady cop busy investigating a murder is a damned unlikely choice for romantic fantasies.*

Sexual ones, maybe. Domestic, no.

Stick to thinking about a kiss, he advised himself.

Not hard, given that luscious mouth and the way a tiny dimple flickered in her cheek when she smiled.

Right now, the dimple vanished and he realized she was waiting politely for...what?

"Uh, excuse me?" he stammered, feeling like a sixteen-year-old with a tight zipper.

"I just said that I'd better be getting home." She made getting-up motions. "I've got an early morning tomorrow."

The reminder of her job made Scott feel all grown-up again suddenly, and not in a good way. Memories of Shelly and the maybe-married man she'd feared—someone Scott knew and trusted—got in the way of fantasies of any kind.

"Can I help you load the dishwasher?" Meg asked, starting to pick up her coffee cup and saucer.

"I'll get it." Scott rose to his feet, too. "I'm glad you took this evening off."

Her blue eyes met his directly. "My pleasure."

No, his. Definitely his.

On the way to the front door, Scott asked, "Working a murder like this, can you ever get it out of your mind? Or do you keep seeing her…"

"Dead?" Meg stopped by the front door, faced him. "No. I guess I have compartments. You have to. Otherwise the scumbags you deal with would leave you feeling dirty all the time. Or you'd get to be scared, not wanting your kid to drive, because after all he might end up like the teenagers in that four-car pile-up out on Highway 2." She shook herself, as if shedding unpleasant memories. "No. Life outside work is one thing, enforcing the law another. Once in a while the two trip over each other, and it's not comfortable."

"You mean, you have to arrest someone you know?"

"Well, I guess that could happen, but no, I was thinking of this case, actually." She wrinkled her nose. "Shelly and I have a lot in common. She wanted her father's attention and love so much. I haven't figured out whether she hated him, too, the way I hated my father. I have to keep telling myself, 'She's not me. Don't assume you know what she was thinking.'"

He'd been itching all evening to slip his fingers into her hair. Now he did, smoothing it back from her face. "She's making you remember things you'd rather not, just like Emily does for me."

"Except I might have been remembering, anyway." Meg closed her eyes and turned her face toward his hand. Her voice sank to a murmur. "Coming home does that."

Blood roared in his ears. Her hair felt as shimmery and insubstantial as it looked, so delicate it was an illusion that might vanish when he took his hand away. Her breath, warm against his wrist, shook him to the core.

"Meg," he said roughly.

She lifted her face as naturally as if they'd kissed a thousand times. He found that more breathtaking than shyness or surprises.

He bent his head, touched his lips to hers, felt her tremble. They tasted, eased back, came together again. All so softly, so tenderly. Her shoulders felt fragile. He kissed his way across her cheek to the pulse that beat beneath her jaw. Her breath caught; she gave a ragged gasp when his mouth trailed to her throat.

And when he captured her mouth again, it was with a ferocity and intent that surprised both of them, although after the first start Meg only gripped him and held on, kissing him back with a strange mix of innocence and knowing that was her and her alone.

When he finally lifted his head, they stared at each other, first in shock and then wariness.

Too much, too soon. He thought it; could see she did, too.

A first kiss was supposed to be clumsy, tentative, not all that satisfying. It wasn't supposed to feel as perfect as pouring the foundation for a house an architect had worked on for months. A man might feel randy, or disappointed, or hopeful. But he shouldn't feel his guts turning over because the woman he'd kissed was going to say a casual good-night and walk out the door.

She was opening her mouth to do it when he cut in. "Meg, I enjoyed this. If I promise to get a baby-sitter next time, will you have dinner with me again? I'd suggest tomorrow night, but I know you'd say no. Sunday night?"

Her smile was like dawn in the high mountain country, pure, sweet and mysterious. "You're right. I would've said no. I'm too fond of my son. But I would love to do this again Sunday, whether you get a baby-sitter or not."

A moment later she was gone, and Scott felt a kind of anticipation he hadn't known in years. Since seeing his son's cold body, he had learned he could get through any one day, as long as he never thought of having to get through tomorrow, too. He had, for him, a rare poetic image: the days were like stepping stones through a tangled garden. To endure, he'd had to concentrate on each one, refusing to let himself know that it wasn't a single stone, but instead the beginning of a path that would lay itself unceasingly before him. *Today* was flat, hard, sometimes rounded, sometimes sharp-edged. He didn't give a damn what tomorrow's stone looked like.

He didn't know how to go on and on anymore; didn't care what was around the curve.

Hadn't known how. Hadn't cared.

Suddenly, thanks to Emily with her big brown eyes and Meg with her too perceptive questions,

Scott found he did care. Sunday was beyond the next curve of the path, and he wanted to get there as much as he'd ever wanted anything.

He wanted to live.

CHAPTER TEN

JEFFERSON ROBB, Shelly's English professor, proved hard to nail down. He was sick; his colleagues had to take over his classes. But he wasn't answering his phone or his doorbell at home, and he wasn't in the hospital.

"Bastard's hiding out," was Ben's opinion.

And Meg's. But, in fairness, she felt compelled to say, "He might have been feeling too crummy to answer the phone. Or he could have been visiting family when he got sick..."

Ben sneered. She gave up.

"Okay. You want to scale the back wall of his house and peer in his bedroom window?"

He growled something she took as an admission that no, doing so would be stupid.

"Do you really think he killed Shelly?" she asked.

They were on their way to Robb's place again, Ben driving—when they were together, she'd conceded to his male need for control and usually became the passenger. Meg figured with her behind the wheel, sooner or later they'd have an accident when she was distracted by him squirming and slamming his foot down on an imaginary brake when he wasn't offering helpful comments on approaching traffic.

"Who better to have killed her?" he asked.

"I don't know." Meg sighed. "Her lover at the ski area."

"The one nobody seems to know anything about?"

"Except Tony."

"You have only Tony's word for it."

"Why would he lie?" she asked.

Ben didn't answer. He didn't *have* an answer. She knew, because they'd had this conversation before. Several times.

A phone rang, and both Meg and her partner reached for their cell phones. "Mine," she said, and pushed Send. "Patton, here."

"Meg, this is Jack Murray."

Her heart raced. "Jack. Is something wrong with Will?"

"Why would you think that? I haven't seen him today. I'm just wondering…well, if you'd have dinner with me tonight."

She was speechless for a moment. "Dinner? You mean, like a date?"

She'd seen Scott again last night. This time per his request she'd dressed to the nines and they'd had an elegant candlelit French dinner at Maximillian's, after which he'd kissed her on her doorstep. Kissed her very nicely, thank you.

Scott McNeil was plenty to handle at one time.

Sounding uncomfortable, Jack said, "I just thought we should talk. About Will. How he feels about all this, what kind of time I'm going to spend with him. But if you're busy…"

"No." She glared at Ben Shea, who was quirking one of his thick dark brows interestedly her way.

"Dinner sounds fine. Seven? Sure." She disconnected.

"Was that Police Chief Jack Murray hisself?" the detective asked, tone mocking.

"None of your business."

His face went expressionless.

"Yes." Her mouth clamped shut. She made herself add, "He's…uh, Will's father."

"So I've heard."

"You listen to gossip?"

"Don't you?"

"Sometimes," she admitted reluctantly.

Ben pulled into the driveway of Jefferson Robb's modest house in old town Elk Springs. Gray clapboard with white and black trim, the little bungalow wasn't that different from the house Shelly had grown up in. Or Meg, for that matter. She should have felt at home.

Instead, she was in a bad mood. She didn't want to have dinner with Jack tonight. They'd argue again about the past; he'd try to twist the way she remembered it, convince her he'd been capable of self-sacrifice at seventeen, which she doubted. She'd be jealous because Will took her for granted and was infatuated with his father.

And she'd wish she was with Scott instead.

"Coming?" Ben stood with his hand on his car door, preparatory to slamming it.

Meg went.

Professor Jefferson Robb answered the doorbell so fast, he had to have seen them coming up his cracked concrete walkway.

"Officers?" he asked, pretending to look puzzled.

Meg didn't buy it for a second.

She showed her badge. "We need to speak to you about a student of yours. Shelly Lange."

"I heard about her death. Tragic." He shook his head, dark wavy hair going silver at the temples. "By all means. Come right in. I won't get too close to you. I've had a nasty flu. Probably past being contagious now, but you never know."

The front door led right into the living room, which even to her less-than-critical housekeeping eye was untidy. Newspapers littered the floor, books and dirty dishes heaped the coffee table and end tables. At least two cats fled the room at the sight of visitors. If Meg wasn't mistaken, their unseen litter box could use a change.

"Mr. Robb—"

"Doctor," he interrupted, then chuckled. "Not that it matters. But 'mister' makes me want to turn my head and see if someone else is behind me."

I'll just bet, she thought uncharitably. Jefferson Robb was a tall, strongly built man, clean shaven with finely chiseled features, a rich voice, and just a little paunch above the waistband of his trousers. She noticed only because he tugged his sweater-vest down self-consciously.

"Dr. Robb," she corrected herself, "tell us about Shelly. Was she a good student? Conscientious?"

He waved them to the sofa and said patronizingly, "Oh, not capable of great depth of thought. But willing and smart enough. Turned in her work on time. I detected an eagerness in her that I hope I encouraged."

"You had her in your class last semester, as well?"

Yes, indeed he had. Oh, yes, her *B* first quarter

had risen to an *A* second quarter, and he credited himself with inspiring her to greater effort.

"Dr. Robb." Meg paused for effect. "We've received an allegation that the *A* you gave Shelly was in fact payment for physical favors from her."

"What?" he spluttered. "Ridiculous! Who told you that?"

"Actually, other students have since substantiated the story. Your...body language toward her was apparently quite revealing."

Sweat beaded on his high forehead. "What you're suggesting would destroy my career! Are you reporting to the college administration?"

"No." She gentled her voice. "Dr. Robb, we're trying to get at the truth about her death. Your professional ethics are not our concern."

"Oh, God."

With melodramatic suddenness, he buried his face in his hands. Those hands were long-fingered, elegant. She imagined him on stage, but doubted he was pretending.

"Dr. Robb," she prodded, her tone neutral now.

"My wife left me because of her." He lifted a distraught face. "I had to cleanse my conscience. I told Jeanette. She wouldn't listen when I told her it was over. That it wasn't about Shelly. I just...lately I've been overwhelmed by everything." He flung out an arm, compelling Meg to look around at the modest living room, the trappings of small-town middle-class life.

Not an irrelevancy, she guessed, but the crux, for him. He wouldn't be the first man his age to have a midlife crisis. Most people had to come to terms at some point with where life had taken them. Robb had a Ph.D., apparently. Had he dreamed of full professorship at Harvard? Yale? Regular publications in literary digests?

Instead, he found himself teaching at a two-year college, which even Meg knew was the bottom rung of the academic ladder. He'd probably never written a great novel. This house was the most he could afford.

"She was so beautiful," he mumbled, and she realized he was actually crying now. "She admired me, flattered me. I did inspire her, she claimed. How could I resist?"

"Seducing her?" Ben asked in disgust.

Jefferson Robb looked up wildly. "She seduced me! She kept coming to my office, sitting on the edge of my desk, touching me... Oh, God," he said again. "I've lost Jeanette."

They untangled his story, which erupted from him in angry, fearful and grieving bursts. Shelly *had* earned the *A,* he insisted; she'd worked hard for it, whatever other jealous students insisted. He'd seen dramatic improvement in her work.

They'd had sex only three or four times, always in his office, with the door locked. Staring, remembering, he said, "Right on my desk. She just sat there, and lifted her skirt, and she didn't have any underwear on. Not that first time." The stare swung blindly until it encountered Meg, focused with difficulty. "You see? It was her. But I should have resisted. I admit it."

He'd been going to end the affair, but hadn't had a chance. After the Christmas break, Shelly had appeared to lose interest. She didn't come by his office, and he could hardly say anything to her in class. His hints that she wait afterward were ignored.

He'd been relieved, her professor claimed, but Meg had her doubts. Why had he wanted Shelly to stay after class if he didn't want to continue sexual relations?

Two weeks ago he'd apparently talked in his sleep. His wife probed, and he confessed. She immediately packed up and left him. Except for a few trips to the grocery store, he'd been holed up here ever since.

When asked, he said that Jeanette Robb had gone to her sister's in Redding, California. He knew she was there, because he heard her voice in the background when he called, saying that she didn't want to talk to him.

Anguished eyes lifted again to Meg. "She would never...*kill* someone!" He said it with such astonishment. An impossibility. "Not Jeanette. She carries spiders outside rather than step on them. You can't seriously think..."

No, Meg didn't. If events had occurred that Monday evening as she imagined, Shelly had driven around with her murderer for some time, persuaded him to leave her daughter behind, perhaps sat there without running while he unbuckled the car seat and set it on the icy ground. She had struggled, fallen, tried to escape once they had parked at the Puma Lake trailhead and he led her into the woods. She had known then, if she hadn't sooner. Another woman might have shot Shelly as she fled through the heavy snow, but could she have yanked Shelly to her feet, shoved her on, dominated her physically? No.

Jefferson Robb, however, could have done all of that.

And yet, why would he have? He'd already confessed to his wife. What more did he have to lose?

His job, Meg reminded herself. Would Shelly have tried blackmail?

And murder, of course, was not a crime of logic. When he saw his world crumpling, he might have turned his rage on Shelly, the seductress. He might have decided it was all her fault, that she should pay, that her death would absolve him.

"Dr. Robb, where were you last Monday evening?"

"Monday?" He looked around as if for enlightenment. "Was that when she… Oh. I was here, of course. I told you. I haven't gone any place."

"Did you speak to anyone on the phone?" Meg asked patiently.

"Monday." With a shaking hand, he reached for a mug of coffee that sat beside his chair. He stared into it and then set it down without sipping. "I called Jeanette. Spoke to her sister."

"And do you have a cell phone?"

"Yes, but I didn't use it. Why would I? The phone's right over there."

He didn't seem to realize that, as far as Meg was concerned, he could have used the cell phone without anyone ever knowing. He could have called from the Puma Lake trailhead. "Dr. Robb," Meg asked, "when did you meet Shelly Lange for the first time?"

"When?" He stared, understanding coming only slowly. "Why, September. When she enrolled in my course."

"So, she already had her daughter."

"Yes. That is, I didn't know she had one, un-til…" His fingers clenched on the arms of the chair. "When we were making love, I found that she…that she was nursing. I hadn't known…"

"Very well." Meg closed her notebook and rose to her feet. "Dr. Robb, please don't leave town. We may well have further questions."

He didn't see them out, his bonhomie gone like his wife.

"You're NOT GOING to wear that, are you?" her son, the critic, asked the moment Meg stepped out of her bedroom.

She glanced down involuntarily. The slacks were the same ones she'd worn to Scott's, and she liked the crocheted linen vest over the untucked white silk shirt. "What's wrong with this?"

"It's…" He shaped something formless with his hands. "It's *baggy*."

"Yeah? So?"

"Don't you want to look pretty?"

Well! She'd actually been rather pleased by what the mirror showed her. Under the hurt pride, how-ever, suspicion niggled.

"Why would I want to look pretty?" Meg's eyes narrowed. "William Patton, you aren't getting ideas, are you? Your father and I are old history. We are *not* getting back together."

His chin thrust out, but he backed into the living room. "I didn't say that."

"But you were thinking it, weren't you?" An ob-servant parent would have seen this coming, she scolded herself. One not working twelve-hour days and trying to conduct a romance, too.

Flinging himself onto the couch, her son said sulkily, "I just thought…when he asked you out…"

"We're going to talk about *you*. About his visitation rights. For Pete's sake, Jack probably has a girlfriend. *I'm* dating someone, in case you hadn't noticed."

"Yeah, like *twice*." He sneered. "You're not exactly married, you know."

"No, I'm not, but I won't be marrying your father, either. So forget it." She waited until he met her eyes. "All right?"

He rolled his eyes and shrugged. "Yeah. Whatever."

This was the first major teenage attitude she'd gotten from Will, but she let it go. She'd made herself clear; message sent and received. She could even sympathize; from his point of view, think how great it would be to have newfound father marry his mother, forming the great American family.

The phone rang. Will rolled from the couch and bounded for the kitchen. Meg stared after him in astonishment. Back before they'd come to Elk Springs, that behavior had been typical of him. Nobody, he seemed to believe, would bother to call his mother; ergo, the phone must be for him. He'd always seemed so disbelieving when he had to hand it over to her. But so far he apparently hadn't made any friends in town, and usually couldn't be bothered to pick up the phone even when she was in the shower.

She heard the murmur of conversation from the

kitchen, then he bellowed, "Mom! It's Aunt Renee!"

"My eardrums," Renee groaned when Meg took the phone.

Meg grinned. "They thicken once you have kids. Kind of like developing callouses."

"It's called 'going deaf.'"

"Well, yeah, now that you mention it."

"What I called for," her sister said, "is that we thought it might be fun to have a potluck tomorrow. Abby's coming."

"I can't take the day off…"

"Dinner at seven," Renee said persuasively. "Will tells me you're dating someone. You can bring him. And his kids, if he has any."

"Come on." Meg leaned a hip against the counter and watched her son pretend an interest in the contents of the freezer. Frosty air poured out. "Surely Will told you every gory detail."

"Well, he did say that you were out with the guy who found the baby. Scott McNeil, the general manager of the ski area."

"And Abby gave you the rundown on his looks, career prospects and general character."

"Hunky, excellent, and she doesn't know him well enough to say for sure."

"What a family." Meg shook her head. "I'll ask him. He may not want to declare himself that far. Coming to meet the family… I don't know."

"Family," her sister mused. "Somehow, it was hard to think of us that way, with just Abby and me. Now, with Daniel, too, and you and Will…"

"I didn't forfeit my right to be included?" Meg asked, tone light although the question wasn't.

"What are you talking about?" Renee sounded outraged.

"I was kidding."

"You weren't."

The doorbell rang. Meg covered the phone. "Will, can you get that?"

Dumb question. He was already gone.

"I'm sorry," Meg said to her sister. "I'm having dinner with Jack, and he's here."

"Dinner?"

"You mean, he didn't tell you?" Meg asked wryly. "There's something you don't already know?"

"I guess not." Renee sounded awed. "Jack?"

"Don't you get ideas, either," Meg warned. "We're discussing visitation."

"Uh-huh."

Argh. "I'll ask Scott. If he's home."

"Okeydoke," her sister said cheerily. "You can have Will call me."

Renee hung up and poked her head into the living room. Will was going through the motions of sinking a basketball shot and Jack was laughing, head thrown back and teeth white. Shirt open at the throat, he wore slacks and a sportscoat that hung the way it was meant to from his broad shoulders.

Shoulders *she* had once gripped as he kissed her, she thought, with that sense of disorientation earned by visiting the past.

If it weren't for Scott, would she be thinking like Will?

"Hi, Jack. I've got to make a quick call."

His gaze swept over her. "No problem."

Scott answered at home on the second ring. "McNeil, here."

"Hi." Glancing at the door to be sure neither Jack nor Will had followed her, she spoke softly. "This is Meg."

Scott's voice warmed. "I was just going to call. Any chance you and Will would like to go out for pizza?"

"I'm sorry." She was, despite the handsome man waiting out in the living room. "Will's dad is here. We need to talk. You know. About visitation and stuff." Meg was immediately annoyed with herself. Why hadn't she just said, 'I'm having dinner with him?' But no, now she felt as if she'd lied.

Scott seemed to sense that, because his tone became expressionless. "Oh? No problem."

"Any chance you're free tomorrow evening? Renee is having a potluck. I mean, you don't need to bring anything. I will. But I thought it would be fun if you and Emily could come."

"You sound like you're suggesting a fate worse than death," he said, amusement coming through.

Meg took a deep breath and laughed at herself. "It's just that there's something about inviting a guy to come meet the family. I thought *you* might think…"

"I didn't think," he interrupted her. "I'd like to come. Are you sure your sisters won't mind if I bring Emily?"

"Are you kidding? You'll have to pry her away at the end of the evening. I think Renee is starting to get ideas."

"Ah." That gravelly note of amusement still lingered in his voice. "I'd better tell Emily to be on her best behavior, then. Wouldn't want her to scare your sister off. Be responsible for her never having children.''

They set a time, Meg called Renee back and then returned to the living room. Jack half sat on the back of the sofa while Will chattered. Meg felt a pang that was becoming familiar. Ever since the move, he hadn't talked to her like that. Her inquiries about how school was going were returned with a grunted, ''Fine.'' If she asked whether he'd made friends, she got a shrug and, ''Not really.'' He didn't become animated, not the way he was right now.

Did he resent the hours she was working? Her dating when she didn't have time for him as it was? Or was he just reaching an age when he needed a father more than a mother?

Jack saw her and smiled the crooked, slow grin that had turned her stomach into knots when she was sixteen. ''Ready?''

''Ready,'' she agreed.

She felt guilty as all get-out when they left Will standing alone in the living room, even though he looked far from unhappy. In fact, his expression as he waved goodbye was irritatingly smug.

Sitting in the car, she waited until Jack slid in behind the wheel. ''Maybe we should invite him. Make it a family outing.''

Buckling his seat belt, he shot her an unreadable glance. ''I was hoping to talk to you alone.''

What did he have to say? Meg worried. ''Oh. Okay,'' she agreed. As he backed out of the driveway, she saw Will standing in the front window watching them go.

On the way, Jack asked about the Lange murder. He was familiar with the father's oddball church.

"They're narrow-minded," he said. "I think they're folks who came together because they share the same intolerance and desire to punish themselves and everyone else in the name of the Lord, but they're not one of those nutty sects with some messiah, either. Making a kid pray until he faints and then punishing him is one thing, but I think they're sincere in their belief in the Bible and the Ten Commandments. You getting any hint Lange sexually abused his daughter? Is that what you're driving at?"

"The thought crossed my mind," Meg admitted. "But we've talked to other members of the church who believe Kenneth Lange is a good Christian who wanted what was best for his daughter. The bishop told Ben Shea he spoke to Lange at about nine o'clock, like the wife said. They claim not to have a cell phone. While my guess is that she'd lie for him about some things, I think even she'd balk at having her husband bedding her daughter."

"And nine o'clock lets him out?"

"Looks like it," Meg said.

He pulled into the parking lot of Maximillian's. "This okay?"

"Fine," she said brightly. Like she was going to admit she'd been here last night.

The maître d' arched a brow at her, but was far too tactful to comment about her succession of men. Meg pretended to peruse the all too familiar menu, then ordered beef bourguignonne, a change from last night's duckling Rouennaise. She might as well enjoy. Hey, how often did men want to wine and dine her at a place this fancy?

The waiter brought wine, uncorked it and waited for Jack to sip the first glass and nod his approval. He and Meg chatted for a while. Meg was pleasantly surprised by Jack's intelligent, open-minded views. Yet, as they compared anecdotes from their police work, she sensed in him the violence and intolerance learned from her father.

The conversation reached a lull; Meg toyed with her food, feeling the increased intensity in Jack's dark gaze. She was braced for his abrupt decision to finally get to the point.

"My parents liked Will."

She met his eyes squarely. "He's a nice boy."

"That's to your credit."

"How nice of you to say so." Meg tried valiantly to keep the sarcasm from her voice.

"Was he okay with the visit?"

"His exact words, I believe, were, 'They're cool.' Said with enthusiasm. He's never had grandparents, you know."

"He could have had them."

She closed her eyes. "Do we have to do this again?"

Jack continued ruthlessly. "Why didn't you tell me you were pregnant?"

"I was going to." Her mouth twisted. "When I got done panicking. I was trying to talk to you that day. Only, instead…"

He finished, "We made love."

"I don't know about the love part," Meg said flatly.

The waiter appeared, to be sure they didn't need anything; Jack curtly expressed their satisfaction.

The moment the man was out of earshot, Jack said in a hard voice, "I guess it wasn't love, or you wouldn't have walked away without a word, would you?"

Her temper began to rise. "How many times do I have to say it? I wasn't walking away from you."

"I think you were." Lines deepened on his face. "Your dad scared the hell out of me. What kind of man did I look like?"

She wanted to tell him that wasn't it, but in all honesty couldn't. If he'd stood up to her father, maybe she would have decided to trust him. Maybe she'd have turned to him and his parents, or at least stayed in touch.

"You were a teenager, not a man." They both needed to remember that.

"I had no business getting you pregnant if I couldn't take care of you and the baby."

"Maybe so," she said wearily, "but neither of us had the sense to be careful. Any more than teenagers in general have the sense to drive within the speed limit, not take pills some other kid hands them…" Meg gestured helplessly. "Jack, don't beat yourself up forever over something that happened when you were in high school."

"What makes you think I'm beating myself up?" He glowered. "I'm just asking why you let one incident change both our lives. Why you didn't give me a chance."

"Because I didn't dare." She lifted her hands, let them fall. "Jack, I wasn't thinking about you. That sounds awful, but remember, *I* wasn't even seventeen. I'd just finished hearing you tell my father you'd never call me again. What was I supposed to do?''

A muscle in his jaw worked. "I never forgave myself for crawling away from him. Leaving you to face him alone. And then, when you were just gone the next day…"

"You were mad at me?"

Jack swore. "No. Only at myself. But I didn't know you were pregnant. To go all these years and never tell me…" He shook his head.

"I thought you'd probably be married, have other children…" Meg gave a small shrug. "I wasn't so sure you'd welcome the news that you had a son."

"It's taking some getting used to." He took a long swallow of wine. "But he's a good kid. I can see myself in him. The best part. Will's no coward."

She tried again to convince him that he hadn't been, either. Only outmatched. Her father had been a big, powerful, angry man; Jack, a gangly teenage boy who'd never dealt with anyone like Ed Patton before. He hadn't grown into it, the way she had.

And she realized, in retrospect, that he had attracted her in the first place because he was so different from her father: laid-back, uncritical, a good athlete but not competitive enough to be a great one. She had loved him because of his nature, and yet that very nature meant he would never be able to stand up to her father.

She couldn't say any of this, however, because her impression was that the Johnny Murray she had loved as a teenager had set out to change in himself the very qualities that had made him loveable to her. And now it was too late; Jack Murray wasn't her father, but he had certainly learned harshness from her father. Or perhaps he had learned it on his own; self-contempt was a sharp prod.

They resolved nothing; how could they? Jack paid the bill and left a generous tip. He opened the passenger door for her, closed it when she was settled in the car. He went around, climbed in behind the wheel and shoved the key into the ignition.

But to her disquiet, he didn't turn it. Instead he looked at her, his face etched in lines of torment by the inner fire she hadn't—couldn't—quench.

"I loved you. I would have married you."

She swallowed. "We were too young."

"Maybe." He let out a ragged breath. "I don't know whether to be glad you brought Will home, or wish you'd stayed away."

"I needed...closure."

Jack gave a humorless laugh. "You sound like some damned pop psychology book."

"I think you need it, too."

"Great," he growled. "Give it to me."

"I can't," she breathed, unable to look away from his dark eyes.

"Yes. You can."

Just like that, he reached for her, his hands gentle despite his mood as he tipped her face up and kissed her.

Meg stayed passive, let him claim her mouth, but she didn't respond. On the heels of Scott's kiss the night before, this was a strange experience. Their mouths touched, pressed, moved; Jack's shaven jaw scraped her cheek. But that's all it was: she felt more emotion when she hugged her sisters.

As suddenly, Jack broke off the embrace, releasing her. They stared at each other.

He cleared his throat. "Well. That was more fun fifteen years ago."

"It was, wasn't it?"

He actually laughed. "I figured it was worth a try. You have to admit, the two of us together would have been convenient."

"For Will," Meg agreed.

"Ah, well." He started the car, laid an arm on the back of her seat as he looked over his shoulder to back out. "You don't mind my seeing him regularly, do you? Maybe take him camping when summer rolls around?"

"Of course not. He's got a huge crush on you, you know. He can't believe he has a father. Just…deserve him, okay?"

Jack shifted into gear. In the diffused lighting from the street lamp and dashboard, his expression was dead serious. "I didn't deserve you. I won't make the same mistake with our son."

CHAPTER ELEVEN

UNDERCURRENTS TWISTED and sucked beneath the surface of this family gathering. The most powerful and obvious to Scott was the fact that Meg's son hated his guts. Heck, it wasn't even an undercurrent; white rapids ripping over jagged rocks was closer to the truth.

He felt obligated to keep trying with the kid, although he wasn't getting anywhere. At the moment, they were beside each other dishing up from the array of offerings on Daniel and Renee Barnard's dining table.

"Your mom tells me you're quite a basketball player," he said.

The boy's shrug was the essence of youthful sulkiness. "I used to be okay."

Scott pushed the potato salad on his plate aside to allow room for Boston baked beans. "You're not playing this year?"

"The season was half over when we got here." *You must be stupid not to know that,* was clearly implied.

"Yeah? So? Did you ask to join the team?"

"It's full." Sullenly.

In other words: no.

They'd reached the end of the table and Scott's plate was overflowing. "Well," he said, with an effort at friendliness, "from what your mother tells me, it's their loss."

Ignoring him, the kid added two rolls to the mountain on his plate. He looked too stringy to put that kind of food away, but Scott seemed to remember being hungry all the time at that age.

Will gave him a dirty look, then slouched away. Daniel Barnard's big yellow Labrador retriever clicked after him, apparently choosing him as the best bet for handouts.

Scott caught Meg's eye. She'd already dished up and was sitting on the couch. Patting the spot beside her, she smiled invitingly. He glanced around for Emily, who was being entertained by Meg's two sisters.

The fact that they were on one side of the big living room and Meg on the other was the surface ripple from another of those undercurrents Scott sensed. The three women were polite enough to each other—everyone had been all smiles when he, Meg and Will arrived—but none of them was totally comfortable, not the way family should be. Too quickly, Meg had ended up talking to Daniel Barnard, Renee and Abby cuddling Emily.

Scott paused above the two women, his hands full with food and a can of soda pop. "Let me set this down and I can take her over now."

Neither of them even bothered to look up. Renee cooed at the little girl, who grinned back. Abby dangled a ribbon with bells until Emily's plump hand seized it and shoved one end into her mouth.

Rescuing the ribbon, Abby said, "You can't have her. We're having too much fun."

Renee bent forward and kissed the fuzzy corkscrew curl on top of Emily's head. "Eat. Take a break. Abby's right. You can't have her back yet."

Shaking his head, Scott joined Meg and Daniel, who sat with his plate balanced on his knee, watching his wife and sister-in-law.

"You were right," Scott told Meg. "I think they wanted Emily, not me."

Saved from homeliness by friendly blue eyes, the big rancher chuckled. "Renee's getting ideas. I can tell. Well, hell," he said in an easy voice. "She's the one who wanted to wait, not me. I'm all for populating the Triple B with little Barnards."

"Being a cop and a mother at the same time isn't always easy," Meg remarked between bites of fruit salad.

"Yeah, that's why she wasn't in any hurry." Daniel shrugged. "Maybe she still isn't."

The three looked in unison at Renee, who was now holding the baby. Emily grabbed Renee's nose and gave a deep belly laugh. Renee pinched her nose in return and laughed just as joyously.

"Yeah?" Scott said. "Don't count on it."

"Where's Will?" Meg asked, craning her neck to see as far as the dining room.

"I saw him go into the family room. I figured maybe he was going to turn the TV on." Daniel downed some beer. "He's not in a good mood."

Get it in the open, Scott decided. "I'm afraid it's me."

Meg's hesitation was brief but noticeable. She must have realized she'd given herself away, because she made a face and said in a low voice, "Yep. In a manner of speaking. He just doesn't seem to like me dating. I'm afraid he has visions of me marrying his father.''

"Jack Murray?'' The rancher almost choked on his roll. "What would make Will think anything like that?''

"It's a common fantasy for a kid with a single parent.'' Meg sounded wry, resigned. "If the parents have divorced, they're going to get back together. If the father has never been around, he's going to sweep in, romance mom, become the perfect dad. Here's Will getting to know his for the first time…'' She made a face. "It'd probably be surprising if the idea didn't occur to him.''

Scott watched her narrowly. How did *she* feel about the idea? She and Jack Murray had gotten together for dinner; was there more to it than she'd said? He'd had the feeling she wasn't saying something yesterday, but told himself he was imagining it. She'd kissed him like she meant it Sunday night; she'd invited him today, hadn't she?

And why the hell was a fourteen-year-old kid barely getting to know his father? What was wrong with Jack Murray? Scott would have given anything to watch his son grow up, and Murray had thrown the chance away.

"He'll get over it,'' Daniel said comfortably, digging into his food.

Meg looked at Scott, her eyes troubled. "I know you're right,'' she said, but she didn't sound as if she believed it.

Too harshly, Scott said, "If Murray didn't bother to take any part in raising his son, why does Will give him the time of day now? Much less want you to marry him?''

Barnard looked startled, and Meg's eyes widened. Hastily she said, "It was...complicated. Not all Jack's fault." Looking at her brother-in-law, she gave her head a small shake, and Scott couldn't help wondering what she was warning him about.

"Not *all* his fault?" he echoed.

"I'm the one who took off." She stared down at her plate, voice stifled.

Belatedly, Scott realized this wasn't the time or place to say what a bastard he thought Jack Murray was for not helping his girlfriend raise their son. Bastard? The word hardly did him justice. Scott made a sound in his throat.

"I'd better check on Emily," he said abruptly.

Meg raised her head and gave a twisted smile. "She's happy. Look."

Scott didn't even have to turn his head; Emily's giggle wafted across the big room.

Playing host, Daniel asked Scott how he'd gotten into the business of ski areas, and he let other worries go to concentrate on a fine meal and the kind of casual conversation that built friendships.

"I was a ski bum," he admitted. "My dad hooked us on wilderness life, though he didn't like lifts and grooming equipment and the necessity of logging mountainsides to open the ski runs. He cross-country skied, but me—once I discovered speed and moguls, hell, I was an addict. I went to the University of Vermont so I could ski and get an education at the same time. After that—well, I'd been a lift operator and run the groomers while I was a student. I went into public relations, financial..." He shrugged. "What you don't realize is that pretty soon you won't have time to ski."

"Do you mind?" Meg asked.

He smiled faintly. "Skiing turned into work. For maybe five minutes a day, when we have some new powder snow or the skis carve right, I remember. Most of the time, I'm too busy checking out the job the workers are doing, watching for reckless kids on boards or blindspots to get any pleasure from going down the hill."

"Would you go back if you could?" she asked softly. "Do something else, so skiing was still fun?"

Scott shook his head. "I'm lucky enough to do what I love for a living. Sometimes it's not as much fun as it was when it was just a hobby, but I remember often enough. I consider myself a lucky man."

"Amen," the rancher murmured, and their gazes met for a brief moment of communion.

As soon as he'd finished eating, Scott insisted on taking Emily upstairs for a diaper change and a try at getting her down to sleep. She'd be cranky in no time and wear out the welcome for both of them if her routine got too messed up.

It took half an hour of rocking and turning country-western tunes into lullabies, but the house was well enough insulated that he couldn't hear voices from downstairs and Emily finally nodded off.

Renee had blown up an air mattress on the floor. Scott swaddled the baby in the afghans his hostess had left neatly piled, then checked to be sure Emily couldn't get into anything if she woke up and he didn't hear her right away.

Downstairs he found that Meg had disappeared.

"She's talking to Will," her youngest sister said airily. "So, what's this I hear about a new lift at

Juanita Butte dropping over the ridge past Outback?''

He lounged in an easy chair and pretended that he didn't wish like hell he could hear what was going on between Meg and her son.

"You know all the environmental laws," he said. "We are thinking about it. The studies and permits will take a year or more, though."

He'd already known Abby Patton, even wondered a little about her. She was a beautiful woman, slim and strong and vibrant, eyes as blue as a Siamese cat's. Her pale gold hair was thicker than her sisters', just long enough to shimmer like aspen leaves in a breeze when she shook her head, to provide her something to brush back with a deliberate slow movement, drawing attention to a lush mouth and delicate jaw and a dimple that came more readily than Meg's.

Abby was too young to interest Scott no matter what, but she wouldn't have, anyway. She was too conscious of her beauty and its effect; everything she did and said was too deliberate. Her playing with Emily was the first time he'd seen her let go and act silly, laugh like a girl instead of with throaty, sensual intent. She was cool, this woman, her real emotions held back. A man too blunt to play games, Scott was wary of Meg's youngest sister.

He liked Renee better, felt at ease with her. She and Meg were more alike, he thought; strong women with soft hearts and sharp minds. The middle sister, Renee had hazel eyes and the same straight, fine hair as Meg, but somehow their similar features had made two distinctly different women. An occasional gesture or smile, a turn of the head, and he saw the other, but for reasons that puzzled Scott, Renee would never have been sexually attractive to him while every time he saw Meg he imagined her long legs bare and wrapped around his, her breasts freed for his mouth and hands to explore.

Funny thing, the trigger that turned a man on. Once he saw Daniel looking at his wife, and he knew that even after a few months of marriage the rancher was thinking the same things Scott was about Meg.

In the middle of that thought, Meg wandered back into the living room, but some tension around her eyes derailed his idle fantasies. His muscles tightened as he prepared to stand, but just then Renee called from the dining room, "Meg, is that you? Come on. We haven't talked yet. Let's put the food away and catch up at the same time."

The three adults left behind chatted idly. Daniel explained that his mother was over in Portland visiting his sister Mary.

"She likes playing grandma," he said with a smile.

Scott glanced around with pleasure at the big, spare room. He liked the texture of the Berber carpet and the soft leather couch and chairs, the bird's-eye maple of the coffee table, the few paintings and drawings against white walls. He didn't like clutter. This room—this house—suited him fine.

After a bit he slipped upstairs to check on Emily, who still slept soundly. She was mostly a noisy sleeper, today being no exception. She slurped on her fist, grunted, wriggled, then relaxed again. He could never resist taking a minute to watch her sleep, face round and dimpled, unmarked by the trauma she didn't know she'd experienced.

Tenderness bumped up against him, as tangible as Emily's solid little body when she slept on his shoulder. She hadn't been with him that long—just over a week, but already she felt rooted in his heart, as if she were his.

The past few days he'd been wondering if maybe she could be. The adoption agency probably had a long list of ideal couples just waiting for a baby. Did the fact that Emily already knew him and lived with him count for anything, or would she be handed over to whoever had been waiting longest? Heck, maybe they'd turn him down anyway because he was a single man who worked long hours.

And maybe one of those perfect couples would be better for Emily. But he loved her, and that mattered most, didn't it? Scott hadn't gotten past thinking; nobody was worrying about Emily's final placement yet anyway. For one thing, they might find her father.

If he wasn't a murderer, it could be that he'd want his daughter, and then Scott would have no choice but to hand her over.

As he came down the stairs, he heard Renee's voice from the kitchen.

"Do you remember what you asked me the other day? About whether I'd ever had a case that was so personal it gave me trouble?"

Meg murmured assent.

"Well, I lied." Meg's younger sister spoke abruptly, with a hint of defiance. "Yes, I solved it, but not before I'd met Daniel, fallen in love, trashed most of Dad's stuff and realized I was wasting my life waiting for you or Mom to come home."

Silence fell briefly; even the clink of dishes stilled. Then Meg fixed on one part of that list.

"You trashed Dad's stuff?"

Scott stopped where he was on the stairs, knowing he shouldn't be listening but unable to help himself. Meg Patton was taking root in his heart, too, just as quickly as Emily had. Her place there scared him as much as Emily's, maybe more. At least Emily herself was uncomplicated. If the state agency let her, she would happily stay with him and love him. Meg, now—he didn't have the slightest idea how serious she was about him.

Whoa! he told himself. *You've dated twice. Kissed twice. You don't even know if* you're *serious. Don't get ahead of yourself.*

"Yeah," he heard Renee say, "it just all got to me one night. I was living in that damned house as if Dad were still walking in the door every day at five-thirty demanding dinner. I didn't change anything. I was afraid to. I couldn't even bring myself to sit in his chair. A few times I'd swear I saw it rock out of the corner of my eye. I moved the TV out into the kitchen, hurried through the living room when I had to. I was just…existing. One night Daniel decided to exorcise Dad. He threw his recliner off the front porch. When it crunched and splintered, I wanted to scream with joy. I didn't see any reason to stop there. Everything went. I even pulled up the carpet. When I was done, it seemed like there was nothing left of him."

"Good for you." Meg's voice was slightly muffled, and Scott guessed that she was hugging her sister. "I used to wish he'd die. That someone would shoot him in the line of duty. I don't know what I thought would happen to us, but at least *he* wouldn't be part of it."

"You, too?" Renee asked. "I felt so guilty for thinking of him dead! For wishing…"

"What about Abby? How'd she feel?"

"I don't know." Renee sounded worried. "He was easier on her. Mostly, she had him wrapped around her little finger. I don't think she loved him, but she didn't seem to hate him, either. Do you think that's healthy, not to be passionate one way or the other? I mean, this was her *father!* The only parent she remembers."

"I've wondered…"

Increasingly conscious of what they'd think if they caught him hovering up here, Scott started down the last few steps. On the way up he'd noticed the basket sitting there, but he'd forgotten and managed to kick it. A hairbrush and a bottle of fingernail polish clattered onto the floor.

Both sisters appeared in the doorway to the kitchen.

"Sorry," he muttered. "I wasn't paying attention."

"Did you put Emily down?"

"Yeah, I was just checking on her. She's out like a light."

"Why don't you come in the kitchen?" Renee suggested, as if he hadn't interrupted anything. "I was just telling Meg about how I met Daniel. His dog brought home a human skull."

The grotesque image made him curious enough

to intrude. "That would make you sit up and take notice," he said, following them. "What can I do?"

Renee handed him a dish towel. "Why don't you dry as I wash the pans?"

Behind him, Meg puttered around the kitchen putting food away in the refrigerator and wiping counters. As they worked, Renee told the story.

Daniel had thought the skull belonged to his senile grandfather, who had wandered away one snowy night and was never found. But Lotto, the dog, had brought home other bones, as well, and taken together the coroner could tell that the skeleton was that of a young man—and one who had been murdered ten to twenty years before.

"But he didn't seem to be anybody who'd been reported missing." Renee went still for a moment, hands in the dishwater, unfocused eyes meditative. "That ate away at me. Nobody caring enough to report him missing. I started wondering if first Mom and then you, Meg, had really left and just never bothered to call or write, or whether you weren't dead somewhere in an unmarked grave. Jack kept wanting me to drop the case—it's not like we aren't always busy enough that he needs every officer, and it was an old crime. But I just couldn't let it go.

"Daniel didn't like me too much at first, because I was out here bugging his mother all the time. With his dad dead, she was the only one who'd remember ten, fifteen years before. Thank goodness she's forgiven me—we're just about best friends now. I finally figured out that the dead man was Gabe Rosler, the son of the neighboring ranchers. You might remember him, Meg."

She paused in the act of putting tin foil around a

pile of ham. "Was he a year or two younger than me? Kind of a strange kid? Yeah, I think so."

"His father killed him," Renee concluded. Her voice sounded odd. "Pretty well my worst nightmare."

"I'm sorry." Meg went to her in a rush, and they hugged, wet hands and all. "I should have called. I know I should have called."

Feeling as out of place and about as comfortable as a skier after his first lesson suddenly stranded on a forty-five degree hill, Daniel grabbed another pot and pretended not to notice the two women's damp eyes.

They murmured a few watery *sorries,* and *It's okays,* then apparently remembered his presence and backed awkwardly away, returning to their tasks. He saw Meg tangle some cling wrap, wipe away a tear and then start over. Renee swished around in the dishwater without accomplishing anything for a minute.

Finally she asked, "Are you getting anywhere with finding out who killed Emily's mother?"

"Well, we've eliminated some people. Shelly's parents, for one. Aside from a phone conversation at a critical time, his feet aren't big enough."

Scott swung around to stare at her. "You didn't say anything. Did you get any kind of decent casts of those footprints?"

"Better than you might think." She gave him a warning look. "This is just between us and the wall. Okay? But, yeah. The print isn't clear enough to tell brand of boot, but we can eliminate some. The last time I went to the Langes', I saw his slippers. Size nine. He's not a big man. Those weren't his tracks."

"So now what?" he asked.

"So now I keep digging." Meg closed the refrigerator door. "I hope you'll make it clear to your people that you want them to cooperate with the investigation. At least one person has hinted to me that she knows something she isn't saying."

He frowned. "I'll have her into my office. Who is it?"

"Let me approach her again, not send you crashing down on her."

That stung. "You think I'm a tyrant?"

She squeezed his arm, a light comforting touch, as she passed him on her way back to the kitchen table. "No, but you're the boss. No one doubts that for a second. Telling tales on another employee is awkward, you have to admit."

Scott grunted reluctant agreement.

"I'm going back up there tomorrow," Meg continued. "If I talk to enough people and I'm persistent enough, something will give. It always does."

Then why did so many murder cases remain unsolved? he wanted to ask, but guessed the answer might be—because a Patton wasn't investigating them. These two sisters had that in common: they were dogged once they started on something.

"I worry," Meg said then, out of the blue, "that I'm identifying too much with Shelly Lange. That's why I asked whether you'd gotten too personal about any case, Renee."

"You're identifying with the victim?" her cop sister echoed. "Why more than usual?"

"Oh, it's all mixed up. Partly me having just come home, which set me to thinking about Dad and our childhood." Meg took a dried pan from Scott's hand and absentmindedly hung it on a wrought-iron rack over the kitchen island. "Partly it's Shelly's relationship with her father. It seems to be the key to her behavior. She never got his attention or approval, so she's been looking for both from other men ever since. But, see, that's where I start wondering... Am I reading something into the choices she made that isn't there, because I figure she must have felt about her father the way I did about mine?"

Soapy water was gurgling down the drain. Renee turned her back on it to face her sister. Drying her hands on a dish towel, she said, "But you didn't go looking for approval from other men." Sudden uncertainty gave a hitch to her voice, uneasiness to her sidelong glance at Scott. "Did you?"

Meg looked from one to the other of them, then laughed. "You ought to see your faces! Do you think I'm going to admit that I was wildly promiscuous after I ran away from home?"

Scott decided then and there that he wouldn't let it matter if she had been; God knows he'd done and—most of all—said things of which he was ashamed. Meg was who she was now, not what she'd been at seventeen, trying to care for a baby and scrape up the money for rent and food.

Renee gave it a moment's thought, then a brisk, knowing nod. "No. Of course not. You would have been promiscuous in high school if you were hunting for a sugar daddy." Her amused gaze slanted toward Scott again. "Sorry, Scott. I don't suppose your relationship was quite ready for this."

"Oh, I don't know," he drawled, lifting a brow

at Meg. "I'm a man. It's never too early for sex. Isn't that the stereotype?"

"You wouldn't be here today if I thought you were a stereotype," Meg snapped.

Renee flung the dish towel at her sister. "Hey, give him a break! I set him up."

Turning away with a sniff, Meg said, "Well, I'll tell you what. I can't figure out how Shelly found the time for men."

"Maybe there weren't any," Scott heard himself saying. "Maybe her image was all smoke and shadow."

Meg stuck out her lower lip while she thought. Scott wanted to kiss her.

"I don't think it was faked, not totally," was her conclusion. "Everyone seems to agree that she lit up for men. In her world, women were just…there. Wallpaper. Even though she was vibrant and beautiful herself, the reality she grew up with is that men are dominant, women are important only as they relate to a man. Alice Lange as good as admitted to me that she exists only to support her husband. Just for a minute, when we told them what happened to Shelly, I saw some fire, but it was dead ten minutes later when she was more anxious to alibi Lange than she was to mourn her daughter."

"I still can't remember Shelly's mother," Scott admitted, "and I lived next door to the Langes for two years."

"Exactly." Meg pulled out a stool and perched on it, knees boyishly apart although she wore a long swirly skirt and a skimpy top with spaghetti straps under a white cotton shirt.

Knowing she wore no bra under there might be

why his imagination wasn't having any trouble undressing her.

Renee boosted herself up onto the counter and sat with feet swinging. "Okay. So your theory is, Shelly had to be like Mama and find a man to worship and obey?"

"Something like that." Meg sounded troubled more than eager. "Maybe she'd have been okay if her father had ever validated her by spending time with her and expressing pride in her, but he didn't. So she's been looking for a substitute ever since. Maybe she loved sex. Maybe it was just the price she paid. But boys her own age wouldn't do. She needed a man who was older, in a position of authority. A guy her own age was better than nothing, which is why she had boyfriends, but as one woman told me, Shelly was always looking over their shoulders for someone more important. The professor was worth going for aggressively. Question is, who else was?" She leaned forward, voice going quiet, intense. "And who satisfied her drive enough that she chose to get pregnant by him?"

"You think it was a choice?" Scott asked.

"On some level."

Renee was nodding. "Yeah. I agree. Don't you think *you* made a choice with Jack?"

"I'd have denied it then, but now…" Meg made a face. "Sure. You're more likely to be careless when you're ambivalent about the outcome."

"But there's no sign of the baby's father in Shelly's life?" Renee said. "No child support? Photos? Nothing?"

"Not that we've found so far. Certainly no financial support."

Scott had been brooding about something else entirely. "She really liked Penny," he said. Seeing Renee's puzzlement, he added, "My ex-wife. Shelly used to hang out at our house. She'd get all excited and giggle when I came home—flutter her eyelashes at me, talk loudly, get me to admire her nail polish. That kind of thing. But she spent time with Penny. If it weren't for Nate, if Penny and I had stayed put, I wonder if Shelly's life would have come out different."

Compassion made the blue in Meg's eyes so vivid they seemed bottomless. "Shelly wasn't your responsibility."

"No. Of course not." Absorbed in their grief, neither he nor Penny had given a thought to the neighbor girl who seemed to have too much time to spend at their house. They had abandoned her from the moment they laid their son to rest. Why hadn't they wondered about Shelly's life in that house where a mother was home, but seemingly not present? Could they have made a difference?

Oh, hell, Scott thought. There was no way now of knowing whether Penny had meant anything to Shelly. After the move to Elk Springs, his wife been a housewife, just like Shelly's mom; maybe that put her in the same category—dependent on a man. But Shelly had seen Penny argue with him, tease him, defy him. Maybe...

He swore silently. All he needed was one more burden of guilt.

Meg let out an exasperated huff of breath and for a wild moment he thought she'd been reading his thoughts. But, no, she was looking past him at the doorway.

"I suppose I should go see what my oh-so-charming son is up to. And here I thought I was raising the one teenager who would never suffer this kind of ridiculous angst."

Her sister hooted. "You would! Meg, Superwoman! You always did think you could do anything." But her laughter was affectionate, running deeper and quieter than the studied politeness earlier.

Meg seemed to recognize that, because she only gave a Big Sister look and said, "Wait'll you have kids."

"Go." Renee hopped down from the counter and flapped a hand. "I'll finish up in here."

"I'd better check on Emily," Scott said guiltily. Except as an abstraction, he hadn't thought of her in half an hour or more. What if she was screaming upstairs, scared at waking in a strange place, without the familiar white-painted crib?

He'd have sworn she had slept better once he'd picked up her very own crib from Shelly's apartment; Emily was more likely to be cooing and cheerful when she woke up than she had been those first days in the rented crib. Once, he'd come in to find her chatting to the yellow and pink ducks stenciled on the headboard, her bright eyes fastened on them as if they'd come to life. "Your mama painted those," he'd murmured as he picked her up. "Aren't they pretty?"

But Emily left Scott's mind again the minute he followed Meg and realized they were briefly alone in the hall. Behind them, dishes clinked in the kitchen; ahead, lazy voices drifted from the living room. But nobody could see them here.

Meg had—he hoped—the same thought, because she turned to face him.

"Scott, I'm sorry," she said in a rush. "Will's a great kid. He's not usually…"

"It's okay." Scott wrapped a hand around her nape, under the silky fall of hair. "He's a teenager. They're entitled. He's used to just the two of you. Of course he resents me."

She turned her head enough to kiss the bare skin on his forearm. "If it weren't for Jack…"

"Why are you even giving Murray a chance now? You must have come back to Elk Springs just to make fatherhood convenient for him. Is knowing him that important to Will?"

Some emotion flitted across her face. *Guilt?* he thought, then couldn't believe it. Resentment, maybe.

"I'm the one who didn't give Jack a chance." She said it apologetically, without her usual conviction. She didn't even believe herself. "I've lived all over the world, you know. I should have made it my business to get home to Elk Springs sometimes, but… My father was here, and… Life gets complicated."

Why should she have had to do all the work? Scott had heard good things about Jack Murray, but did people know he had a son he hadn't made any great effort to see? Scott growled in the back of his throat.

"You've had to do too much alone," he said.

"No!" She stiffened under his hand, and that elusive emotion ghosted through her eyes again. "It's been all joy. I wouldn't have wanted to lose Will every summer, the way some single mothers do."

"*All* joy?" His voice had gone husky. He
kneaded her neck, feeling the delicacy and strength
both. He wasn't troubling to bank the fire anymore.
"There weren't times you would have liked a helping hand?"

"How could Jack have helped me?" Meg fired
back, eyes hot with—what? Then the expression on
her face changed, blazed with hunger. "Let's not
talk about it. Kiss me good-night now. While we
have the chance."

To hell with Jack Murray. Fool that he was, he'd
lost not only a son, but this incredible woman, too.

"With pleasure," Scott murmured, and captured
her mouth with his.

Quivering with tension, she rushed into the embrace as if she'd been waiting forever for it. Her lips
parted, her tongue met his, her arms came fiercely
around his neck.

Desire slammed into him. Scott backed her into
the corner by the stairs. One hand tangled in her hair
while the other gripped her buttocks and lifted her
against him. The tenderness of those other kisses
was missing; flat-out *wanting* had shoved it aside.

And he wasn't alone. She was sobbing for breath
and rubbing against him, as lost in the need as he
was.

But he couldn't quite forget where they were. God
Almighty, if Will came on them—saw his mother
taking a man's hand and laying it on her breast...

A groan tore its way from Scott's chest and he
weighed her small breast in his palm with pleasure
and regret.

"Sweetheart," he said, low and rough against her
neck.

"Kiss me," Meg demanded raggedly.

One of the hardest things he'd ever done was lift his hand from her high, firm breast and smooth her hair back from her face. "Meg, anyone could come along. Including your boy."

Her eyes had gone cloudy with wanting; the focusing came slowly, as reluctantly as he called her back.

"Oh, my God," she said. "Will."

"We'll take this up another time." Scott kissed her smooth forehead, intending to let her go. But, oh, the way her face tilted up! Somehow his lips found the bridge of her nose, her closed eyelids, her cheekbone, her earlobe...

"Scott," she whispered. "Emily is crying."

"What?" Then he heard it, the thin frightened wail. He swore under his breath, rested his forehead against Meg's. "Yeah. Okay."

"And there's Will. I should find him."

"I know, I know."

"I wish..." she barely breathed, not finishing.

"I wish, too." He kissed her, quick, hard, then made himself retreat a step. "Someday we'll be alone."

"You think?" She backed away.

"I don't think. I know," Scott promised.

She must be visible to the people in the living room now. "I'll hold you to it," Meg said, so softly Scott just heard her. And then she disappeared to find her son.

All he could think about as he headed up the stairs was how soon they could be alone.

And that Jack Murray was an even bigger fool than he'd thought.

CHAPTER TWELVE

FINDING TIME to be alone wasn't as easy as it should have been. Between work and kids, Meg and Scott couldn't manage it.

Dinner, yes—Scott brought Emily over to Meg's condo and they talked in the kitchen while she cooked and Will hunched over the computer in the next room playing some grisly game. The clash of metal occasionally resulted in blood-curdling screams. Will was currently hooked on this game, and Meg had carefully *not* looked at it; she knew she'd hate it. And she knew, too, that he was playing right then so that he could chaperon Mom. He wasn't about to go to his bedroom and leave her even briefly alone with Scott.

A quick lunch in Scott's office on Thursday—that one was too short to be satisfying, especially since his secretary interrupted twice. A lift had broken down, skiers were stranded on the chairs. The Chief of Operations, Mark Robillard, just wanted Scott to know. They were working on it. About the time Scott started getting restless, Trish stuck her head back in.

"Up and running, Mark says. Folks were cheering."

"I'll bet they were," he muttered. "But give 'em

an hour or two to stew, and they'll be down here demanding ticket refunds.''

''Will you give them?'' Meg asked.

''Probably.'' He grimaced. ''They weren't up there more than half an hour, but... We want them back.''

''Said as a good businessman,'' she teased.

''That's what I am.''

He'd been working on a new brochure. Layouts were spread across his desk. By this time she recognized the dark decisive handwriting in every margin. The sketches, however...

''Well, you're definitely not an artist.'' She tapped one. ''Is this a Christmas decoration?''

''A tram.'' A smile tugged at his mouth. ''Don't be insulting.''

She sighed and stretched. ''You're right. Otherwise you'll start speculating aloud on why I'm not better at *my* job.''

He stood, too, and wrapped big hands around her waist. ''Hadn't occurred to me. Has somebody been on your case?''

''Mmm.'' Meg kissed Scott's hard, scratchy jaw. His hands tightened; a rumble started in his chest. It was like making a cat purr, she thought with amusement and the stirrings of the hunger that cramped in her womb every time she saw him.

''Who?'' He nibbled on her earlobe.

Brain fogging, knees weakening, Meg had to think. ''The sheriff himself. He wants results. The high school is having problems with gangs—can you believe it, in Elk Springs? Anyway, they want me there. He didn't cut us off yet, but he will if we don't make an arrest soon.''

"That's ridiculous," Scott began.

"No." She laid a hand on his cheek. "If a murder is solved at all, it's usually right away. We wouldn't file this one yet, anyway, but I don't want to make it a part-time pursuit. Ben may have to. There was a shooting at the truck stop last night. One dead, one in critical condition. The witnesses don't agree on how it started or who pulled a weapon first."

His phone rang; she felt his muscles jerk in reaction, but he made no move to reach for it.

"Answer it." Meg gave him a gentle push. "I've got things to do, too. Places to go, people to see."

Scott hesitated, then grabbed the phone. "Yeah? Can you hold on a minute?" He covered the mouthpiece, stopping Meg before she went out the door. "I'm having a staff meeting at three. You want to stop by? Say a few words?"

Look for a murderer? she thought, but only nodded. "Sounds good."

On the way out, Meg told herself it didn't matter that she hadn't yet told him that Jack had never known about Will. A chance would come, but she wanted to be alone with him, have some uninterrupted time. Her decisions weren't ones he'd accept without question; she knew that. He felt too much anguish at the loss of his son.

She'd never meant to lie. He'd misunderstood her, and she hadn't corrected him, and then suddenly she *was* lying. Doing so didn't come naturally to her, and now the consciousness of the lie dogged her as insidiously as her fear in the early days that her father would find her anytime. But what could she do about it? This wasn't the kind of thing you just blurted out.

Or was that simply an excuse, because she was afraid he'd hate her for what she'd stolen from another man?

In the outside office, Trish was talking on the phone at the same time as she worked on the computer; two Hold buttons flashed. She didn't even notice Meg, who told herself to put aside personal problems. She had a job to do.

And Trish could wait. Meg went looking for other fish to fry.

So far as she could determine, the community college had been a bust. Shelly had been a model student. Her boyfriend had been no more than casual, another Tony Rieger. Jefferson Robb had been Shelly's only handsome male instructor; the others were either female or edging toward retirement.

Robb didn't work in Meg's mind as the murderer. Yeah, on the surface he blamed Shelly for the seduction, but it was his own weakness in succumbing that tormented him. He'd already lost his wife a week or more before Shelly's murder. Revenge as a motive never satisfied Meg.

People were more likely to kill to protect something—or someone—precious to them.

His job? In a fog of despair over losing his wife, would Robb have cared enough about his tenure at the college to kill? Had Shelly threatened it in any way? Would a woman hungry for a man's approval have dared blackmail him?

Maybe. But Meg didn't think so, although Ben Shea didn't agree. He'd taken an acute dislike to Jefferson Robb.

Portland police had interviewed Robb's wife and her sister, plus some neighbors. The wife had definitely arrived several days before Shelly's murder and had stayed put. The neighbors were sure. And the sister agreed that he had phoned on the night in question; he phoned every evening at more or less the same time. She was getting tired of it. She'd never believed in answering machines, but she was about to go buy one.

No, Meg still thought the answer lay here, at Juanita Butte. Where Shelly had worked when she got pregnant; where she had been afraid of someone.

Meg stopped by the ski shop this morning, but she'd already talked to the three employees working. Rental shop—ditto. At the ski instructors' hut, she hit the first pay dirt of the day.

A young woman she'd never seen before said, "Shelly Lange? Oh, sure. I remember her. She was really murdered? I mean, it's so scary!"

"That's one way of putting it," Meg said dryly. "Do you have time for a few questions?"

She had a lesson to teach at two; until then, she was all Meg's. The instructors' hut wasn't very big. At a counter in the front room, new students could sign up for lessons. In back, wet gloves made ragged lines on the plywood floor in front of a potbellied wood stove. A couple of sagging couches were good enough for breaks; right now, several guys who didn't look a heck of a lot older than Will seemed to be amiably arguing about a Lakers basketball game.

Meg and the young woman—Rhonda Buchanan—chose to go outside. The day was hazy but warmer than it had been—twenty degrees instead of eight. Meg pulled on her gloves and tucked her chin inside the collar of her olive-green parka.

The area was relatively quiet today—it was Thursday, over a week since Shelly's murder. Lift lines were almost nonexistent; a few clusters up the hill suggested ski classes. A couple came laughing out of the lodge and unlocked their skis, stamping into them not far from Meg and Rhonda.

Watching with a trace of envy as they skated toward the roped-off entry to the chair lift, Meg said, "I'll have to get up here skiing."

"What?"

"Nothing." She sighed and sat on a bench. Her butt was immediately cold. "Were you friends with Shelly?"

Rhonda had given her a few lessons; Shelly hadn't skied all that much before she took the job here. "Can you imagine?" Rhonda marveled. "She said her dad wouldn't spend the money."

"I don't think the Langes are well-to-do."

"But *everyone* around here skis!"

"Not everyone. I grew up in Elk Springs, you know." And her father wouldn't pay for lessons or lift tickets, either. *God damn waste of time,* he'd called the sport.

"Well...most people."

"I'll give you that." Meg didn't want to argue. "So, did you and Shelly talk?"

"Oh, yeah!" About lots of things, Rhonda insisted. Books, politics, environmental issues. "Not just makeup and who was hot," she said earnestly.

But she wasn't disappointed to find out that what Meg most wanted to know was who Shelly had thought was "hot."

"Mr. McNeil," she said, blushing enough that Meg guessed she felt the same. "Mr. Robillard—

she liked the older guys. Oh, and I saw her one time hanging all over Evan Hannah. He's the head of the ski patrol. I mean, I could see her point there.''

"Anyone else?"

There were a few others—all cases of Shelly admiring from afar, Rhonda thought. "And that guy from Mechanical, you know about him, don't you? Tony something?''

"Tony Rieger. I've talked to him."

"Well." Rhonda ruminated. "I can't think of anybody else."

"The only one you actually saw Shelly with was Evan Hannah?" Meg asked, to be sure.

"Besides Tony."

"Right. Besides Tony."

With two o'clock looming, Rhonda left Meg to her meditations. She'd beard Hannah now, she finally decided, then Trish. Bottom numb, she trudged awkwardly back to the main lodge. The ski patrol was on the bottom floor.

Another of those tanned, blond gods with flashing white teeth was behind the counter. "Evan? Oh, jeez. I don't know where he is. Can I help you?''

"No, I have a question specifically for him," Meg said patiently.

"Well, I know he's coming down from the mountain for some kind of meeting with the general manager. McNeil," he added helpfully.

"I'll catch him before then," Meg said.

To fill the time, she went back up to turn the screws on Scott's secretary. Trish had her hands on the computer keyboard, but no phone receiver crooked between her ear and her shoulder. Hearing

Meg's footstep she glanced up, looking instantly wary at the sight of the uniform.

"Deputy Patton. Scott says he suggested you stop by for the meeting at three. That'll be at the end of the hall in the…"

"I wanted to talk to you first."

The secretary sighed and let her hands fall from the keyboard to her swollen belly. "About who I saw Shelly with, right?"

"Yep."

Trish squirmed. "It just feels…"

"Like tattling?"

"Yeah, I guess so."

Meg pulled a rolling secretarial chair over and sat gingerly. No feeling in the nether regions yet.

"Trish, I need to find out who Emily's father is. If he didn't kill Shelly—great. But why hasn't he come forward?"

"Maybe he doesn't know he's a father."

"Maybe. But this is a small town. Wouldn't you think he'd have followed up to see why she quit working here?"

"Not if they weren't seeing each other anymore," Trish said stubbornly.

"But everyone in Elk Springs knows now. Shelly was killed and she left a six-month-old baby. An honorable man would have come forward and said, 'I was having sex with her. The baby might be mine.'"

"Unless…" Trish nibbled on her lip, her eyes worried. "Unless he's married."

"If he's married," Meg pointed out, "he may well have an alibi for the time Shelly was murdered. We won't have to tell his wife anything. I promise.

Adultery is his business." She paused, then added with quiet force, "Murder is mine."

The secretary heaved a breath. "Okay. I know you're right. And what I saw…it may not have meant anything. I mean…he's not that kind of guy. He *is* married, and he's always calling his wife and bragging about his kids."

Meg hid her impatience. "He?"

"Mark. Mark Robillard. Chief of Operations."

"Ah."

Trish eyed her suspiciously. "You don't sound surprised."

"Someone else mentioned his name. Also…" she spread her hands. "He fits the profile."

"You mean…he's the kind Shelly liked?"

No, what Meg had really meant was that Mark Robillard had the motive to kill if Shelly had threatened his secure family and job in some way. Blackmail? An insistence on resuming the relationship? A half tearful, half spiteful threat to tell the whole world how he'd slighted her?

It didn't matter *how* Shelly had threatened him, only that she had. And that his family was precious to him.

Under questioning, Trish told her about seeing the two of them in front of a convenience store at the High Mountain Resort, ten miles south of town. Mark was putting Shelly into a car and kissing her.

"He was supposed to be out of town," Trish said unhappily. "And…oh, it was just chance that I was there. I was meeting a friend…they have some really great boutiques there, you know—well, maybe you don't since you're new around here."

Ski season hadn't opened yet, Trish remembered.

Shelly had been working at the shop from early summer; this had been just after Labor Day weekend.

"You don't think…" she asked doubtfully.

Damn right she did, Meg thought, her hunting instincts sharpened. But she reassured Trish, left her momentarily confident she'd done the right thing in talking.

Robillard might not be the only one who fits the profile, Meg reminded herself. *Evan Hannah might, too. Remember, he was seen with Shelly, as well. There might yet be an unknown who had the same motive. Don't jump to conclusions.*

She went straight to the staff meeting. Both Robillard and Hannah were present, along with a half dozen others, all department heads. Advertising, Financial—the one woman, Mechanical, Snow Removal, Parking… The list went on: an attorney headed the legal department, security, ticket sales and lift operation fell under the Chief of Operations. Scott oversaw and approved all their work.

The group listened attentively as Scott stood at the head of the lone table in the bare-bones conference room and reminded them that the police required their cooperation.

"Deputy Patton has found a few employees reluctant to be frank with her. Please urge everyone to help her in any way they can. Assure them that their jobs will not be put in jeopardy because they pass on either substantiated evidence or rumor."

"Thank you," Meg said, when her turn came. She let her gaze run down the table. "Most of you I've met. Mr.… Hannah, is it?"

Perhaps forty, he was dark-haired, deeply tanned

and fit. It struck her how attractive all these men were, given that they were essentially corporate executives. A daily game of racquetball wasn't required to keep any of them in shape. If they didn't ski as part of the job, they did for pleasure.

"Mr. Hannah, could I speak to you afterward?" Meg asked. "Since we didn't have a chance earlier?"

"Sure, no problem," he said easily.

After giving a basic rundown on the progress of the investigation, she excused herself and waited outside. The meeting continued for another fifteen minutes. At last the door opened and they filed out, each nodding as he—or she—passed.

Meg saw nothing different in Mark Robillard's manner. Not that he was easy to read. A dour expression must keep his underlings intimidated.

"Evan's waiting for you," Scott said in a low voice as he followed Robillard out. "Did Trish get the message to you that Will called?"

"Did he say…"

"Not an emergency. Trish discovered that much. He said he guessed it could wait until you got home tonight."

"Oh." How strange. Meg glanced at her watch. School was out for the day. Would he have called for permission to go to a new friend's house?

Would he ever *make* a new friend?

"I'll use your phone after I talk to Mr. Hannah, if you don't mind."

"Of course not." He didn't touch her, not with the attorney and the chief financial officer apparently waiting for him.

Hannah sat with his big brown hands clasped behind his head. He started to rise when she entered the conference room, but Meg waved him back.

Liking his twinkling eyes and rakish smile, she decided to take the most direct route.

"Mr. Hannah, are you married?"

His eyebrows shot up, but he answered after a barely discernible pause. "Yes. I am."

"Children?"

"Teenagers." One corner of his mouth lifted in a rueful smile. "I've recently become an idiot."

She almost rose to that, admitted to being the parent of a fourteen-year-old, but she kept her face impassive.

"Mr. Hannah, did you know Shelly Lange?"

He sounded cautious now. "By sight."

"Not feel?"

Hannah flattened his hands on the table and shot to his feet, his eyes narrowing in quick anger. "What the hell does that mean?"

Meg didn't alter her pleasant expression. "I've been told that you were seen with Shelly. She was 'hanging all over you,' according to the witness."

He swore. "I usually think of myself as a gentleman, but I'm going to be straight with you here— Shelly Lange 'hung all over' anything in pants. I wouldn't have had her working for me! She had a way of backing me into corners. She imagined that I was battling secret lust for her, Deputy Patton."

"She was a beautiful young woman."

He made a disgusted sound and abruptly sat back down. The chair legs screeched across the floor. "Do you know how many beautiful young women work here? Women make up half the ski patrol. Some of them look goddamn nice in their stretch pants. Do I notice? I'm a man. Sure I do. Would I act on it? Nah. See, I've got something better at home. I have a gutsy broad who knows everything about me. I've got two kids who won't turn out to be worth crap if I don't set an example for them. You think I'm going to blow the things that really count for some hot young thing?" He glowered. "Let me put it this way. My kids may think I'm an idiot right now, but they're going to figure out one of these days that they're wrong."

Meg had to suppress a smile. "Mr. Hannah, where were you on the evening of Monday, January 14?"

"You should have asked that in the first place." He'd relaxed again; his eyes even held a hint of that twinkle. "I was coaching a freshman girl's basketball squad at the high school. We had a game. Beat Medford 24-18. Went for pizza afterward."

"I'll need to confirm that."

"Well, I can't say I'm thrilled at the idea of you asking questions about me, making the folks at the school wonder."

"I'll do it discreetly," she assured him.

He grimaced. "That it, then?"

"That's it." She allowed herself a smile. "Thank you, Mr. Hannah. By the way, we have something in common. I have a fourteen-year-old son."

"Yeah?" He frowned. "Patton. My daughter's a freshman. That name rings a bell."

"We just moved here a couple of weeks ago. His name is Will."

A flash of recognition was followed by a broad grin. "Big dark-haired kid? Yeah, yeah. I saw him shooting some hoops the other day. My daughter says he's 'hot.'"

"I don't think Will's of an age to appreciate that," Meg told him. As they scraped their chairs back and walked out of the conference room she got the particulars on who his daughter was so that she could ask Will later.

Upstairs she called Will from Trish's desk. All he wanted was permission to take the school rooter bus to a basketball tournament Friday evening.

Except, of course, he was already backpedaling. "If you want me to stay home, I don't have to go..."

"Why were you thinking about it in the first place?" Meg interrupted. "Considering you haven't been to a single game since we moved here?"

She could see him shrugging as well as if he were here. "I played a pick-up game with a couple guys today. One of 'em was the big star forward. A junior." He was trying to sound sarcastic, indifferent to the importance of these other boys, but she heard the pleased undertone. "They said I should be on the team next year. I just figured I should watch them play once, see if they're any good or if they're crap."

"Yeah, I think you should," she agreed. "Then why the hesitation? You never seem to have that much homework."

"Well, if you want to do something..." Even he knew that was lame. His voice trailed off.

It came to her in a blinding flash: he didn't want her to be alone with Scott.

Followed by: she could *be* alone with Scott. A whole evening. She could do something with a man she hadn't done in… Well, years. So long that the whole idea scared her even as she felt a cramping of pleasure and excitement in her belly.

"Go," she said in the no-nonsense voice she used when she meant what she was saying, no argument allowed. "You know, you might even get to know some of the other kids."

The rolled eyes came through as well as the shrug had earlier. "Mom, I don't need a social director."

"Well, then, get a life," she said unsympathetically. Before he could hang up and go off to sulk, she had an idea. "Do you know a Marie Hannah? Your age?"

"Why?" Nobody could be as suspicious as a teenager.

"I hear her dad coaches the freshman girl's basketball team. I just want confirmation that he really was at a game on January 14, and that when they went out for pizza afterward he was with them. Can you casually ask around and find out for sure?"

"Oh, yeah. Sure," Will sneered. "Casually."

"Don't be a brat. Can you or can't you?"

Heavy sigh. "I'll try."

"Good. See you in a couple of hours. Put the manicotti in the oven at five-thirty—375 degrees."

Her son grumbled agreement.

Scott wasn't in his office; Meg didn't know whether to be disappointed or relieved. She left a note on his spindle. *Dinner tomorrow night? No Will. Meg.* Summed it up nicely, she thought.

Mark Robillard had just left, his secretary a floor down told Meg. There was some problem up on the Sugar Bowl lift. But Meg could catch him if she hurried.

She hurried.

In front of the lodge, Robillard was just dropping his skis to the snow and was talking on—not a cell phone, a walkie-talkie, she thought. He held it in a gloved hand. Meg noted the glove: black leather, comfortably shaped to his hand.

"Mr. Robillard."

His eyes focused on her. Looking less than pleased, he said into the walkie-talkie, "Gotta go, Clint." Brief pause. "Yeah. Do your best. I'll be up in a minute." With a practiced flick, he stowed the antenna and shoved the walkie-talkie into an inside pocket on his parka. All deftly done, considering that most people were awkward wearing gloves. "More questions, Detective?"

Tension around his eyes; he didn't like her here. But then, most people didn't like cops asking questions. And she was probably fouling up his busy day.

"I hear you had a lift shut down earlier."

He shrugged. "It happens."

"People error, or mechanical?"

"Mechanical. Usually is."

He spoke dismissively; she didn't really care about the answer, had merely wanted to establish a conversational tone.

The nearby lift growled and clanked as chairs swung along the cable, empty on the way down and around the pole at the bottom, a few filled for the ride up.

Somebody bumped Meg from behind. "Oops!" a young guy said. "Sorry!" His snowboard was propped casually on his shoulder as he dodged skiers and other boarders coming down from the hill.

She lifted a hand. "It's okay." Concentrating on the man waiting silently, she said, "Mr. Robillard, can you give me a minute?"

He shot a look at his watch. "I'm here, aren't I?"

She'd been going to suggest they talk somewhere more private. Irritation drove her to the point. "You were seen kissing Shelly Lange. When you were supposed to be out of town for the weekend."

For a moment he stared at her without any change of expression. Then a nerve twitched below his eye; he swallowed. "My wife," he said hoarsely. "I don't want my wife to know."

"Will you tell me about it?"

He looked around blindly, goggles shoved up on his head, his poles planted in the snow to each side of him. His lips, cracked and dry, had the look of a man who'd been out in the weather too much. His dark hair grayed at the temples. The five o'clock shadow on his cheeks glinted gray mixed with the darker beard growth. A handsome man, but one edging into his forties.

"She… It didn't last long. A few weeks." His Adam's apple bobbed again, but with every word spoken, Robillard collected himself, overriding the distress. "My wife and I'd had had a rough patch. Oh, hell. I was flattered. Shelly was young and pretty. I didn't know then that she was cheap." He said it with contempt, this man who had cheated on his wife, lied to his children. "If he wore pants, she'd spread her legs for him."

"You're saying you weren't alone?" Meg asked neutrally.

"Alone?" The Chief of Operations gave a harsh laugh. "Every time I saw her she was coming on to some other man. Ask around, Deputy Patton. I'm telling the truth."

"Did you see her with another man while the two of you were...dating?" How delicately put, Meg congratulated herself.

His jaw muscles flexed and anger was dark in his eyes. "Damn right, and she had a pack of lies! Apparently she thought I was stupid."

"Did you end the relationship?"

"Yes."

"Because?"

"I don't share."

"Not because of your wife and children?" *Who had to share?* she thought but didn't add.

His eyes narrowed; his gloved hands locked around his poles. "I don't make a habit of this."

She chose to ignore that. "Given the timing of your affair with Shelly Lange, has it occurred to you that her daughter, Emily, could well be yours?"

"She could be anybody's."

"Did Ms. Lange ever tell you that she was pregnant with your baby? Did she claim Emily was yours? Did she ask for child support?"

"No. No to all three questions." His hard, cold facade was back, if she had ever truly cracked it. "I never saw her again after she quit working here."

"Would you submit to DNA testing to determine paternity?"

He made a harsh sound; now she had shaken him, at least a little. "How can I, without my wife finding out? What the hell would I do about it if the kid was mine?"

"Are you aware that Shelly Lange's parents have no interest in adopting the baby?"

His jaw worked. "No."

"She will grow up with no biological family if her father is not found."

"I...can't." Voice raw, Robillard forced out each separate word.

"Mr. Robillard," Meg said formally, "do you want to reconsider your account of your activities on the evening of Monday, January 14?"

Pure fury boiled in his eyes. "No! I was home with my wife. She'll tell you. Now, if you have no more questions?"

"Not at the moment," Meg said, standing back. "Please don't leave Elk Springs without informing me."

His head bent; he stamped into one binding and then the other. Meg waited where she was until he looked up, the tic jerking beneath his eye.

"Don't tell my wife." Now, finally, torment made the plea sound real. "Please don't tell my wife."

Without a trace of emotion, Meg said, "I can promise you only that, if you didn't kill Shelly Lange, I'll do my best to keep what I know from your wife."

He squeezed his eyes shut briefly. "That'll have to do, won't it?"

She watched him push himself forward with his poles, take a few skating steps, quick-step around the barrier that, on busier days, would keep the lift line orderly. His movements were as natural as if he were walking down a street.

An important man here at Juanita Butte, Meg

thought again. An attractive man, but outwardly cold, unlikely to be attentive, charming, to a young woman. Not easily won even by pretty Shelly Lange, and therefore a satisfying emotional surrogate for the father whose attention she had never won.

Yes, Meg mused, she could easily see Shelly trying to hold Mark Robillard by having his baby.

Unfortunately for her, Meg was beginning to suspect that he was also a man who would kill rather than lose what he had.

Now all she had to do was prove it.

CHAPTER THIRTEEN

"ROBILLARD? What was it, two months ago? Yeah, sure," agreed the woman patrol officer who stood in Meg's office doorway. "I went out on the call. I remember it. Second domestic disturbance at that address, wasn't it? Has there been trouble again?"

"I'm investigating a murder," Meg said. "Mark Robillard's name came up. I ran a background check, and guess what."

Patricia Barr nodded. "Amazing, isn't it? House like that, nice family... Last thing you'd expect."

"I haven't seen the house yet." Meg waved at a chair. "Got a minute?"

Already she had to move a stack to allow the other cop to sit down. These—she glanced at the top notes ruefully—were contacts she'd meant to make as the new Youth Services Officer. Before she'd found something else to do.

The stack went on top of her filing cabinet.

"Okay, I read your report," Meg said, settling back in her office chair, "but I see no charges were filed. With the change in laws, that's unusual. I wondered about your impressions."

The other woman was about Meg's age, plain but for thick dark hair and warm eyes. "Husband and wife met me at the door together. He's handsome, smiling. She's all made-up though it was late evening, smiling, bustling around, wanting my partner and me to take a cup of coffee, a cookie—it was like we were making a social call. They have a little girl, who came in blushing to tell me that Mommy and Daddy were having a fight and Mommy got mad and threw her hairbrush at the wall and it scared her. She thought something bad was happening, maybe some stranger was in there with Mommy and Daddy, so she remembered what they said at school and dialed 9-1-1.

"The parents had a story about what they were arguing about—something silly, but the kind of thing you do get mad at your husband about. They pretended to be proud of their daughter, even though they were embarrassed, too. I noticed the wife was cradling one arm when she thought I wasn't watching, so I got her aside, but she looked me right in the eye and insisted everything was fine. On the surface, it looked like a genuine mistake, even though it was the second call. The first one hadn't panned out, either."

That time nobody had been home by the time the responding officers arrived. A neighbor had called; she'd heard crashes, a man bellowing, a woman's scream. But the house was dark and deserted when the unit got there; the Robillards claimed the next day that they'd been out all evening. Maybe a young couple had parked out front and had a fight? they'd asked. Or some teenagers were having a beer party?

"Tell me your gut feeling," Meg said now.

Patricia Barr's expression hardened. "That the bastard had been hitting her, and the kid panicked. Maybe he'd scared the hell out of her by the time we arrived; more likely, he fooled her into thinking she hadn't seen what she thought she'd seen. But I'd bet my next paycheck Robillard is abusing his wife. They were all smiling, but let me tell you, the tension in that house raised the hair on my arms.''

''That's what I wanted to know,'' Meg said, thanking her.

Her blood sang with a kind of fierce pleasure. She was closing in. Not someone who ever would have enjoyed hunting animals, Meg thought nothing on earth gave the satisfaction her job did. When she wound up a case like this, it was a puzzle coming together, a scumbag off the street, emotional healing for the victims—a rush of adrenaline for her. The good kind.

Today it had a sexual edge. She and Scott would be alone tonight. They'd planned the time to do something that should be impulsive, hot-blooded, the furthest thing from deliberate. She'd made love—no, had sex—with only two other men since Johnny Murray. Both times she'd been dating them for a while—longer, she thought, than she'd known Scott McNeil. In neither case had she made a decision—*I care enough about this man, I want him enough*—to go to bed with him. They had simply been kissing, her blood had heated—she was a healthy young woman, for all that she was the mother of a kindergartener, then a fifth grader. She'd found herself naked, grappling with the man.

And in each case, she had shortly thereafter broken off with him. Sexually, the experiences had been reasonably satisfying. And yet…and yet they left her feeling naked in ways she didn't want to examine. She had made herself too vulnerable. Sex wasn't enough, on its own; Meg was old-fashioned, maybe, but she wanted more, thought it ought to *mean* more. Like forever. And she couldn't trust herself and Will to either of those men.

Any more than she had been able to trust Johnny.

Meg wasn't a fool; she knew she both hungered for a man's love and distrusted it because of her father. And yet she'd grown up with love: her mother's, her sisters'. She rather thought she was a good mother.

She was convinced that somehow, someday, there would be a man she could trust. She'd always worried about how she would know.

And now she did.

Breathtaking, but true.

She'd only known Scott a couple of weeks; they had dated—what?—five or six times. And here she was, deciding in cold blood to bare herself emotionally and physically. To trust that he was steady, loving, faithful; that he would listen to her, talk to her, feel the same fire for her that she did for him.

All this, so quickly, Meg thought in awe.

The next second, a wave of panic struck. Dear Lord, what if she was wrong? What if he wasn't ready to love anyone again? He was a man; just because he kissed her like that didn't mean he was handing over his heart and soul.

What if, when the moment came, she couldn't take that leap of faith? What if she chickened out? Or did it, and felt herself freezing inside just as she had the other times?

What if she wanted Scott to be that man, and he wasn't?

The phone rang. Meg took a breath to steady herself, to shove the fear back down, and answered.

"Butte County Sheriff's Department. Patton here."

"We still on for dinner?" Scott asked.

"Oh, yeah," she said, and felt her deep-down certainty tumble like desire through her veins.

THANK HEAVEN she hadn't suggested cooking for him again; a nice sit-down dinner in a restaurant was an interlude, a sort of airlock between job and intimacy, between the hunt for a killer and the acceptance of falling in love. Meg needed this in-between, to be sure she wasn't letting on-the-job adrenaline push her into anything foolish.

But before the conversation got entirely personal, she had some questions to ask him.

They'd gone Mexican tonight, the restaurant small and stuccoed, the waiters and owner all family with strong accents. Scott ordered the chicken fajita, Meg a chimichanga. They sipped margaritas—she would allow herself only one; tomorrow, she didn't want to be able to blame alcohol for her decision, either.

Only herself.

Business first, Meg reminded herself.

"Scott, I'm assuming you were wearing gloves when you found Emily. That you had them on when you picked up her car seat and buckled it in."

Not what he'd expected, clearly, but he showed only a flicker of surprise. "That's right. Remember, it was a cold night."

"What kind of gloves?"

His brow rose.

"I mean…leather? Gore-Tex? Some other synthetic?"

Scott didn't even have to think. "Synthetic. I keep that pair in the pocket of my parka. They're black, nothing special. They're in the car."

"Definitely not leather. You're sure."

"Positive. Are you going to tell me why you're asking?"

She had to, before she could ask him to do something for her. "We lifted some prints from Emily's car seat. No…" Meg stopped him before he could speak. "Not fingerprints. Glove prints." She went on to explain that leather had patterns as distinctive as did human skin. "They're not something we can run through an FBI computer, obviously, but once we have a suspect, they can be used to convict him."

"But you don't have a suspect…" Scott stopped.

"Yes," Meg said quietly. "I do."

Their waiter set their dinners in front of them. "Hot plates," he warned them. "More margarita?"

"No. Thank you." Gaze never leaving Meg's, Scott covered his glass with his hand; Meg shook her head. The waiter went away, leaving them alone at their corner booth with the one fat candle flickering inside amber glass.

As soon as she was sure she wouldn't be heard, Meg said, "I've got to tell you, this is a gut feeling as much as anything."

Will had eliminated Evan Hannah as a suspect; he'd called from school at lunchtime today to tell her that "this girl he knew" said that Hannah was at the game and the party afterward. "He's so cool!" she'd told him, a pronouncement that Will had wickedly mimicked.

Now, Scott waited, not touching his meal. "Who?"

"Mark Robillard."

Almost any other man she'd ever known would have been bent on denying her answer. Would have been angry that she'd even presented it.

But Scott was too smart, and too controlled. "I've worked with Mark for seven years. He's a friend. No, not a friend, but close enough." His eyes bored into her, giving her the feeling of being turned inside out. "Why?" he asked simply.

"Why did he kill her? Or why do I think he's the one who did?"

"Both."

She told him both whys. Robillard had had an affair with Shelly Lange; she had been afraid of him, had broken it off, had been wary enough to stay clear of him for a while. But then she had done something—asked for child support, perhaps. And he would not let anyone, much less a young woman, threaten him. For that's how he'd seen it.

"He admitted to having had an affair with her. He isn't interested in finding out whether Emily is his," Meg said. "My guess is, he knows quite well that she is. His wife has taken a lot from him, and probably blamed herself the whole time for upsetting him, but even he must know that this would be the last straw. She might leave him, take the children. And what if he lost his job when you found out he'd slept with an employee? He couldn't let any of that happen. So he killed Shelly."

Scott rubbed a hand across his face. After a minute he asked, in a voice stripped of emotion, "And how are you going to prove that he did?"

"I need you to do something for me."

She saw him weighing it, deciding. "What?"

"He carries a walkie-talkie."

Scott took a swallow of his margarita as though he needed it. "Yeah?"

"Yesterday Robillard wore black leather gloves. And he was handling the walkie-talkie. The plastic should take a print well."

"He may have other gloves."

"He may," Meg agreed. *Please, no, or else he'll walk.* "Do you?"

"I usually stick to one pair for a few months."

She leaned forward. "I want you to lift that walkie-talkie without him knowing. If he sees you or guesses, he may get rid of the gloves."

"You could take them..."

"Not without a warrant. And I can't get that without something solid. Like a match on the prints. If I don't get the warrant, the evidence can't be used in court."

He jerked his head; rubbed the back of his neck. "Yeah, okay. I see. I'll do it."

"I'm sorry," Meg said softly.

"If he did it, there's nothing to be sorry for." He sounded cold, distant, but the look in his eyes betrayed how he really felt.

Meg began eating. After a minute, Scott did, too. The silence lasted several minutes.

Meg broke it. "Where's Emily tonight?"

"Um?" Scott looked up. "With Marjorie. My housekeeper. I'm not ready yet..."

"To leave her with a teenager?" She didn't give him time to think about pretty, bouncy Shelly. "I don't blame you. Will's a smart kid. Really. But he does the dumbest things.'' She told tales on her son, then. About the time he'd had a friend dangle him by the ankles from a hotel balcony so he could scare the cheerleaders staying in the room below his; about Will sneaking a buddy onto the base without a pass; about him refusing to turn in a single assignment for an entire quarter in one class because the teacher had ticked him off.

''And then there's this thing with Jack...'' *Nice segue,* she told herself. Now all she had to do was say, *Oh, by the way, I've been fibbing to you. I cheated Jack out of fourteen years of his son's life.*

''Will came up with it by himself?''

She looked sharply at Scott, alerted by something in his tone. Was he jealous? ''Darn straight he did.'' Incurable honesty jabbed at her. ''He might have had help from Jack. I'm not sure. Jack took me to dinner one night. He even kissed me.'' *Do you have to be* that *honest?* Meg asked herself. Answer: *Yes. And you can't stop here.* ''No fireworks went off. As Jack said, the two of us together again would have been convenient. For Will.''

Scott didn't react in any predictable way. He didn't ask *when* she'd kissed Jack. She saw no sign that his male ego was injured, or that he was ready to rev the engine, so to speak, with Jack in the car beside his. Maybe, she thought in amazement, he was that rare man who drove more or less within the speed limit, who didn't want to punch every jerk who challenged him...

''Why did the two of you break up in the first place?'' he asked, his gaze resting thoughtfully on her face.

''I got pregnant.'' Now was the time to tell him.

It wouldn't have been so hard if she'd been sure in her heart that she'd done the right thing back then. But she'd taken to wondering: had she hugged Will to herself entirely out of fear? Or because she was mad at Jack and she didn't want to share?

"The moment of truth," Scott murmured. Paused. "People around here respect him."

Meg was supremely conscious of the irony. The moment of truth was still ahead of her.

Edge into it, she told herself.

"We were both afraid of my father," Meg admitted. "We were kids. Too young to have a baby. No sixteen-year-old wants to tell her parents. But this was different. I was afraid my dad would kill me. I always wondered if he hadn't murdered my mother."

Scott swore. "You're serious."

She told him more about her childhood, about the mother who left without a trace—thanks, it turned out, to Chief Patton, who'd had the mail delivered to a post office box so he could intercept his ex-wife's letters. Scott needed to know all this, or he couldn't understand why she'd done what she'd done.

"And yet," Meg mused, "as Abby pointed out one day, our father provided a home, he went to parent nights at school, he even took me shopping for my first bra..." After telling her she ought to be ashamed of herself, not covering up any better than that.

"Do you think he loved you?"

"I truly don't know." She tried to smile and failed. "He was so full of hate and anger, there wasn't room for much else. If he felt affection, he hadn't a clue how to show it.''

"That's a sad epitaph.''

"No kidding,'' she said on a spasm of pain that surprised her. She had thought she'd come to terms with her father's memory.

Taking a deep breath, she said, "Scott…''

But he wasn't looking at her. He'd spotted the waiter and lifted his hand to signal for the bill. He came, smiling, to the table. The moment was lost.

Scott paid and before Meg knew it, they were walking out. Panic knotted her stomach. She still hadn't told him. On the drive home…

But in his Jeep it was dark, and she wanted to be able to see his face.

Another excuse.

When we get there, she decided, and let the conversation stay desultory.

Emily had slept through the night finally. A critical step had been taken toward construction of the new lift at Juanita Butte. Small subjects. Nothing either of them wanted to linger over. Just words to fill the dark car, to let Meg, at least, think about something besides the solid bulk of the man beside her, about what she was going to do.

He pulled into her driveway and turned off the engine. In the silence both sat still for a moment, looking straight ahead. She couldn't do it, not now. It wasn't that important; it could wait. He'd understand.

Scott spoke first. "Can I come in, Meg?''

"Yes.'' What had happened to her voice? "Yes. Please.''

He hadn't moved; both his hands were curled

around the steering wheel. He sounded just as odd as she had. "I'm falling in love with you."

"I...hoped you were."

His head turned; in the dim light from the street lamp and her porch, he looked searchingly at her. "What about you?"

"Yes." Oh, Lord, she was actually blushing. "I mean, I feel the same. It's fast, but...right."

What little he could see must have satisfied him, because he nodded. "Just so we both know what we're getting into."

She swallowed and nodded, too.

Scott took the key from the ignition and got out. Meg followed. He took her arm and steered her up to her own front door, as if she wouldn't make it alone. He waited while she unlocked, let her open the door, step inside, set her purse down on the small hall table.

Then he said in a hoarse voice, "Meg?" And when she turned and saw the look on his face, she stumbled into his arms.

Those first kisses were pure, raw emotion. She hadn't had to take off her clothes to offer herself up. The comforting part was that he was doing the same. This wasn't sex; oh, no. It was lovemaking from the start.

His hands were powerful, lifting her, holding her against the hard, muscled length of his body. Meg kissed him back with what felt like unpracticed fervor, but otherwise all she could do was hold on. Her knees were threatening to buckle; her whole body had gone weak, pliable.

She should have hated the contrast with him, the difference in strength, the aggressive way he took what he wanted from her, while she—the woman—gave. Maybe that's what she'd resented before, not understood, not wanted to be part of.

But this—it wasn't like that. She saw that, just as Scott lifted her in his arms.

"Which bedroom is yours?" he asked, voice guttural, eyes molten silver. Mercury.

She kissed his throat and felt him shudder. The reaction made her happy, so she did it again, this time licking his skin, tasting skin and salt and something that stung. Aftershave, maybe. An interesting and erotic combination. Meg rather liked it, so she kept kissing him, nibbling her way up to his ear.

Scott was groaning as he shouldered open her door, carried her across the room and lowered her to the bed.

"I want you," he said just before his mouth ravaged hers.

And that, Meg thought dreamily, as his big body bore her down, was why she didn't mind being outmatched, in a sense. Need meant vulnerability, even weakness.

And miraculously, Scott McNeil wanted her, needed her, was maybe just as scared by what he felt as she was. His muscles tightened under her hand; his skin shivered; he took a ragged breath. He was vulnerable. To *her*.

She quit thinking after that. Maybe for the first time in her life, Meg let herself be swept away. No wariness, no part of herself one step removed. She just felt, touched, cried out, and said his name. Over and over.

When she closed her eyes, images were burned onto her eyelids: his hands, big and dark on her breasts. His body, so beautifully muscled. The fiery chestnut of the soft hair that curled on his chest, down his belly. His mouth, suckling her nipples, kissing her belly button. His face, skin stretched tight, the sweet smile coupled with the fierce need in his eyes as he entered her.

It was a dance. Music: two flutes, achingly high, teasing notes around each other. No, a symphony, the final movements crashing around her with inescapable power and glory. Or perhaps it was a battle, hot, sweaty, needy, each trying to master the other.

If so, she won; she lost. All Meg knew was that her body reached for the glory, and found it.

Afterward, she settled against Scott's side, her head pillowed on his shoulder, and she had no regrets.

IF HE'D KNOWN it could be like that, he wouldn't have wasted half a lifetime existing when he could have been searching for Deputy Margaret Patton.

Thinking that way felt ridiculously adolescent, but right this minute he didn't give a damn. He was too happy.

She lay cuddled up to him, her head nestled on his shoulder, her satin sheet of pale hair flowing over his chest. They'd made love twice now. The clock was ticking, and he had to go soon. He just didn't want to.

Meg began drawing some mysterious picture on his chest with one finger. She was smiling as she did it. Scott kissed her head and with startling suddenness she rolled on top of him.

Her grin was all joy. "What do you say, big guy?

I'm game if you are..." Until she saw the clock. "Oh, no! Will."

"Don't we have half an hour before you have to pick him up?"

"But I have to get dressed. And I don't want to be late." She sighed and eased down in Scott's arms, settling for a long sweet kiss.

He slapped her bottom, dumped her off him and jackknifed to a sitting position. "How am I going to convince your son I'm not so bad?"

She scrambled off the bed, too, and went to her dresser. "Just be yourself. He'll see."

God, she was beautiful! Long legs, tiny waist, an elegant stretch of back and hair that had slid through his fingers like water. He forgot about getting dressed himself and just watched her, until she'd squirmed into a pair of panties and then jeans and tugged a sweatshirt over her head.

Turning, she smiled at him, face soft. You'd figure she was a teenager in those tight jeans and bare feet until you looked at her eyes, smart and sensuous.

"You planning to shock my son?" she asked, with a tilt to her head.

"What?" He looked down. "Oh. Yeah."

He'd never wanted less to get dressed; staying here right now would be good, maybe making love with her one more time before they fell asleep, waking in the night to the weight of her against him, seeing her eyes heavy with dreams in the morning before she remembered her responsibilities and worries.

Instead, he got dressed and followed Meg into the kitchen, where she poured them both coffee. Scott had barely taken his first sip when they heard a key in the front door. "Did Will get a ride?" he asked.

"He doesn't know anybody." She eased toward the door, moving like a cop.

The door slammed. "Mom?"

"Will."

Scott could just see her from where he stood, the tension in her body visibly gone although she didn't move. Her voice was easy.

"Somebody gave you a lift?"

"Yeah. We got back early. Jason—you know, that junior I told you about? He doesn't drive yet, but his dad was already there."

"How'd it go? The team any good?"

"Actually, not that bad. They won..." The boy reached the doorway and saw Scott. He was too young to hide his displeasure. "*He's* here."

She laid a hand on her son's shoulder, her fingers tightening. "That's right. Scott's here."

Will took a longer, harder look at his mom, whose mouth was swollen from kisses, whose cheeks were rosy red, whose feet were bare and who didn't wear a bra beneath the sweatshirt. Anger and hurt sparked in his eyes.

"Dad wanted to see you again," he said loudly.

Her apologetic gaze met Scott's. "Your father and I said what we had to say. It's you he comes to see."

The kid oozed out from under his mother's grip and slouched into a chair across the table from Scott. "Maybe because *he's* always around," he said rudely.

"Will Patton." Meg's voice cracked, and the

kid's spine straightened in automatic response. "That's enough out of you. Apologize. Now."

His chin jutted. "I didn't say anything!"

"It's okay," Scott began, until one razor-sharp glance from her shut him up.

"Now," she commanded.

"You never listen to me!" he cried.

Her eyes closed briefly, but her voice didn't soften. "An apology, please."

In an abrupt, violent movement, he grabbed the napkin holder and flung it. Made of teak, it cracked and skidded across the kitchen floor. His voice rose; cracked just like the wood, like the little boy he didn't want to be. "You've never given Dad a chance! If you'd ever told him about me, we could have been together all along!"

In the stunned silence, Meg shot another lightning glance at Scott. "You don't know anything about it," she finally said icily. "Now, apologize."

The boy's face worked. "I'm sorry, Mr. Mc-Neil." Rising to his feet, he knocked the chair back. "But I do know what I'm talking about! You always said—"

"Later. Not in front of company. Go to your room."

A sob wrenched him. "You're…you're just like *your* father!" he exclaimed, and rushed from the room.

Meg sagged into a chair. Tears glittered in her eyes. She tried to wipe them away.

"I'm sorry. I—I don't know where that came from. We…we used to be such good friends."

He seemed to be watching her from some great

distance, as if through binoculars. His heart was being squeezed in a fist.

"What did he mean?" He sounded strange to his ears, his tone so…unemotional. "When he said, 'If you'd ever told him about me'?"

Tears spilled over as she stared at him, stricken. Abruptly she buried her face in her hands. Watching her cry, Scott knew he should go to her, hold her, comfort her. But he couldn't seem to move.

"He never knew you were pregnant, did he?" That same dispassionate tone reflected the peculiar flattening of his emotions.

"No." Slowly she looked up, eyes red and puffy, her nose running. "He—my father caught us together. He beat up Johnny—Jack. Jack left me alone to face Dad. After…after he was done with me, I packed up, stole money from him, and ran away."

"When did you tell him?"

"I…"

"When?"

She took a shuddering breath. "Two weeks ago. When I found out my father was dead and came home to Elk Springs."

"My God." Disgust—no, rage—roughened his voice. "For fourteen years, Jack Murray didn't know he had a son."

"I—I was afraid." She was pleading. "Of my father."

Scott shoved himself to his feet. "Do you have any idea how much you took from him?"

Now her mouth trembled. "It's not like with you. Jack wasn't ready to be a father. He would have told mine. I might have lost Will!"

The sense of betrayal damn near swallowed him.

"I thought you were courageous. Beautiful. Generous. I'm having trouble believing you'd rob a man of his son, but I guess it goes to show that I don't know you very well."

Meg rose, shaking, crying, to her feet. "Scott, I've been trying to make you understand. Listen to me! Please!"

"No!" Throat raw, he moderated his voice. "Maybe another time, but not now. God. If I'd lost Nate because a woman had been so petty…"

"It wasn't like that," she said again, but he could see that even she didn't believe it. "Scott…"

"No." He took one last look at her face, the delicate bones, the shimmering blue eyes, the moonlight-pale hair, and groaned. "If you'd told me yourself… But you knew what I'd think, didn't you? I've lived all these years with my chest cut open because I lost my son. And you did that to a man. Knowing." He shook his head, staggered, blundered toward the door.

He heard a cry behind him, but he kept going.

How could he have been so wrong?

CHAPTER FOURTEEN

WILL'S CEREAL sat untouched in front of him, probably getting soggy. He watched Meg sit down with her toast and coffee across the table from him.

"Mom, I..." He gulped. "I mean, I..." Whatever it was, he couldn't get it out. All he did was stare at her like a dog waiting to be hit.

Any other day in her life, Meg would have been hurt that he would ever in a million years look at her that way. She would ache for him, as any parent would. Today... Today her emotions were as arid as desert sand. She'd cried them out last night; they'd seeped into her pillow and out of her soul. Once before, she'd thought she had cried every tear she would ever cry. Now she knew she had been wrong, but she also knew it might be years before she could summon another tear.

But she also knew none of this was Will's fault. It was hers. Hers for long-past mistakes, hers for ones just made.

"Eat your breakfast," she said gently.

"Mom, I didn't mean..."

"I know you didn't."

"*How* do you know?" he wailed like the little boy he'd once been, the one who didn't understand why his best friend's dad wasn't coming home from Kuwait.

"Because…" Well, how did she? "Because you're you."

To her shock and discomfort, this big tough teenager was actually crying now. "But I've been a jerk lately!"

She didn't have the energy for this, for him, but she had to find it somehow. "Yes, but it's understandable. This move…finding your dad…family…me working so much…" Meg sighed. "I would have wondered what was wrong with you if you'd taken it all in stride. You're a kid. And you know what makes kids act the way they do sometimes?"

By rote he said, "Hormones."

"Right. You've found your dad, he's really cool, you suddenly think we could be like Colin's family. But we can't, Will. I don't know how to tell you any better than that, but we can't."

He wiped away the tears and lifted his chin, his red-rimmed eyes steady on hers. "But I'm not really a kid anymore. It's not like I'm going to…to hate Dad or anything if he…well, did something bad. Back then. So why won't you tell me?"

She had talked about his father when Will was growing up. Funny things he'd done, his interest in living creatures too small for the naked eye to see, the way he threw the football. She'd wanted her son to be able to grow up knowing his father was a good man; to know that the part of himself that came from his father was worth having and valuing.

Maybe that was another of her mistakes. Maybe she'd created a perfect father in Will's mind, Michelangelo's *David* on a pedestal. And now she was refusing to love that perfect man, which made her seem either foolish or perverse. Perhaps it *was* time for him to know that Jack had feet of clay, too.

"All right." She sat back in her chair and looked her son in the eye. "Your dad let me down badly. I know now that he *couldn't* stand up to my father; he was only a few years older than you are. But then...then all I knew was that he didn't. He promised my father never to call me again, to cross the street if he saw me coming. He abandoned me to my father's anger and brutality."

She saw by the shock in Will's eyes that he'd expected something else, something more easily explained away.

Meg got up from the breakfast table and went around to his side just to kiss his cheek. He gripped her suddenly in a strong, awkward hug, his face momentarily buried in her stomach. She stroked his hair and closed her eyes, but although they burned, no tears came.

"I know," she said, when Will looked up, "that you want your dad to be everything that's noble, courageous...good. What you have to understand is that nobody is born that way. He's changed. Some of the change came about because of that terrible scene with my father, and because I ran away and Jack knew that I'd needed him and he'd let me down. If I'd had more faith in him, I might have waited to see if he *would* change. But because I was pregnant with you and scared of my father, I didn't think I had that luxury. And, of course, I was mad and hurt and melodramatic about it all. After all, I was a teenager. And you know what that means."

He grimaced. "Hormones."

She held Will's shoulders. "So, maybe I should

have given him a chance. For his sake as much as mine. But I didn't, and we can't go back. Neither of us will ever know if he would have come through back then, when I needed him. And though I can see now that he's not the same man, I can't ever forget he let me down, and he can't ever forget it, either. We're working on coming to peace with what happened, but it's not something you forget." Meg searched her son's face. "Do you understand?"

"I—I think so." The desperate need for reassurance made him look so young, but the way he let her words sink in, accepted them—in that, she saw his growing maturity. "I wish you'd told me," he said gruffly.

"I wish I had, too." She kissed his head again, closing her eyes to breathe in his essence. *My little boy.* "But maybe neither of us was ready."

"Yeah. Mom." He looked up again, his eyes stricken. "What are you going to do? About...about Mr. McNeil?"

"I don't know." Her approximation of a smile hurt them both. "I just don't know."

"I GOT THE WALKIE-TALKIE," Scott said without preamble the moment she'd identified herself after answering the telephone.

Meg closed her eyes, grateful he couldn't see her. "I didn't know if you'd still do it."

"Shelly Lange's murder has nothing to do with you and me." He sounded cold, indifferent. "I want to know who killed her."

"Then...thank you. I'll head up there right now."

"I'm on my way to town, anyway. Shall I bring it by the station?"

"No." She gave him directions to the crime lab shared by city and county.

"Then I'll see you shortly," he said, still as if he were speaking to a total stranger. "I hope like hell you're wrong."

"I hope I'm wrong, too," she said, but knew herself to be lying.

She had looked into Mark Robillard's eyes.

SCOTT SET DOWN HIS CUP of bad coffee when Ben Shea and Meg turned expectantly. The three had been waiting in the lobby for the fingerprint tech to do his stuff.

He'd lifted the expected jumble from the black plastic walkie-talkie, he announced.

"Some fingerprints, mostly gloved," he told Meg and Ben Shea.

Scott stood grimly behind them, listening, but also bitterly conscious of Meg Patton, who was acting as if they'd barely met, as if last night had meant nothing. She'd agreed with obvious reluctance to let him wait with them.

"You'll need expert corroboration," the fingerprint guy continued, "but in my opinion they definitely match those we took from the car seat."

If anything could have knocked memories of last night off the front burner, that was it. *The glove prints matched.* Scott let out a harsh breath.

This had to be a nightmare. He'd worked with Mark Robillard for the past seven years, since Juanita Butte was nothing but a scar on the mountainside. He'd had dinner with Mark and his wife; Robillard had stood beside Nate's grave. He'd offered gruff sympathy when Penny walked out.

People you knew didn't kill.

"Crooks in books and on TV always wear gloves so they *don't* leave a fingerprint," he said, knowing his voice was too loud but not giving a damn. "How can you be so sure?"

The fingerprint tech glanced at him with one of those looks that said, "Who is this guy?" but he answered. Hell, he was probably thrilled to get to explain his job.

"If you want to commit a crime," he said, "wear latex. You know, the kind doctors wear. Just be careful not to rip them. There've been cases where the perp did tear one and left a partial..." He seemed to realize he was wandering from the point. "The thing is, leather is organic. It's skin, just like our fingertips. It's distinctive. Now, a glove print isn't proof that a particular pair of hands was wearing the gloves on that one occasion, but what's this guy going to claim? He lent them to someone? He misplaced them, but found them the next day lying in the parking lot?"

"Anything you can tell me about the hand?" Meg asked thoughtfully. "Would they be different if someone different was wearing those gloves?"

"Depends." The tech rattled on at some length, but the gist was that he'd bet on the same hands. A smaller hand would have gripped at a different point on the leather finger of the glove. Ditto a bigger one, squeezed into the gloves. He grabbed Detective Shea's hand and held it next to his own, showing how the size of the pads varied, the strength, the way they closed on an object. "Like I said, we've got a dandy match here," he said. "Whether it'll stand up in court... I hear it can go either way."

Meg and her partner huddled over how to handle the next step and finally decided to leave it until morning.

"He's not going anywhere," Scott heard her telling Shea. "I shook him for a minute the other day, but he's used to controlling people. He was sure he had me convinced. I'd put money on it."

Scott muttered an oath. "I can't believe it."

Both turned to look at him. "That's because he's good. We ran a background check on him," Shea said. "There have been two domestic disturbance calls to his house. Both times he walked. The cops weren't convinced, but the wife was charming, they were apologetic, once they even had one of the kids take the blame."

"You're sure." He was numb.

For the first time, Meg spoke directly to him. "That he murdered Shelly? One hundred percent. No. Am I sure in my own mind? Yeah. We found where Robillard had been taking Shelly last summer. I tracked down the people who own the neighboring cabin—they live in Springfield, so they'd never read about the murder. We faxed photos, they remember Shelly and Mark Robillard. They saw them looking happy, but she had bruises a couple times, too. They thought she was scared of him."

Scott's jaws clenched. "Then why wait until tomorrow?"

Ben Shea spoke up again. "We need to sell it to a judge. Get a search warrant." He glanced at his watch. "It's after hours now. No reason to rouse Her Honor at home."

"So you do nothing?"

"We'll put it together in the morning."

Scott wondered distantly if Shea knew there was trouble between his partner and Scott. Detective Shea was a hell of a lot more chatty than usual, picking up the conversation before silences had a chance to congeal.

From the minute Scott arrived, Meg had been civil, cool, willing to look him in the eye. He couldn't tell if she felt a thing.

She had to. However collected and apparently serene she was today, yesterday she had sobbed out his name, first in passion and then hurt. He didn't like thinking of that last sight of her face, eyes huge, tear-drenched and full of pleading. He wondered if Meg Patton had pleaded for anything since she was five years old and wanted an ice cream cone. Scott could see her, a gawky twelve- or thirteen-year-old, gazing at her father with cool reproach and disdain when he wanted her to cry. From things she'd said, Scott guessed her father had hit her, and he could just see it, her lifting her head with stubborn pride no matter what the bastard did.

It took you to make her cry. You to make her beg, his inner voice observed with disgust. *You couldn't even listen.*

And why should he? She'd done the unthinkable, denied the boy's father the most precious part of both of their lives. What she'd taken could never be restored. It might be defensible if Jack Murray had abused her or been a drunkard or a druggie.

Yeah, that insidious voice retorted, *but you don't know what he* did *do. You didn't listen to her side.*

She lied, he thought harshly.

Did she? Or was it just none of your business

until you started kissing her? And then when it was
you wouldn't listen.

"God damn it!" Scott exclaimed, and then felt
like a fool when the two cops stopped walking and
turned around to stare at him.

For just a second, he saw something human in
Meg's eyes. Sympathy, maybe. Understanding. She
thought he was mourning the loss of a friend—the
discovery that a man he'd thought he knew was evil.
But the moment was brief. Walls slid into place; her
gaze was cool, inquiring.

"Never mind," Scott muttered.

They'd reached the parking lot, where he had
parked right next to the Butte County squad car.

They stopped there, waited for him. "Mr. Mc-
Neil," Shea said smoothly, "I'd like your assurance
that you won't say anything to Mark Robillard. It
might be better if you can avoid even seeing him,
without being obvious."

Anger, hot and welcome, shot like a knife blade
between Scott's ribs. "You think I'm going to rush
up there and tell him you know he murdered Shelly
Lange? And, oh, yeah, you're coming for him tomorrow?"

"You wouldn't be the first person to decide there
has to be another explanation. That if you just ask,
your buddy will straighten it all out."

Eyes watchful if brighter than they should have
been, Meg stood silent beside her partner. In daylight he saw how tired she looked, shadows and puff-
iness beneath her eyes, skin tight over elegant
cheekbones.

He refused to feel guilty.

"I won't say anything," Scott said curtly. "I was

fond of Shelly when she was a kid. I'm not about to foul up your investigation.''

''That's what I wanted to hear,'' Shea said in the tone of an adult congratulating a kid for using his head for once.

Scott let the irritation slide away. He didn't give a damn about Shea. He'd save his anger for Meg Patton, who offered him a vague nod and opened the passenger side door on the patrol unit.

At the last minute, she glanced back. ''Thank you for doing this, Mr. McNeil.'' Without waiting for an answer, for *You're welcome,* she climbed in and slammed the door, looking straight ahead as she waited for her partner to join her.

Shea gave him an odd, direct look over the top of the vehicle. He shook his head and got in, too.

From that moment, Scott might as well have been invisible. The patrol unit backed out of the parking slot. Through the windshield, he could see them talking, neither of them even glancing his way. He was still standing there when they drove away.

He wouldn't feel guilty. Anger was a waste of energy. Which left...?

Searing emptiness he'd prayed never to feel again. It was like losing part of himself. Not his ''good right arm.'' No, he hadn't lost anything that obvious, he could go through the motions, he looked the same in the mirror. Inside was different.

Inside he hurt, and knew something irreplaceable was gone.

What was left of his heart.

THE HOUSE WAS EMPTY and quiet. Meg found the note scrawled on the white board on the refrigerator.

"Mom, I'm shooting hoops with some of the guys at the H.S. Open gym until 6:00."

She sank dispiritedly into a chair at the kitchen table. Will was finally making friends. Before she knew it, he'd never be home. And then he'd be gone to college, and she would be really alone.

All of her felt leaden. Even her mind moved slowly. No, she thought at last, being alone wasn't what she minded. It was the contrast between what-would-be and the glorious what-could-be she had briefly imagined. Just last night.

Could it be that recently? she wondered, the amazement dulled by the lassitude that had hit her the minute she walked in the door.

A nap. She needed to sleep.

But, despite last night's lack, she wasn't really sleepy.

Something else, then. A pile of chocolate chip cookies and a glass of milk. Or…ice cream. Chocolate mint. A bowl so big she'd gain five pounds just looking at it.

But she wasn't really hungry, either. And getting out a bowl, dishing up, all seemed to require too much energy.

She wanted Scott. Will. The mother of her distant childhood memories, not the one dying attached to monitors in the hospital. She wanted home. Family. Not to be alone.

Staring blindly, Meg thought, *Renee.*

Pictures tumbled through her memory: a little towhead toddling after her; herself walking a nervous kindergartener to class the first day of school; the two of them, almost teenagers, giggling over a dirty joke; and Renee, big-eyed and solemn, flopped on Meg's bed listening and nodding sympathetically as Meg ranted and raved about their father.

On the very thought of her sister, Meg was out of the chair and heading for the phone. It was only four. Would Renee be working? Home?

She tried there first. Renee answered on the second ring.

"Renee, this is Meg."

Her sister heard the ache in her voice. "Something's wrong. Meg, are you all right? Will? Will's not hurt, is he?"

"No. No, it's nothing like that." Closing her eyes, Meg leaned her forehead against the cool wood of the kitchen cupboard. "Can I...can I come over? Are you busy?"

"Don't be silly. Of course you can. Unless you want me to come there?"

"No. I don't mind." The exhaustion retreated; she would make it. She had a purpose. Someone who cared.

Maybe.

Renee met her at the door. She took one good look at Meg and held out her arms.

Meg found out she'd been wrong. She could still cry.

AN HOUR LATER she articulated one of her worst fears.

"I thought...maybe you hated me."

"Never!" Renee launched herself from her end of the couch to hug Meg with fierce strength. "We're sisters! I just...I was so scared without you! And I missed you so much!"

Meg gave a watery sniff. "But you were mad, too, weren't you?"

"Of course I was!" Renee pulled back to gaze earnestly into Meg's eyes. "But I never, ever, quit loving you. That day you walked into the station was one of the best of my entire life. I'd dreamed of it so many times, just looking up and there you were. And then it happened, and you were home. I feel like…" She gestured helplessly. "I don't know. As if some circle is closed. My life is complete. Like at my wedding. It didn't feel right, not having you there."

Meg was the one to hug her sister this time. New tears wet Renee's shoulder. "I wish I'd been there. If I'd just come sooner…"

"But you didn't know Dad was dead."

"No, but…" Meg sank back, grabbed a tissue and blew her nose.

Hearing something new in her voice, Renee followed suit, then waited.

Meg sighed. "I think maybe Scott's right. Could I have been petty enough to want to keep Will from Jack just because I was angry at him? Because I felt betrayed? I'm thirty-one years old! I knew Jack wasn't a kid anymore. Why didn't I quietly contact him years ago? Why didn't I stand up to Dad years ago? Once I was a working, responsible adult, no court would have taken Will away from me. Maybe I still could have rescued you and Abby. I just…" She bit her lip. "I keep thinking back. *Why?* And…and I don't know. It was like…I wouldn't let myself even consider the possibility. I couldn't trust Jack, I'd tell myself. I couldn't take a chance. Dad would find a way to hurt me, I just knew he would.

It was too late for you guys, I convinced myself. And so...I didn't do anything.''

Meg had never let herself face the pain she'd caused so many people by her choices. Will must come first, she had always believed. But how could contact with his father, with his aunts, have hurt her five- or eight- or twelve-year-old son?

No. By that time, she wasn't afraid for Will. She was just afraid.

''I think,'' her sister said softly, as if reading her mind, ''we've both let Dad shape our lives in ways we never realized. You and I, we fought so hard. We would have both denied we feared him. I never, never, let him see my fear. He'd hit me, and I'd stare back at him until he hit me again. Oh, what pride I had in defying him, in seeing his frustration! But in the end, it took me six months after he died to change even one tiny thing in the house, because... I don't know. Because he'd come back and torment me some more? Because secretly, I was terrified of him. I'd just never admit it to him or myself.'' She reached out and took Meg's hand. ''And maybe you felt the same.''

''Yes. Yes, I did.'' Meg blinked back moisture. ''That's the real truth. I got away, and I was afraid to come back. Even for your sake. Oh, Renee, I'm so sorry!''

They hugged again, wept some more. Daniel strolled in and tried to tiptoe back out, but Renee said, ''It's okay, Daniel. We're just...venting. Meg, where's Will?''

''Oh...'' She glanced at the clock. ''Home, I hope. I'd better call. No, he'll be getting hungry. Maybe I'll take him out for pizza.''

"How about if we all go out for pizza?" Renee looked at her husband. "Mario's. Even if we do have to wait at this time of year."

They smiled at each other, and Meg had a feeling she was missing something.

"Why not?" he said. "Shall I pick up Will? Meet you ladies there?"

Meg phoned her son, who said, "Yeah, cool."

On the way, Meg updated her sister on the murder investigation and the plans for tomorrow.

"You don't think he kept the gun, do you?"

"Probably not," Meg conceded. "Chances are it's buried under ten feet of snow somewhere out in the woods. But you never know. He wouldn't be the first perp to be arrogant enough to figure no one would ever suspect him."

"But now," Renee pointed out, "he knows you do."

"Maybe. An affair and murder are two different things. He knows we're talking to other people, too."

Meg turned into the parking lot next to the restored brick building that housed Mario's. Daniel wasn't there, yet. Neither woman reached for her seat belt clasp.

"Are you watching him?" Renee asked.

"You kidding?" Meg stared at her in astonishment. "Do you guys in the city P.D. have that kind of budget?"

"We wish." Her sister gave an odd sort of shiver. "I just have a bad feeling about this guy. Like you said, he has a lot at stake. Be careful when you make that collar, okay?"

"I'll be careful," Meg promised.

"And give McNeil time." Renee touched her hand lightly. "He'll come to his senses. If he doesn't, he's not worth losing sleep over."

"Right," Meg said wryly. "I'll remember that."

But probably not tonight, which she would spend asking herself the same questions again. Why had she kept Will from his father? Was Scott right in thinking her petty, even cruel?

Her father must be chortling in his grave, Meg thought with sudden bitterness. How he would enjoy knowing that, after all, she had been afraid of him! That, because she let her fear rule her, now the man she loved was rejecting her.

Oh, yes. Death hadn't stopped Ed Patton. He had reached from the frozen earth to punish his wayward daughter.

WILL LIFTED HIS SKIS from the rack atop his father's blue Toyota 4x4. It was Sunday morning and Mom had to work again, but Will's dad had agreed to take him skiing. A bank of snow towered fifteen feet or more above this stretch of parking lot. Blue sky arched overhead, and the glitter of morning sun reflecting off snow dazzled Will's eyes.

"This is going to be great!" he said, blinking from the brilliance and turning to watch his father lock up. "Mom keeps promising to bring me, but she's always working." He eyed some older boys who were passing, and said enviously, "I want to learn to snowboard. I'll bet it's even better."

"Living here, there's no reason you shouldn't," his dad said. "Your mother working today?"

"She's *always* working." He lifted the skis to his

shoulder and added grudgingly, "I mean, she's got that murder investigation. I guess she can't help it."

"She getting anywhere?"

"I think so." They started the length of the parking lot. His skis dug into his shoulders and his boots weren't that comfortable—they weren't made for walking anyway, and rentals never fit quite right. Maybe now his feet were done growing and Mom would buy him his own equipment. "She and Aunt Renee were talking about it last night. Mom said something about getting a search warrant today."

"Ah." His father wore all black except for a white hat; even the band on his goggles, pushed up on his head, was black. *Darth Vader,* Will thought. Or like George Clooney in *From Dusk to Dawn.* Really cool. His best friend Colin's dad had had a pot belly and always wore these super ugly plaid shirts.

Impulsively, Will blurted, "Do you ever wish you and Mom had gotten married? I mean…stayed together. You know." His father's arched brow had him stuttering. "I mean…"

"I know what you mean."

They turned from the parking lot and climbed the snowy, boot-packed slope to the lodge and ticket booths. He didn't say any more for a minute, and Will thought he wasn't going to.

Finally he said, "Your mom didn't give me a choice back then. For a long time, I was sorry. But when I think back… We were so young. Who knows what would have happened?" He stopped by the ticket booth and thrust the base of his skis into a snowbank. "Water under the bridge," he concluded.

"But neither of you is married," Will persisted.

His father gave him a look that wasn't unkind but didn't lift Will's hopes any, either. "Whatever we had together is gone. The years do that. Even to married people, if they aren't careful."

Not until they had their lift tickets, had shuffled through the line and were on the chair, swinging out over the snowy slope, did Will say, "Do you ever want to get married?"

This time his father laughed. "Why the obsession with marriage?"

"Mom's dating this guy," Will said glumly. He swung his skis, one tip up, one down, careful not to rock the chair.

Jack squinted and seemed to be studying the summit. "Seriously?"

"I don't know." A lie: his mother really liked the guy. That's what had scared him. Into telling McNeil something Will knew he wouldn't like? He swallowed. "Maybe. He's an okay guy. I guess. It's just..."

"You thought maybe your mother and I would get back together."

The chair clanked past a lift pole.

"Yeah."

"Well, we're not." His dad straightened. "We're almost there."

Like Will couldn't see the lift house coming up. He rolled his eyes. Ski tips up; the chair lurched, and he and his father stood and skied down a short incline to the top of the run.

Both pulled their goggles over their faces and gripped their poles.

But his father didn't take off right away. He ignored the skiers pouring off the lift behind them, parting to go around them, giving them looks as they passed.

"Will," his father said. "I'd like to live with you. But your mother and I...it's just not going to happen. This guy she's dating...I hope she finds happiness. I hope you let her."

He had to say that. After Will had already fouled everything up, made Mom cry.

Will couldn't think of anything to say.

A second later he was watching his father's back as he drove into the first mogul.

CHAPTER FIFTEEN

WILL TOOK A HUGE windmilling fall on the sixth run. Clambering up, he had to spit snow out of his mouth and shake it from under his collar. His goggles had to be unburied. He put on one ski, did a hopping turn and sideslipped to the spot where the other one was sticking out of the snow.

"You okay?" his father called from down the hill.

"Yeah!" He waved. "I'm the Herminator!"

The best part of the Olympics had been watching Austrian Herman Meier's fall in the downhill. Everyone thought he was going to be dead or something. Instead he went on to win two gold medals in the Super G and the giant slalom. Talk about comebacks.

At the bottom Will took off his hat to shake the snow from it. "Did you see me?" he asked. "I mean, I was flying!"

"Spectacular fall," someone said quietly from behind him.

Will swung around so fast he crashed down. Again. But this time—jeez!—in the lift line! Some guys further back laughed. And it hurt.

With as much dignity as he could, considering, Will got back to his feet. "Mr. McNeil," he said stiffly.

Neither man laughed. Scott McNeil's gray eyes were steady, nonjudgmental. "Will," he said with a nod. "Murray. We've met."

They all shuffled forward. The line was short; Will's and his dad's turn was next. The chair was coming. In a rush, Will said, "Mr. McNeil, are you by yourself? Can I ride up with you? Is that okay, Dad?"

Jack Murray took a second, sharp look at Scott, and inclined his head. He skated into place and sat as the chair moved under him.

When Will and Scott McNeil followed, the guy operating the lift greeted him. Will bet he was extra sharp helping people when his boss was around.

They settled into the chair and let it swoop them forward and out over space.

After a moment, when Will didn't say anything, McNeil pointed up the hill. "We're planning to put a new lift down the other side of that ridge. It'll open some pretty steep terrain." He talked about it: the numbers here over Christmas break, the competition between skiers and boarders, the racing— "Are you interested? We have a junior program."

Will could tell McNeil was filling the silence to be nice, which gave him this crawly feeling of shame. The guy probably *was* okay; Will knew he hadn't given him a chance.

Finally he interrupted, saying hurriedly before he could chicken out, "What I said the other night— about Mom not ever telling my father about me…"

Those clear gray eyes trained on his face. "I could tell you're angry about that."

"No." Will watched skiers swooping down the wide smooth slope beneath them. "See, I'm really not. I mean, my dad's great. I'm glad I know him now. But Mom...the thing is, we were cool together. You know? She's the best.''

"Your father might not agree," the man beside him said dryly.

Starting to feel desperate, Will said, "But he's not that mad at Mom. It's...it's weird. Like he understands why she never told him about me. I think..." Mom might kill him for this—she said you never tell family secrets to outsiders—but Will thought this once it was justified. "Mom says he—my dad— let her down really bad back then. *Her* father hurt her. She says Dad has changed, but that she couldn't take a chance then that he would, or else she would have lost me. And she says not for anything would she have let her father raise her kid. And so you see..." He took a nervous glance toward the approaching lift house. "She did it to protect me. And...and I think you should know. That doing what was right for me is all she cared about. And if that's wrong..."

"My son died." McNeil sounded hoarse. "He wasn't even six months old."

Will gave him a startled look. At the last second he saw the net below them and he lifted the tips of his skis.

"I expected to see him grow up." They both rose to their feet, let the chair nudge them forward. "If I found out my ex-wife had lied, that Nate hadn't died after all... That all those years were gone, for whatever reason..."

Will stopped beside the man he was pretty sure his mother wanted to marry. He could only think of one thing to say.

"But if you found out she'd lied to you to protect your little boy? Because that was the only way she thought she could?" Will swallowed, lifted his chin. "Wouldn't you want her to put him first? Even if…if it meant you couldn't see him?"

Scott McNeil stared at Will. His voice sounded odd. "Why are you saying this?"

"Because it's true. And—" he looked down, poking at one ski with his pole "—because Mom never cries. But she did after you left. For a long time. And I know it's my fault."

"No. Not your fault. Mine."

"I'm the one who opened my big mouth…"

"But I wouldn't listen to her."

"Well…" Will looked over to where his father waited, watching them. "You still could. When you're sorry, Mom never stays mad. At least, not at me, but I bet…"

"She might not hold a grudge against me, either." McNeil gave this twisted smile that almost hurt to look at. "Thanks, son. We'll hope you're right."

With that he took one skating step, skied past Will's dad with a quick word and kept going, shooting right over the brink and straight down The Wall, just whisk, whisk, whisk, these little snappy turns that were so pretty to watch, they took Will's breath away. And he'd thought his dad was good!

"What…what did he say?" Will asked his dad as they both watched.

Jack Murray smiled. "He told me I have one great kid."

"WHY…I DON'T KNOW WHERE he is," the secretary said worriedly. "Mr. Robillard's wife called just a minute ago, and he talked to her and then he went running out of here. I asked him if his children were all right, but he didn't answer!'' She looked from Ben to Meg. ''Did something bad happen?''

Damn it! Meg thought furiously. Atherton and Dailey had jumped the gun and served the warrant on Robillard's wife early. They'd *agreed,* all of them, to exactly coordinate the two searches so neither Robillard could warn the other; they'd checked their watches. What in hell had gone wrong?

''I'm sorry,'' Meg said formally. ''To the best of my knowledge, his children are fine. But we do have a search warrant for Mark Robillard's home and office, and I suspect his wife warned him we were coming.''

They overcame her shock, presented the warrant and hastily checked: no gloves. Ben swore viciously.

''Let's find him,'' Meg said. ''We must have just missed him on the way in. Where does he park?'' she snapped to the secretary as they raced past.

''The employee lot...'' Her voice trailed them.

He drove a one-year-old Toyota 4x4, green; their warrant included it.

''If he ditches those gloves, we don't have a case,'' Ben growled as they bounded down the stairs.

Stating the obvious had never been her favorite hobby. ''Unless Atherton or Dailey have big mouths, he doesn't know we want gloves or why.''

''They're usually good. God damn idiots.''

People turned to stare as they sprinted past the clothes and rental shops. Down the hall. Ben slammed open the back door. They slipped and slithered along the path between banks of snow until the parking lot opened before them. Sun glinted off windshields; roof racks obscured their field of vision.

Ben swore again. "It's a big lot."

The only named slot was the general manager's: Scott's. Robillard's 4x4 could be anywhere.

"A ton of people work here." She thought quickly. "You get the car and try to block the highway, if we're not already too late. Radio for a patrol unit to head up the mountain loop highway looking for him. I'll hunt here."

He didn't argue, just took off at a run. Miracle of miracles, was he learning to trust her? Meg wondered wryly. Or did he just not trust her behind the wheel?

She edged between parked cars. Bumped her hip on one. The parking lot was slippery, as if the sun had varnished the packed snow. She should have worn boots; hadn't expected to be doing anything more than walking into the lodge, maybe waiting for Robillard to come down from the ski hill.

Movement flashed to her left. She swung around, pulled her revolver.

A young brunette got out of a car and slammed the door. Meg must have made a sound, because she turned, saw the gun and gasped.

"Go on, go on," Meg held her finger to her lips and gestured toward the lodge. The young woman took off at a trot.

Meg dodged through the next double row of cars, her frustration growing. Where was Robillard? Would he have parked elsewhere? Or wasn't he run-

ning, after all? He must know it would be futile. Her
mind worked feverishly as she scanned the lot.

*What was Robillard doing? What was he think-
ing?*

Metallic green caught her eye; no, it was a van.
Next to a tan Bronco; half the population of Butte
County drove utility vehicles.

Only part of her mind was on the search. The
other part was still thinking motive, behavior.

What if Robillard had kept the murder weapon—
had had it all along? Maybe after the call from his
wife he'd taken off to toss it in a snowbank, or figured he could throw it out the window of his vehicle
halfway to town, if he could slip past them now.

He wouldn't know they were after the gloves.

Meg banged her shin against the bumper of a
pickup and mumbled a curse. If she weren't careful,
she'd shoot herself in the foot. Or take out somebody's windshield.

She looked one way up the next row, then the
other.

And saw him hurrying toward her, maybe fifty
yards away. Wearing a parka, hands black-gloved.
He spotted her at the same moment and plunged
between cars. Paralleling him, Meg pursued.

"Stop!" she called.

The green Toyota was parked in the next row. As
she slid and almost fell, she saw Robillard fumbling
with something. Keys. Must be keys. He disappeared behind his vehicle. Unlocking it.

She headed right down the middle of the row.

He'd parked nose out. She was thirty yards away
when the Toyota rocketed out of the slot directly
toward her. Why hadn't he gone the other way?

He'd seen her; she knew he had. He could have reached the exit either way, and he didn't know Shea waited for him there.

The sun reflected off the windshield. She couldn't see him, only the blinding glare.

He was accelerating, the snow tires gripping the icy surface with ease. She was smack in the path of the 4x4, the footing slick as a wet bar of soap.

Too late, Meg realized: the bastard was going to run her down.

HE'D GOTTEN ONLY ONE RUN, and his pager was already beeping. Trapped in the lift line between two packs of teenagers, Scott felt tension eat at his stomach the second he saw the number: Robillard's office.

He grabbed his phone and dialed even as he automatically moved forward in line.

"Oh, Mr. McNeil!" cried the secretary. "I don't know what to do! It's terrible, and I don't understand, and…"

Usually unflappable, capable of handling a multitude of minor crises in her boss's absence, she babbled on. Something about a search warrant, a call from Mark's wife, him taking off—he'd looked so upset, and he hadn't said where he was going—and now the cops had gone after him.

"Oh, please. What should I *do?*"

Cops. Her story hit Scott, a slam in the gut. Not "cops."

Meg.

No simple serving of a warrant. Somehow Robillard had known what was coming and taken off.

Meg was after him. After the man who might have murdered Shelly.

Scott swore, inciting another burst of worries from the secretary. He ignored them, thinking hard.

Meg wouldn't be alone, would she? No, Melissa had said "cops." Plural.

He still didn't like it. If Robillard would drag Shelly across the snow, shove her down into that snow well and shoot her in cold blood despite her pleas, why wouldn't he kill a cop if he thought he could get away? *God.*

"Nothing, Melissa," Scott snapped. "Don't do anything. Don't call anybody. Sit tight."

Shoving the phone in his pocket, he backed up, bumped one of the kids. "Excuse me."

He lifted the bright orange rope that prevented skiers from cutting the line and skated under it. He scanned the area in front of the lodge.

Nobody was running. The ticket booths were busy. People were coming out of the lodge, going in, putting on skis. A mom pulled two little ones in a blue plastic saucer, all of them laughing. A teenage girl threw a snowball at a boy. A couple, leaning on their poles, talked intensely, even hotly.

All normal. He'd had momentary visions of a hostage situation, a shoot-out among the families skiing at Juanita Butte. Thank God they evaporated.

He used the drop-off from the lift line to send him shooting past the nearest ticket booth. From here the ground rose to the back of the lodge. He'd never climbed so fast on skis; sweat blurred his vision.

Scott reached the back of the timbered lodge and

poled forward to the edge of the snowbank. From this vantage point he could see the parking lots.

Somebody ran between cars, yelled something. Olive-green uniform, pale blond hair. Meg. She had her gun held two-fisted.

Oh, crap. There was Robillard, farther down the same row. He dove in behind his Toyota. Meg was running toward him, yelling.

Scott had never felt so impotent in his life. Even when his son died. That had happened behind his back, the soft breaths stopping sometime during the dark hours, when Nate was alone, asleep, unknowing—or so Scott prayed. But this—God Almighty, this was spread out before him, too far away for him to help, but all crystal clear, brutally real.

That SOB drove straight for Meg.

With a bellow, Scott shoved off the top of the bank and arced through the air. Still on his skis, he hit the icy parking lot with a force that slammed through his body like a pile driver, but he stayed on his feet. The momentum kept him shooting across the ice toward the drama ahead.

For a second Meg's stance widened; Scott thought she was going to shoot the oncoming vehicle.

And then she must have realized, as he did, that the Toyota was going too fast, too straight. It would hit her even if she killed Robillard.

She scrambled, slithering, crashing to her knees. She wouldn't be able to get out of the way. The 4x4 was too close, really moving now.

Scott wouldn't make it, couldn't do any good if he did. His throat was raw from the bellow rending the air. "No! Meg! God damn it, no!"

Somehow she got to her feet and flung herself sideways. Just as the Toyota reached her.

He heard a dull thud. She fell to one side, flopping on the ice.

Rage filled Scott. He had his skis off before he knew what he was doing. Grabbed one of them, hoisted it in both hands above his head as if it were a javelin. Waited. If he could kill with this ski, he would.

Wait. The Toyota came on. Robillard would run him down, too. One more second.

Now!

Weight behind it, Scott slammed the butt of the ski into the windshield, aiming at the driver behind the wheel. The force flung him to one side as a crazy web of cracks bloomed. The glass had stayed intact. He'd failed. The vehicle's momentum slammed the ski against his head. The side mirror got his ribs. Already vomiting, fire lacing his torso, Scott was on his knees on the icy lot when the smash of metal shook the ground. He rolled onto his side and saw the Toyota sliding, entangled with another car, shoving it. Robillard had lost control. Maybe slammed on the brakes in the icy lot. Now more metal screamed as they hit a van. The domino effect.

His stomach heaved; pain lanced his ribs—or his belly, he didn't know. Only dragged himself to his knees. Meg. Meg was hurt. He pushed up. Wobbled to his feet.

And saw her. Walking toward him.

Her face—something was wrong with it. Blood and swelling. And she limped. But she was walking. Steadily. Alive. In better shape than he was.

Scott crumpled to his knees again, grabbed a bumper for support.

"You're hurt!" She reached him, crouched, and he saw the terror in her eyes. For him.

"Okay," he managed, although the effort of speech made him want to throw up again. "Robillard."

"I've called for backup and an ambulance." Her hand touched him, softly. A woman's hand. Loving.

Her other hand held a long-barreled black gun.

"Go," he said.

She walked away. "Robillard," she called. "Don't move. I want to see your hands."

A man lay halfway through the now shattered windshield. Blood trickled down the green hood onto the snow.

Meg reached him, checked his pulse. And lifted a gun from the bloody hand.

"I'M NOT ABOUT TO STAY in the hospital if I don't have to," Scott growled from inside the turtleneck he was yanking over his head, half an inch at a time. Who would think broken ribs could hurt so much?

"You won't be able to hold Emily," Meg pointed out, from her unseen spot beside his bed.

"Watch me."

"You're bullheaded."

"Damn right."

His head emerged from the turtleneck and he discovered he had visitors. Her son and Jack Murray. He had a hazy memory of them in the parking lot along with EMTs and cops and... Hell, half the skiers up at Juanita Butte had clustered around, it had seemed like. He hoped he was exaggerating; he hadn't been at his best about then.

"You're okay?" Will said, eyes bright and interested.

"'Okay' being relative," his mother said dryly.

"Mr. McNeil looks better than you do," her son told her.

She gave a crooked smile, all she could manage with one side of her face skinned, purple and swollen. "Thanks, buddy. I am stingingly aware—a pun, get it?—that I don't look my sharpest." She pretended to think. "Hey, was that a pun, too?"

"Jeez, Mom." Will rolled his eyes. "You're the one who is always telling me to take *some* things seriously."

"Oh, I took this seriously." Meg's eyes met Scott's, and he saw a shadow of her fear in them.

"It's almost too bad Robillard lived," Jack commented. He'd been paged on the hill, too, by a dispatcher who knew where he was. *Officer down.* Every cop within twenty-five miles had come running. He and Ben Shea had been the closest.

"Oh, no," Meg said softly. "I want him to stand trial. To have lots of time to think about Shelly Lange. Remember her face, hear her sobs, see her blood. Fifty years would be good."

Scott couldn't look away from the courageous woman who had yet to remind him of what an idiot he'd been. But he had to know. "The gun matches?"

"They're still messing with it," Murray said, "but I hear it looks good. The bastard would be sent away for trying to kill a cop anyway."

"He might wriggle out from under that, though,"

Meg said. "Claim the sun was in his eyes and he didn't see me."

"It was morning. He was heading west."

She cocked her head, winced. "Still. How can we prove what he saw or was thinking?"

"Thanks to good, solid police work, you'll get him for Shelly Lange's murder." The Elk Springs police chief clapped her lightly on the back. "You want me to take this kid away?"

Meg looked up at her son, and suddenly her eyes were misty. "Nah. I'll keep him. But thanks, Jack."

They looked at each other a moment; smiled, nodded. Scott knew what she was thinking: if she had died today, Will would have had a father. A good one.

"Then I'll see you all later." Jack said something quiet to Will and left.

Meg sat on the edge of the hospital bed beside Scott and went right back to her original point. "Will Marjorie keep Emily tonight?"

Talk about bullheaded. "I'll manage."

"Will? Can you wait outside for a minute?"

"Yeah. Sure. But you know, we could, like, stay with Mr. McNeil. And get up with the baby and stuff." He flushed. "I mean, if he wants us."

Meg's smile was radiant. And, apparently, painful, because a whimper escaped her. "Took the words out of my mouth. But do me a favor, kiddo. Whatever you do, don't make me laugh."

He opened his mouth as though the challenge was irresistible, then took a good look at his mother and closed it again. "I'll, um, be out in the waiting room."

Meg waited until the door closed behind him.

Head bowed, she said, "I was going to make the same offer. Unless there's someone you'd rather have. No strings attached. I'm not asking you to change how you feel. But…" Her gaze turned up to him, her eyes so huge and blue he felt as dizzy as if he were staring up into the heavens. "Let me help. You're hurt because of me."

"I thought you were dead." His voice was hoarse. He forgot the pain in his ribs. He reached for her, felt a rush of gratitude that she came into his arms without protest. Against her hair, Scott said, "The way you hit. Bounced." A shudder walked up his spine. "I wanted to kill the bastard. I've never wanted to kill before."

"The fender grazed me. That's all." She seemed unaware that she was patting him, tracing the line of the bandages wrapping his rib cage, checking for other damage. "When I saw you…"

"Will talked to me today."

Meg tilted her head back. "Just now? That was nice of him, wasn't it?"

"No. Earlier. We rode up the chair together. He told me you'd been justified in keeping his existence secret. And he said…" What the kid had said sliced into his gut, worse than the scraping edges of broken ribs. Scott swallowed. "He asked me a question. What if Nate could have lived, but only if Penny hid him from me? Wouldn't I have wanted her to do whatever she had to do to protect him?"

Meg went completely still in his arms.

"Yes." Scott's voice was as raw as Meg's cheek. "Yes. Of course, I would have. I would have done anything to protect Nate. Just like you did what you had to for your son."

She tried to argue, to tell him that she thought maybe she'd been a coward, unwilling to admit that she was so afraid of her father she was irrational. Scott wouldn't listen.

"You did what you thought you had to," he repeated. "You've raised a great kid. I was…lashing out from my own misery. I couldn't see beyond my own loss."

"Damn it," the tough cop in his arms mumbled, "I'm crying again. That's all I seem to do these days."

"In between having wild sex and arresting murderers."

She lifted her head and looked at him straight on, new tension humming through her, causing the faint tremor under his hands. "Do you mind? That I'm a cop?"

"No." He tried a smile of his own, though it didn't match either his voice or the anxiety suddenly swelling under those tight bandages. "Meg… I know it's too soon. We hadn't met a month ago. We've had—what?—three, four dates."

"Yes," she said.

"Three? Or four?"

"I wasn't answering that question."

The anxiety was transmuting to hope, as painful in its way. "I'm going to try to adopt Emily. I don't know how you feel about that. Maybe it's stupid, but I believe Shelly meant for me to have her. And for Emily to have me."

"I think—" Meg's smile was as soft as a mountain dawn "—that it would be wonderful if you adopt Emily."

"I'll share her if you share your son." That was as close as he dared come to what he was thinking.

"Deal." Meg feathered a kiss across his cheek, then groaned. "That hurt. I can't even kiss the man I love!"

"You love me." He turned his head so that their mouths touched. He nibbled gently on the good side of her lips, on her earlobe. "Did you really say it?"

"I said it." She gave a huge sigh. "You could try."

He swore, and his voice went rough again. "God, I love you. It's too soon, but will you marry me anyway?"

Bruised and swollen, her face shone. "Yeah. Don't tell Will—we'll have to get him used to the idea first—but, yeah. Of course I'll marry you."

His mouth swooped for hers, stopped short, and Scott groaned. He couldn't kiss her; he sure as hell couldn't make love to her. Not today, or tomorrow.

But soon enough, he thought with satisfaction and a huge welling of life and joy he'd never expected to feel again. They had time, and then some.

"Well, then, Deputy Margaret Patton," he murmured, "shall we collect our children and go home?"

"Oh, yes," she breathed, the tears she hated in her eyes again. "Home, it is."

Turn the page
for an excerpt from
Janice Kay Johnson's
third book in the

PATTON'S DAUGHTERS
miniseries—

A MESSAGE FOR ABBY

Coming next month
from Harlequin Superromance!

HER DEAD DADDY'S pickup sitting beside the road, smouldering from an arson fire.

That was Abby Patton's first thought on seeing it—that it was Daddy's—and now she couldn't get rid of the willies.

The pickup wasn't really his, of course; it couldn't be. Ed Patton had been dead for three years, his Chevy sold only months after he went in the ground. This one was just the same color, the same vintage.

Coincidence, is all.

Abby prowled around the pickup. For sure these plates weren't the ones that had been on Daddy's truck—but then, she'd bet ten to one this pair had been stolen from another vehicle, anyway. Shiny, tabs new, they didn't go with the red dust coating the dented, fading green paint of the pickup.

Firefighters had smashed the passenger side window and pumped foam on the seat, just to be sure a blaze didn't leap to life later. Sweating in the hundred degree heat, wearing their gear, they had made a few choice remarks about the dumb ass who'd gone to all the trouble to rip the stuffing out of the seat, soak it with gasoline and set it on fire, only to roll up the windows and lock the doors.

"Doesn't every school kid know fire needs

oxygen?'' one of them asked, shaking his head. A minute later they'd tooted a fare-thee-well and were gone.

Now, left beside the road with nobody but jackrabbits and the wind to keep her company, Abby said aloud, ''And why bother?'' Why not junk the truck if it wouldn't run, sell it on a lot if it would?

Because setting fires was fun? Because the pickup was stolen and some teenage perp thought he could get rid of fingerprints this way? Or because the arsonist needed to destroy the vehicle for some other reason? There sure wasn't anything in the rusting bed of the pickup.

Before taking a close look, Abby got on the radio to run the plates. While she waited, she leaned against her car door and looked around.

Barton Road was paved, even had a yellow stripe down the middle, but at the bottom of the gravel banks to each side, gray desert scrub stretched away, bordered by ancient barbed wire attached to rotting fence posts. Cattle must have grazed out here once upon a time, or why bother fencing, but this now looked like the pronghorn country it had once been.

She guessed she was five miles outside the Elk Springs city limits, east of town where the land got bleak and flat mighty quick. Just a few miles west, ranches started studding the landscape, including her brother-in-law's, the Triple B. But here no houses were visible, and only three vehicles had passed in the last twenty minutes. Plus, the arsonist could have seen anyone coming far enough away to be gone in a cloud of dust before the passerby arrived.

Some teenage boys out here target shooting had reported the fire on a cell phone. Interesting they'd seen flames. Either the fire setter had just left, or they'd lit this baby themselves.

A voice crackled from the receiver. "Marshall Patton, the plates belong to a blue 1997 Chevrolet Lumina, registered to…"

"Whoa," Abby interrupted. She repeated the plate number. "You're sure about the vehicle?"

"Yes, ma'am. The registered owner is Shirley Barnard, address 22301 Butte Road, Elk Springs."

Shock silenced Abby long enough for the dispatcher to say, "Do you need a repeat?"

"No! I…" She swallowed. "No. Thank you."

The prickle of some kind of primitive fear crept up her spine.

A fire set in a pickup that could have been Daddy's decorated with stolen plates belonging to her sister Renee's mother-in-law. And one of Daddy's daughters was an arson investigator.

Coincidence, Abby tried to tell herself again, but disquiet stirred the hair at her nape. She suddenly felt as if somebody was watching her.

She gazed around one more time, but the sagebrush wasn't dense enough to hide a man, and the road stretched bare and shimmery in the noonday sun.

Abby shivered despite the heat. Pulling on latex gloves, she walked back to the pickup. Reaching through the broken window, she gingerly lifted the latch and shouldered open the door.

The interior was filthy and dripping with gasoline and retardant. The upholstery appeared to have been slit with a knife and then ripped open; most of the fabric was on the floor. Blackened from the fire, stuffing cascaded down to the seat covering, exposing springs.

The smell was bad. Really bad. Instinctively Abby began breathing through her mouth. Gasoline, charred plastic and fabric and some sharp overtone that made her think of burning urine. What *was* that stench?

Oh, no.

She lifted the guts of the upholstery and turned it. Burned bits crumpled. She didn't notice, was too absorbed in the dark stain on the woven material. When she let it go, the latex fingers of her glove were pink.

Blood and plenty of it.

HARLEQUIN®
SUPERROMANCE®

PATTON'S DAUGHTERS

by
Janice Kay Johnson

The people of Elk Springs, Oregon, thought
Ed Patton was a good man, a good cop,
a good father. But his daughters know the truth....

Renee, Meg, Abby
Sisters, Cops...Women

They're not like their father. And that's all right with them. But
they still feel they have something to prove to the
townspeople—and to themselves.

Daniel, Scott, Ben—three men who can see past the
uniforms to the women inside. They're willing to
take on—and ready to love—Patton's Daughters.

Look for Janice Kay Johnson's newest miniseries:

August 1999—*The Woman in Blue* (#854)
September 1999—*The Baby and the Badge* (#860)
October 1999—*A Message for Abby* (#866)

Available at your favorite retail outlet.

HARLEQUIN®
Makes any time special ™

If you enjoyed what you just read,
then we've got an offer you can't resist!

Take 2 bestselling love stories FREE!
Plus get a FREE surprise gift!

Clip this page and mail it to Harlequin Reader Service®

IN U.S.A.	IN CANADA
3010 Walden Ave.	P.O. Box 609
P.O. Box 1867	Fort Erie, Ontario
Buffalo, N.Y. 14240-1867	L2A 5X3

YES! Please send me 2 free Harlequin Superromance® novels and my free surprise gift. Then send me 6 brand-new novels every month, which I will receive months before they're available in stores. In the U.S.A., bill me at the bargain price of $3.57 plus 25¢ delivery per book and applicable sales tax, if any*. In Canada, bill me at the bargain price of $3.96 plus 25¢ delivery per book and applicable taxes**. That's the complete price, and a saving of over 10% off the cover prices—what a great deal! I understand that accepting the 2 free books and gift places me under no obligation ever to buy any books. I can always return a shipment and cancel at any time. Even if I never buy another book from Harlequin, the 2 free books and gift are mine to keep forever. So why not take us up on our invitation. You'll be glad you did!

135 HEN CQW6
336 HEN CQW7

Name	(PLEASE PRINT)	
Address	Apt.#	
City	State/Prov.	Zip/Postal Code

* Terms and prices subject to change without notice. Sales tax applicable in N.Y.
** Canadian residents will be charged applicable provincial taxes and GST.
  All orders subject to approval. Offer limited to one per household.
  ® is a registered trademark of Harlequin Enterprises Limited.

6SUP99   ©1998 Harlequin Enterprises Limited

"Don't miss this, it's a keeper!"
—**Muriel Jensen**

"Entertaining, exciting and
utterly enticing!"
—**Susan Mallery**

"Engaging, sexy...a fun-filled romp."
—**Vicki Lewis Thompson**

See what all your favorite authors
are talking about.

Coming October 1999 to a retail store near you.

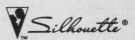

 **HARLEQUIN®**
Makes any time special ™

WIN A
DREAM

In celebration of Harlequin®'s golden anniversary

Enter to win a *dream!* You could win:

- A luxurious trip for two to **The Renaissance Cottonwoods Resort** in Scottsdale, Arizona, or

- A bouquet of flowers once a week for a year from **FTD**, or

- A $500 shopping spree, or

- A fabulous bath & body gift basket, including **K-tel**'s *Candlelight and Romance* 5-CD set.

Look for **WIN A DREAM** flash on specially marked Harlequin® titles by Penny Jordan, Dallas Schulze, Anne Stuart and Kristine Rolofson in October 1999*.

FTD

RENAISSANCE.
COTTONWOODS RESORT
SCOTTSDALE, ARIZONA

K·TEL

HARLEQUIN®
SUPERROMANCE®

Three childhood friends dreamed of becoming
firefighters. Now they're members of the same team
and every day they put their lives on the line.

They are

AMERICA'S BRAVEST

An exciting new trilogy by

Kathryn Shay

#871 FEEL THE HEAT
(November 1999)
#877 THE MAN WHO LOVED CHRISTMAS
(December 1999)
#882 CODE OF HONOR
(January 2000)

Available wherever Harlequin books are sold.

HARLEQUIN®
Makes any time special ™

HARLEQUIN®
SUPERROMANCE®

**Two women—who are going to be mothers.
Two men—who want to be fathers.**

EXPECTING THE BEST by **Lynnette Kent**
Shelly Hightower falls for Denver cop Zach Harmon—but she
figures he's done with raising kids. He has to convince her that
he *wants* to be a father to their baby....
AVAILABLE IN OCTOBER 1999.

THE FAMILY WAY by **Rebecca Winters**
Wendy Sloan is pregnant by her husband—and mourning his
death. She doesn't understand why she's so attracted to the
mysterious stranger who's come into her family's life—the man
who wants to be a father to her kids. Including this new baby...
AVAILABLE IN NOVEMBER 1999.

**Two deeply emotional stories.
Read them both.**

Available at your favorite retail outlet.

HARLEQUIN®
Makes any time special ™

#864 MY BABIES AND ME • Tara Taylor Quinn
By the Year 2000: Baby

She's a goal-setting, plan-making kind of person, and one of Susan Kennedy's goals is to have a baby by the age of forty. That's coming up fast. A couple of problems, though. There's only one man she can imagine as the father of her child. And that's her ex-husband, Michael. She gets pregnant on schedule, but then there's another problem—well, not really a problem. She's expecting twins!

#865 FAMILY REUNION • Peg Sutherland
The Lyon Legacy

Family means everything. Scott Lyon's heard his great-aunt's words forever. But now Margaret's disappeared, and the closer Scott comes to finding her, the more family secrets, betrayals and deceptions he uncovers. And then he meets Nicki Bechet, whose grandmother knows more about the Lyons than she's telling.

Join Scott and Nicki in this thrilling conclusion to the Lyon Legacy as they search for the truth and learn that family—and love—really do mean everything.

#866 A MESSAGE FOR ABBY • Janice Kay Johnson
Patton's Daughters

Abby's the third Patton sister. The baby. The one everyone said was privileged, spoiled. But childhood with a harsh, unapproachable father and only a vague memory of her mother wasn't easy, even if she did make it look that way. So now Abby's determined to live up to her image and have fun. Then she meets Detective Ben Shea—and he has news for her. *Sometimes it pays to get serious.*

#867 A RANGER'S WIFE • Lyn Ellis
Count on a Cop

Lawmen know that everything can change in an instant. The smart ones don't take their lives or their promises for granted. At least, that's what Texas Ranger Ty Richardson believes. Before his best friend, Jimmy Taylor, died in the line of duty, Ty promised to take care of Jimmy's wife and young son. And Ty intends to honor that promise—to help them, protect them, be there for them. But he'll never forget that they're Jimmy's family, not his—no matter how much he loves them both.

#868 EXPECTING THE BEST • Lynnette Kent
9 Months Later

Denver cop Zach Harmon's finished with raising kids. As the oldest of eleven, he spent too much time helping out with his siblings. But then, he never expected to fall so hard for Shelley Hightower—who understands his feelings all too well. *Now* he has to convince her that raising their child together is exactly what he wants to do.

#869 THE RESCUER • Ellen James

Dr. Alexandra Robbins may be a successful psychologist in Chicago, but her own marriage wasn't a success. She's in the middle of a messy divorce. So it's a relief for her to escape to Sobriety, Idaho, and complete her research on type R men—rescuers, compelled to risk their lives to save others. Colin McIntyre, the object of her study, fascinates her big-time, but the more he attracts her, the more frightened of him she becomes. And she doesn't understand why....